RUN, HIDE, DIE

A JIMMY BLUE NOVEL

IAN W. SAINSBURY

For Patrick
1948-2021

CHAPTER ONE

CAUSE OF DEATH was the easy bit: the murdered man had a harpoon sticking out of his chest. He was lying on his back at the side of the swimming pool. The corpse stared at the weapon as if surprised to find it there.

Motive wasn't difficult to find. Detective Chief Inspector Barber could think of twenty people off the top of her head who would be delighted by the man's premature death. Harry Penrose—better known as Harpoon Harry, a nickname Barber guessed would stick now, no pun intended—was someone who inspired intense dislike in almost everyone. The only people who didn't hate Harpoon Harry hadn't met him yet.

Opportunity. That was the tough bit. Harry Penrose died ten minutes before midnight at a rooftop party. Harpooned in the chest, surrounded by thirty-seven witnesses. None of whom saw a thing.

It had been the sort of party where guests were frisked at the door. A harpoon gun would have been hard to miss.

The white-clad forensic team moved through the predawn scene like ghosts. Barber doubted they'd find much. Anyone capable of pulling off a crime like this was unlikely to leave much physical evidence.

The murderer had used a principle beloved by magicians for thousands of years: misdirection. Four to six seconds when everyone looked the wrong way. When they turned back, Harry Penrose was dead, with no sign of his murderer.

Barber looked up from the corpse to observe Detective Inspector Cunningham's approach. He shuffled around the pool, yawning, looking exactly like a man dragged out of bed after a few hours of sleep. Crumpled shirt, crumpled face. DCI Barber, in contrast, wore a suit. Her short hair was brushed, and her shoes were polished. She wanted to yawn, but she didn't.

Cunningham had made the final three in the interviews for DCI before Barber got the job. He'd congratulated her and never mentioned it again, instead choosing to make his disdain clear in a hundred tiny ways every day. When he'd put in for a transfer a month ago, Barber had approved it immediately. Cunningham was a good detective, but he needed to grow up.

"The uniforms haven't found a thing," he said. "Interviews with the guests have drawn a blank. Maybe they're all covering up for the murderer."

Barber raised an eyebrow. "Unlikely." Harpoon Harry Penrose may have been a despicable, psychotic little shit, but the party guests were loyal to his father. They wouldn't protect the killer of Douglas Penrose's only son.

"The bodyguards say no one at the party was armed."

"Not even Harry? The harpoon is his weapon of choice, after all."

Cunningham shrugged. A layer of dandruff fell from his shoulder. "Not even Harry."

Barber walked away from the body and stood at the edge of the building. St Paul's Cathedral, half a mile north-east, still had the power to impress, and London looked at its best in the pastel smears provided by sunrise. Dawn was her favourite time of day. Her lists prepared, items ready to be checked off, the calendar booked up with appointments. At dawn, Barber visualised the new day as a sequence of prioritised tasks, each in its place, awaiting her attention. A semblance of order which rarely survived the morning.

Twenty-six floors below, uniformed officers checked the street for the elusive harpoon gun.

Cunningham joined her at the rail. Not too close. "This is their third pass. It's not there."

"It must be."

Barber closed her eyes and put together a series of images, projecting them onto an imaginary screen. A party, most guests under the age of thirty. Smart suits, little black dresses. Champagne, vodka, tequila, cocaine. A row of Bentleys, Aston Martins and Lamborghinis on the street below. Laughter, music, dancing, drunken flirting. Witness statements put Harry Penrose with the Swifton twins, nineteen-year-old heiresses to an old-money fortune. His phone rang. He turned his back—the girls went in search of more engaging company—and walked to the far side of the pool, away from the music. Next, a flare—fired from where exactly?—ignited the firework display. Everyone looked up. The DJ was the first to notice. From his raised platform, looking out across the dancers, he saw beyond them to the swimming pool and the impaled body floating in it, Harry's white shirt already crimson. The music stopped, and the screams began.

What happened during the few seconds when the fireworks went off? What did everyone miss?

A radio squawked from the top of the staircase leading to the roof. The officer controlling the entrance spoke into her lapel mic, then called over.

"DCI Barber? They've found something."

"The harpoon gun?"

"No, Ma'am. They're bringing it up now."

The 'something' they'd found turned out to be a para-gliding wing, jet black, discovered two streets away.

The young constable who brought it up to the roof waited as DCI Barber stared at the parachute without speaking.

"Probably someone base jumping, ma'am. They film themselves and put it online."

Still Barber said nothing. Cunningham stepped forward and took a handful of the nylon material, as if touching it might tell him something about its provenance.

"Bloody idiots." He released the material, turning to Barber. "We arrest them when we catch them. Most of the time we don't find out until there's a video online of some twat jumping off the Gherkin. I doubt it's connected to this."

Cunningham walked away, hands in pockets.

Barber finally spoke, looking at the constable. "What about you?"

"Um." The constable wasn't sure what her superior meant. "Sorry, ma'am?"

"Do you doubt it's connected?"

"Er. Well, I mean, how could... um. I'm not sure. Ma'am."

"Good. That's a better answer. If you ever want to make detective, remember one thing."

"What's that, ma'am?"

"Everything's connected. Everything."

CHAPTER TWO

Six hours earlier

———

Jimmy Blue called Harry Penrose at 11:33 p.m.

"It's Dan, Harry. I have some news about our little business venture. Good news."

Harry knew Blue as Dan Blanchette, a heroin dealer. The 'business venture' referred to a huge shipment coming in from Rotterdam. Dan, for a substantial finder's fee, had agreed to supply details of when and where the heroin would enter the country. Harry planned to intercept the shipment on its journey to London. Naturally, one of the couriers would be harpooned. Harry wanted to build a reputation.

"What news? When's it going down?" Harry talked like someone pretending to be a gangster. Many sons try to escape their father's shadow. Doug Penrose's shadow was so long that his son considered wholesale slaughter with a theatrical touch the only way he'd ever make an impression. What Harry lacked in intelligence, he tried to make up for with a puppy-like enthusiasm for his vocation. It might have been endearing had his vocation not involved killing people.

Blue checked the wind. Even at this height, barely more than a whisper. The night was warm. Hundreds of feet below, the London roads and pavements released the heat baked into them all day by the June sun.

"Tomorrow. It's noisy at your end. Go somewhere quieter, will you?"

"Sure. Hang on." Harry didn't baulk at being told what to do. He was too excited.

'Dan' had painted Harry a pretty picture of a massive score, a reputation-establishing haul of drugs worth over fifty million on the street. Soon, Blue had promised, when people talked about Penrose, they would mean Harry, not his father. Jimmy Blue hadn't lied. In about three minutes, Harry's legend would be secure.

Through the binoculars, his quarry walked towards the pool.

Time to act.

Blue climbed the railing and threw himself forwards, away from the building, six hundred feet above the pavement.

As he dropped, he kept his eyes on the target. He fell for two and a half seconds before flinging the bunched-up chute up and away from him. The wing snapped taut and he grabbed the brake toggles, heading towards the river before banking, lining up the rooftop venue to the south-west.

It was a short flight. Thermals from the street conspired to lift the pilot higher, so Blue twisted handfuls of lines in both hands, pulling in the edges of the polyester wing to force it to fall faster.

Fifty yards out, he watched Harry Penrose walk the perimeter of the pool, phone at his ear. Jimmy Blue spoke into his Bluetooth mic. "Everyone will remember your nickname forever, Harry. I promise."

"No kidding, Dan. No fucking kidding."

Twenty yards. Blue slid the flare gun from its holster and fired it across the roof towards the west corner and the firework display. He dropped the gun after firing.

Ten yards. Five.

The fireworks ignited, rockets screaming away from the rooftop into the sky above the Thames. Screams, laughter, a few curses from those who knew they weren't due to go off for another ten minutes.

Harry Penrose looked towards the light show.

Jimmy Blue pulled the D-ring that released the wing, falling the remaining eight feet to the rooftop. He used the momentum of his roll to bring him to his feet, pulling the harpoon gun from his back as he rose.

Harry turned towards him. His initial expression of shock and fear was replaced by a look common at parties. *Where do I know you from? Your face is familiar, but I can't place your name.* Not much use in the current circumstances. Jimmy Blue had many names, and Harry Penrose only knew one of them.

Blue fired as he ran, always in motion. He registered the harpoon piercing his victim's ribcage before wheeling left, accelerating hard. He didn't hesitate at the building's edge, vaulting the rail and dropping out of sight before Harry fell into the pool.

There was no finesse about this second jump. As soon as gravity got the better of his forward momentum and redirected him to the street below, Jimmy Blue released the reserve parachute. The eighteen seconds that followed left him at his most vulnerable, floating across the street towards the mouth of an alleyway. He'd heard the first screams already. Some of the partygoers were capable of ignoring their initial reaction to the bloody sight in the swimming pool. They'd search the area; someone might look his way.

By Blue's calculations, there was a very slim chance someone would witness the end of his escape. If they did, the odds they could do anything about it were low. Even so, Jimmy Blue didn't like the element of luck.

London is an old, cosmopolitan city, its residents resistant to overt displays of surprise or admiration. The handful of onlookers who applauded Blue's appearance at street level, the chute billowing behind him as he landed in a bus stop, were probably tourists.

Ignoring them, Blue turned and pulled in the lines, folding the parachute as he jogged into the alleyway. The van waited at the far end. He opened the door, unclipped the harness and shrugged it off, started the engine, and stuffed the chute into the passenger side footwell.

Turning left onto the main road, the van joined the endless stream of city traffic and became anonymous. Blue smiled, tapping the steering wheel in a percussive accompaniment to the music in his mind.

A good night's work, and a message delivered to Penrose senior.

CHAPTER THREE

THE YOUNG CONSTABLE relayed a message from her radio. "Douglas Penrose is downstairs."

Cunningham's face twisted at the name. He hawked and spat, sending a glob of spittle over the edge of the building. "That arsehole. Can't wait to see his face." He smiled, folded his arms, and leaned against the railing.

"Go home, Cunningham," said Barber.

"No, you're all right. I've arrested Douglas sodding Penrose three times now. Anyone who thinks the criminal justice system works should meet that smug bastard's lawyers. I'll go once I've seen Penrose take a gander at something he can't buy his way out of."

Barber shook her head. "I wasn't asking, Detective Inspector. Today, he's not a suspect; he's a father whose son is dead. Go home. That's an order."

She ignored Cunningham's muttered obscenity as he left.

While she waited for Penrose, Barber considered the evidence so far. A parachute, a harpoon, the sheer audacity of the murder. It was extravagant, theatrical. The killer wasn't just doing a job, he was showboating.

A connection tickled the edge of her mind. Nothing solid, not yet, but a connection.

To Barber, the flutter of excitement that woke her in the early hours, or caused her stomach to tighten when she examined a crime scene, had nothing to do with instinct, and everything to do with deductive intelligence. Her methodical approach, her exhaustive interviews of witnesses, her willingness to go back over old cases again and again, paid dividends. Not immediately, but when the connections became clear and answers arrived, they were always worth waiting for. To stop fellow officers looking at her like she was a different species, she learned to call it 'listening to my gut'.

Her gut was talking now. It was telling her she'd already seen this killer's work. She'd seen it in the report from Paris after Rhoda Ilích was thrown from the top of the Montparnasse Tower. She'd seen it at Robert Winter's home after the massacre which numbered paid killer John Strickland among the dead. Winter hadn't escaped for long, dying of multiple gunshot wounds in the Caribbean weeks later. His human trafficking organisation collapsed in the months that followed, and what remained of Winter's crew were picked off in a series of brutal attacks.

When all the evidence pointed to a single assailant being responsible for the slaughter at Winter's house, Barber had started digging. Her gut led her to one of her own DIs: Debbie Capelli. Capelli had pursued Winter for her entire career like a dog chasing a rat, but shortly after the bloodbath at his Elstree house, she disappeared. She resurfaced on England's east coast with a bullet in her leg, and a house full of dead mercenaries. Capelli chose keeping her silence over keeping her job. She was protecting someone behind her convenient amnesia.

Barber's senior officers had steered her away from pursuing the lone vigilante theory. If he even existed, he had done them a favour. Why waste scarce police resources trying to find him?

Barber's gut told her why: this was the same killer. Another criminal organisation, another flamboyant murder. She'd listen to Doug

Penrose. Then she'd have a good dig through Debbie Capelli's old case notes.

———

Douglas Penrose, tall and lean, had the bland features popular in nineteen-eighties American soaps. Barber had never seen him wear anything other than a suit. Tonight's was dark blue. Grey shirt, no tie.

Barber waved the forensic team away before Penrose arrived. She intended to give the man some privacy. Not too much, though. She shared Cunningham's distaste for Penrose. Allowing him up here had little to do with compassion.

Penrose nodded at her as he crossed the rooftop towards the pool. He had been around plenty of death. Although never charged with any crime, it was no secret that Douglas Penrose controlled the flow of heroin and cocaine in the city. Barber's police career began at the same time Penrose tightened his grip on the capital's illegal drug trade. She had set her sights on bringing him down. His name had been on her list of those whose money and connections bought them immunity. With Robert Winter dead, Penrose jumped to the top of that list.

Barber wondered if that suave, unflappable facade would crack when Douglas Penrose saw his son's corpse. He shouldn't be at the crime scene at all. No doubt Cunningham would report this departure from procedure. But grief made people's behaviour unpredictable, and she wanted to be close when Penrose saw his harpooned son. Twenty years ago, such a cynical ploy would have horrified her. Not now. Successfully closing investigations trumped sympathy. Sympathy didn't catch criminals.

She gave Penrose some space while he stared down at his son's corpse. Barber counted the seconds. She hadn't reached ten when Penrose turned away and walked to the west edge of the rooftop, beyond the pool, looking over the edge, scanning the building and the street below. His people must have given their boss an account of the night's events. Doubtless, it would be more detailed than the bare minimum shared with the police. Interesting that his first thought was to check the view.

Barber joined him at the rail. Neither of them spoke for a while. She had interrogated hundreds of suspects. Some needed leading, some required a soft, friendly touch. Others needed to be bullied into giving up information. None of this would work on Penrose, but he hadn't left yet. He must have something to say.

"He was a vicious, cruel, stupid bastard. But he was my son. Someone will pay for this."

Barber kept her face still. She didn't turn to look at Penrose. He sighed.

"His mother was a Catholic. Did you know that?"

"No."

"The first few times Harry got in trouble, she didn't tell me. At primary school, they called her in because he bullied the other kids. She hid it from me. Ashamed of him, I think. When he was in his teens it got worse. I paid off some girl he knocked about on a school trip. Mary believed she was being punished. By God. For marrying me."

Penrose worked his jaw like he was chewing gristle. "When I let Harry work for me, she said I was enabling him. But I was just keeping him where I could see him. Even then, he fucked up. All the time. Every job I gave him, he acted like he was in a bloody gangster film. Beating people up, threatening their families. He didn't have a fucking clue. Then this thing with the harpoon. Stupid bastard. That first guy he..."

Even off the record, there were things Penrose wouldn't say. Barber remembered Harpoon Harry's first kill. A sixteen-year-old dealer, way down the food chain, who hadn't shown Harry the deference he thought he deserved.

"His mother..." Penrose stopped again. He scanned the skyline, gripped the rail with both hands. His face was impassive, but his knuckles whitened and his breaths, she noted, were shorter. "His mother heard about that before me. You remember."

Barber remembered. Mary Penrose didn't take the news of her

son's graduation from bully to murderer well. She hanged herself in the garden.

Penrose looked away from the view and faced her.

"He may have been a liability, but he was my flesh and blood. All I had left of Mary. Now I have nothing. I want the fucker who did this. But I'm a realist, Barber. You know that."

He was in a talkative mood. Barber saw no reason to interrupt and spoil it.

"I'll cooperate with your investigation. And if I find him before you do..."

He didn't have to finish his sentence. But a man like Penrose would never willingly help the police. She looked again at his hands gripping the rail, and her gut provided another insight. Douglas Penrose was fighting to keep control, but not because he was angry. He was afraid.

Barber's stomach muscles tightened. She couldn't stop herself from speaking this time. "Harry isn't the first, is he?"

Penrose looked at her, considered his answer, then nodded and looked back out across the waking city.

"I thought it was a joke. A note on my car, under the wiper. I forgot about it. Then people started dying. Those gang skirmishes in the estates."

Barber nodded. Deaths of North London drug gang members had been up recently. Clashes weren't uncommon, but these were particularly bloody.

"There were notes on the bodies. Same as the one on my car."

Barber was already there. She remembered the note at Marty Nicholson's murder, the first of Winter's organisation to die. She could picture it. Then Penrose said the words.

"Jimmy Blue is coming."

CHAPTER FOUR

BARBER ARRIVED at the sushi bar fifteen minutes late. It wasn't a power play. She'd fired Capelli months ago. Both women understood who held the power in their relationship. No. She wanted her former subordinate to sweat. Give Capelli time to wonder if Barber had something on her. Which she did.

The sushi place hugged a corner in Soho. Small, glass-fronted, all bright lights and white surfaces. Barber stood at the top of the Underground steps and looked across the street, knowing she couldn't be seen in the shadows.

Capelli was sitting at the long bench in the window, dipping raw fish into a bowl of soy sauce, a paperback in her other hand. Barber smiled. If Capelli was panicking, her body language and choice of seat suggested the opposite. She knew her old boss too well.

Capelli didn't respond when Barber stood at her elbow.

"Hello, Capelli. Let's sit at a table."

Best to reaffirm who was in charge. Barber slid onto a seat in the corner without checking to see if the other woman was following. Capelli might be over ten years her senior, but Barber believed in a military-style respect for rank over age. She was the senior officer here.

After a minute, she realised Capelli wasn't coming. She hadn't moved, and was now staring out of the window while sipping green tea. Barber watched her for ten seconds, then stood up. "Fine."

She put a hand on the other woman's shoulder. Capelli glanced up and plucked a Bluetooth bud out of one ear. "Oh, I'm sorry, Maisie. Didn't see you come in. You look tired. Working too hard?"

Maisie? Tired? Working too hard? How dare she? Barber reminded herself that Capelli didn't work for London's police force anymore. Barber's mother saddled her with *Maisie*. She preferred Barber. When pressed, she lied, claiming her first name was Margaret. Barber shook her former subordinate's outstretched hand, forcing a tight smile.

Capelli didn't look like a woman worried about what Barber had described as a 'serious and sensitive matter' on the phone. She looked relaxed. Calm. Happy, even. Well. The results turned up by Barber's investigation would soon change that.

"Let's get some privacy, shall we?" Barber indicated the table.

"Oh. Yes, of course. Tell you what." Capelli tapped her plate with the chopsticks. "I'll finish this, then I'll join you. Won't be long." She replaced the earbud and turned back to her food. Barber bought a coffee, returned to the table, and burned her mouth on the first sip.

Five minutes later, Capelli took the chair opposite. "Hope you don't mind me eating without you. You were late, after all." She put the paperback on the table. *Presumed Innocent.*

Barber wasn't in the mood for games. She took a folder out of her briefcase. "I want to talk to you about Jimmy Blue."

Capelli raised an eyebrow at that. Barber placed the folder on the table.

"And Tom Lewis."

Ah. Better. Microexpressions telegraphed Capelli's shock and dismay.

"What about him?"

"You've protected Lewis since he was twelve years old. Ever since the night his parents were executed."

"So?"

"Hmm." Barber tapped her fingers on the folder. There was no name on the front. She wanted Capelli wondering what was inside. "I've read Lewis's file. Fears of brain damage from the shot to the head. No improvement, even after two decades. During those first few months, you might have hoped he would remember and be your star witness at Robert Winter's trial. But you kept looking out for him years after it became obvious that would never happen. You don't have children of your own, do you?"

Capelli's lips hardened into a thin line. "Oh, spare me the cod psychology, Maisie. I felt sorry for Tom Lewis, of course I did. But he's not a surrogate child. I'm not a desperate, barren woman latching onto some poor basket case who'll be a child forever; I'm a police officer."

"Not any more you're not."

"Thanks to you."

Barber took a sip from her coffee. She'd left it too long now, and it was lukewarm. "Touché."

The first photograph in her folder showed Harry Penrose's body, the harpoon sticking straight up, an exclamation mark at the end of his short, violent life.

Capelli looked at it and shrugged. "I read the papers."

"Jimmy Blue killed him."

Capelli blinked. "Maisie, are you still chasing your theory that one man killed Winter's people? I thought the chief told you to drop it."

That was the problem with ex-police officers. They still had friends inside, telling them things they shouldn't.

"I follow the evidence, Capelli. It led me here. Jimmy Blue is getting more and more brazen. He's out of control."

Capelli pointed at the photograph. "Out of control? Killed the psycho son of the biggest heroin supplier in London in front of forty witnesses and no one saw a thing? Doesn't sound out of control to me." Her hand shook the tiniest bit when she picked up her cup.

"I don't have time for lies, Debbie. I did some digging. About last Christmas. Found a witness and some security camera footage from a service station on the M1."

Capelli became very still and very quiet. Barber pushed the advantage.

"Lewis was with you in Suffolk last year. In the house where you were shot in the leg. On the night four hardened professional killers were picked off by one man. You protected him. It cost you your job. You were lucky to keep your pension."

Capelli didn't bother to deny it. She said nothing for a while. Barber gave her time to think, to wonder how much they knew.

"What are you suggesting, exactly?"

Barber's turn to shrug. "Suggesting? Nothing. I'm telling you what I know."

"Really? Then why are you here? If you believe I've committed a crime, why haven't you arrested me?"

Time to get her on board.

"Because you can help. We're bringing Jimmy Blue in, with you or without you. You can stop it turning into a bloodbath."

"What makes you think—"

"I re-examined the forensic evidence at Winter's house. This time I knew whose DNA to match it to. The hospital freezes blood samples from coma patients, Debbie. For research."

This was a lie, and a risky one with someone as sharp as Capelli. Barber forced herself to breathe normally, and not to speak first. She saw signs of defeat in the lack of eye contact, the almost imperceptible droop of her shoulders.

"I know Tom Lewis is Jimmy Blue," said Barber. She didn't, not in a cast-iron, prove-it-in-court way, but her gut said it was so. And Barber never argued with her gut.

No denial from Capelli.

"I haven't taken this upstairs yet. Our only chance of taking him into custody without violence is to get the help of someone he trusts. Someone he cares about. He saved your life at Christmas, Debbie. Now you can return the favour."

No reaction.

"He'll be treated fairly, I promise. He'll go to prison, there's no avoiding it, but there's clear evidence of diminished responsibility. Severe psychological trauma. He needs treatment, not punishment. But one thing I won't do is leave him on the streets. He's killing people, Debbie. He's been lucky so far, but it's only a matter of time before someone innocent gets hurt. We're going to stop him before that happens. If you're worried about your own involvement, I can guarantee immunity from prosecution, and—"

Capelli sighed. "Stop. Please. Just stop." She took a tissue from her bag and blew her nose, then pressed both fists against the sides of her head and pushed, hissing like a steam iron. Finally, she looked up.

"What do you need me to do?"

CHAPTER FIVE

DEBBIE WALKED three-quarters of a mile to Green Park station, then circled the park, hardly seeing the couples sunning themselves, the children playing, the benches of Eastern European nannies smoking and gossiping while their charges dozed in prams under lacy parasols.

After forty minutes, she took the Piccadilly line to Hammersmith, a five-minute walk from her flat. She used her Oyster card to pay for the journey, touching in and out at the contactless barriers. After turning off her phone and taking out the SIM card , she withdrew a hundred pounds from a cashpoint and used it to take a taxi to Wembley. At a big, anonymous supermarket, she bought a burner phone with five pounds of credit already on it. She found a bench in the shadow of a tree and dialled a memorised number.

"Tom, it's Debbie Capelli. I have to tell you something. It's very important. Can you hear me? Do you need to go somewhere else, or can you listen now?"

The voice that replied was, as always, quiet and tentative. "Mm, yes. I, mm, I can listen. Where, mm, where have you been?"

Debbie had kept her distance from Tom Lewis since the night his alter ego slaughtered four mercenaries in her family home on the Suffolk coast.

"Tom, I'm sorry, but there's no time. I'm not sure if you'll understand, but I need the... the other side of you to hear this. It's really important, Tom. Ok?"

"Mm. Yes. Yes."

"Good. When I hang up, I'll dump this phone, so don't call me back. The police know, Tom. DCI Barber knows about you. About Jimmy Blue. The police are looking for you. You need to get away. Out of the country. You'll never be safe here again. Barber wants me to help catch you. She doesn't know I'm calling. From now on, you can't trust me. If I call you again, or send you a message from my usual phone, it'll be because I'm working with the police. If I say I want to meet, it will be a trap. It will be a trap, and the police will be there to arrest you. Do you understand that, Tom? Do you understand what I'm telling you?"

"A trap. Mm."

Tom's voice remained a colourless monotone. Debbie had little idea of his current level of comprehension. When she had spent time with him at Christmas, Tom's intelligence had fluctuated. Sometimes, he grasped concepts quickly; at others, he struggled to understand the most basic ideas. In hindsight, Debbie suspected Tom faded when his alter ego was near the surface. In which case, was Jimmy Blue listening now?

"Yes. A trap. They'll put you in prison. Please, Tom, leave the country. Please."

An Indian family walked past her, their toddler smiling from the pushchair. Debbie turned away, hunching to hide her face, waiting until they were out of earshot.

"I won't be able to call again, Tom. I won't be able to see you. Don't forget, if you hear from me, it will be because I am working with the police. From now on, treat me like I've betrayed you."

"Betrayed?"

"Yes." Debbie stood up. She pictured Jimmy Blue in her parents' house in Pakefield, the night he had shown her who he really was. A cold predator with no compunction, no empathy. She looked around. There was no one in sight. She hissed into the phone.

"If you can hear me, Blue, get out. Save Tom. I don't give a shit what you're trying to do to Penrose and his people. I only care about Tom, and you're going to get him killed. Get out, please. Please!"

Debbie pulled the phone apart and removed the SIM card. Her vision blurred with tears, but she kept moving, not wanting to draw any attention. She put the battery in one bin, the phone in another, and dropped the snapped SIM into a duck pond. Then she took a taxi to Earl's Court, again paying cash.

From there she walked home to her flat in Hammersmith. She had no idea if she'd done enough.

CHAPTER SIX

BARBER'S OFFICE had no view to speak of. It looked out across a side street to the brick wall of a neighbouring building.

She looked from the window to the clock. Eight minutes past ten. The briefing began in twenty-two minutes, and the operation would be over before lunch.

In the three weeks since confronting Debbie Capelli, Barber had thrown herself and her team into finding out as much as possible about Tom Lewis. She didn't just want to know where he lived, where he worked, where he ate, any pets, associates, friends, or lovers; she wanted everything from the moment he was shot in the head twenty years ago until he gatecrashed Harry Penrose's party with a parachute and a harpoon gun.

There were still some dissenting voices regarding Lewis's involvement with the Penrose murder, but Barber had steamrolled the investigation to this stage. If she hadn't actually burned bridges, she'd certainly lit fires under a couple. She had pushed her theory about Lewis, Jimmy Blue, and his one-man murder spree as far as it could go. Fail now, and her career might never recover. Succeed, and she could write her own ticket.

The results of the investigation sat in a thick folder. Barber was no technophobe, but when it came to assembling evidence, pulling threads together, and making connections that others might have missed, she liked hard copies. Photographs, reports, statements—she spread them across her desk, pinned them on cork boards, and carried them around the room while she was thinking. You couldn't do that on a computer screen.

She drummed her fingers on the folder, staring through the window at the familiar brick wall.

The investigation had been one of the most frustrating of her career. This close to an arrest, Barber usually knew the prime suspect better than her close family members—of whom there were few—or friends—of whom there were fewer. Not this time. Tom Lewis was still a stranger to her. He'd been in a coma aged twelve, followed by a long, painful, slow recovery relearning basic functions like feeding himself, walking, or going to the toilet without help. Speech returned much later, but never completely. Medical reports showed Lewis's mental recovery to be been partial. A senior neurologist put his intellect on par with an average six-year-old. All of which tallied with DI Capelli's regular reports.

Barber leaned forward until her forehead touched the thick glass, three floors above the pavement. London's microclimate had produced a hot, dry summer, and the cyclists who used the side street as a cut-through were red-faced and sweating.

According to the medical evidence, Tom Lewis was incapable of anything more taxing than a game of snakes and ladders. But no one had a better motive to kill Winter and his crew. Revenge, after twenty years of waiting.

Barber flipped open the folder, turning to the section that frustrated her the most. The missing years. Seven of them. Tom Lewis left a job on a building site and, instead of going to the agency for another minimum-wage labouring job, vanished. Completely. Not a single trace remained on record of where he was or what he was doing between the age of twenty and twenty-seven. Fill in that gaping hole, Barber suspected, and everything else would fall into place. She certainly hoped so.

Maybe he was planning another vanishing act. Lewis hadn't been seen since a temporary warehouse job at Christmas. His bank account, containing seventy-four pounds, hadn't been touched. He hadn't signed on with any job agencies. He was a six-foot-three, broad, bald hulk of a man with a big ridge of scar tissue on his head. You'd think someone would remember him, but apparently not. He was a ghost. Sending the most recent photograph they had of Lewis to police stations around the city unearthed a grand total of one potential sighting, from a Hounslow post office employee. Not that it mattered now.

Twenty-seven minutes past. Barber straightened, drank a glass of water, focused on what came next. She would get her answers soon enough. In another three hours, Jimmy Blue would be in custody, and London would be a safer place.

———

The briefing room hummed with conversation and off-colour jokes. The adrenaline always pumped before a big operation. Some officers became more chatty, spoke more loudly. Others retreated into a tense silence. All were affected, even those who'd learned to hide it.

Capelli was in the latter group. She'd found a seat at the back and was using her visitor pass as a bookmark. Barber noted it was a different crime novel to the one Capelli brought to the sushi bar. She glimpsed the title and frowned. *A Big Boy Did It And Ran Away.*

A few officers clustered around their ex-colleague, and there were plenty of smiles, which faded along with the general buzz of conversations when Barber walked in. Capelli had been a popular DI. Barber caught her eye and waved her forward to the front of the room. Behind them, a photograph of Tom Lewis from a cleaning job ID photo stared out at the police officers.

"Good morning. I'll keep this short. You all know what you have to do today. Just a reminder to be on your guard. We don't know what to expect. You all remember Deborah Capelli. As Tom Lewis's liaison with witness protection, DI Capelli knows more about him than any of us. Debbie?"

Barber took a half step back. Capelli kept it short and succinct. This wasn't her first briefing.

"Tom Lewis is thirty-two years old. His mental capacity is that of a child, due to the brain trauma he suffered aged twelve. He finds speaking difficult, he avoids eye contact, his speech is slow and his vocabulary poor. He's easily confused, so make sure you clearly state what you're doing when you approach him. Please. He won't run if you don't scare him."

"Sorry, Miss." Detective Sergeant Sharon Tisley was the class clown. "Isn't this the bloke that's been doing all the murdering? Shouldn't we be the scared ones?"

Barber quelled the chuckles with a raised hand. "The evidence suggests there's another personality, one Lewis has concealed for the past twenty years. When he's Tom—which is most of the time—he presents no threat. You read the briefing document?"

"I did," said Capelli "It was a bit light on background."

Barber feared she might blush. She felt the colour rise in her cheeks, but willed it to subside. "Someone capable of hiding a second personality for twenty years can also cover his tracks. Thank you, Detective Inspector." She waited until Capelli had returned to her seat.

Another voice from the back. "These murders you reckon he's responsible for; drug dealers, human traffickers, rapists, right?" DI Cunningham spoke with his hands in his pockets, chewing gum. His entire demeanour projected lack of respect. His transfer couldn't come a day too soon.

"I'm sorry, Detective Inspector. Did you have a question? Is there something you don't understand?"

"Yeah. I think there is. I don't understand why we're arresting him." He waved the briefing document. "Not much in here that warrants an arrest. Even if you find enough evidence to charge him, I don't know why you'd bother. If he offed Harry Penrose, we should get him knighted. At the very least, take him out for a drink. I'll chip in."

This little speech might have prompted a round of applause with another DCI in charge. Not Barber, though.

"Cunningham, if you have no respect for the law, might I suggest a change of career rather than a transfer? Something low-skilled, perhaps."

He coloured, and when he looked around for support, no one offered it. Good. Barber left a long enough gap to make him uncomfortable.

"DI Capelli texted the suspect two days ago to arrange this morning's meeting." She glanced across at Capelli's stony expression. "Stick to the brief and this should be straightforward. However, if Tom Lewis is the criminal known as Jimmy Blue—and circumstantial evidence strongly suggests he is—he may resist arrest. Be prepared for trouble."

At her side, Capelli shot her a look. Barber remembered the lie about matching Lewis's DNA to the killings. And she'd just admitted the evidence was circumstantial. Oh, well. She was already off Capelli's Christmas card list after forcing her into early retirement; they were hardly about to become confidantes now. She scanned the room, making eye contact with individual members of the team.

"Harry Penrose's killer is someone capable of putting together an audacious, intricate plan. He's also capable of lethal physical violence. He worked his way through Robert Winter's organisation with explosives, guns, knives, and his bare hands. We will not underestimate him. Which is why we have been joined by seven specialist firearms officers for this morning's operation."

Capelli's shoulders stiffened. Barber pointed at members of the armed team. "Jones, Devon, and Ahujah will cover the street from neighbouring roofs. If Lewis produces a weapon, they will shoot. Hollett and McMahon will be in a van parked outside the cafe. Bradford and Welton will cover the rear exit. Beta team, you're inside, at the back by the window, occupying the three tables nearest to Capelli's booth. We won't move in until Lewis sits opposite you. Are we all clear?"

Nods, grunts, a couple of thumbs up.

"Good. Let's go."

CHAPTER SEVEN

DEBBIE LOOKED through the window towards the Thames, which carried its usual mixed traffic of river buses, rowing boats, and working vessels. On the wide path between the cafe and the water, tourists and locals passed, the former taking selfies and buying over-priced ice cream, the latter walking fast, often barking into a phone. Many of them used Bluetooth earbuds with phones now. When Debbie started her police career, people walking around the city talking to themselves usually had a bottle of booze in their pocket rather than a phone, but now half of London did it.

She scanned the faces, but none of them were Tom's. Underneath the table, her hands curled into claws, and she dug her nails into her palms, keeping her face calm, her breaths even. She had done all she could. Her call to Tom meant he wouldn't come, wouldn't respond to the message Barber forced her to send.

Tom. I need to see you urgently. Meet me at the Putney Bridge cafe Wednesday morning at 11:30. Debbie.

She pictured Tom listening to his phone app's expressionless voice read the message aloud. There was a reason she usually called rather than texted. "Not this time," had been Barber's response. The DCI didn't trust Debbie, thought she might slip in some coded warning. She didn't know that horse had already bolted.

Tom's reply had been the letter Y. He knew Y and N, and used them to reply to messages, proud of his ability to understand what they stood for.

That was forty-eight hours ago. Two sleepless nights of wondering if Jimmy Blue was conscious of everything Tom experienced, if he would remember her call.

Surely he wouldn't show up.

She sipped her coffee without tasting it. The plainclothes Beta team were old hands, good at their job. Six of them occupied three tables between her and the main door. They chatted and laughed as naturally as if they were there to gossip and eat granola bars. Through the glass at the front of the cafe, the van with armed officers remained on double yellow lines. Out of sight on neighbouring rooftops, three telescopic lenses watched the street.

What if Tom didn't understand? What if the signal had been bad when she warned him and he hadn't heard her properly? What if Jimmy Blue had become more dominant, and had turned up anyway, arrogantly certain he could elude any trap?

What if? Over thirty years' police work taught her that *what ifs* were only useful in the office. In the field, they were counterproductive. She was here now, a pawn in Barber's operation. She could do nothing to save Tom Lewis if he ignored her warning and turned up.

One of the plainclothes raised a finger, her earpiece concealed by hair normally pulled back into a ponytail. Barber hadn't offered Debbie an earpiece.

The officer spoke quietly and calmly. "Possible suspect, two hundred metres. No weapon spotted."

She listened again to her earpiece. "A hundred and fifty metres. A hundred metres. He's the right build, right height. Bald male. Wait. Confirmed. Scarring on head. It's him. It's Lewis. Sit down."

It took a second for Debbie to realise the last comment was directed at her. She looked in confusion at the plainclothes officer.

"Oh." She sat down. And kept her eyes on the van containing two armed officers prepared to use lethal force. She willed the door to stay shut, at the same time listening for the crack of sniper fire. Debbie's hands stayed flat on the table to stop them shaking. She didn't breathe.

When the door of the cafe opened, she didn't take her eyes off the van. In the corner of her vision, a figure approached her booth. She looked up. Barber.

"We got him," said the Detective Chief Inspector. "He didn't put up a fight. Didn't say a word. Got into the car as meek as a lamb."

Debbie was on her feet again. "He'll be confused by what's happening to him. I'll come in with you, talk to him. He's far more likely to cooperate if I'm there. I'm the closest thing to a friend Tom has."

"No." Barber dismissed her plea with a brisk shake of the head. Debbie recognised the gesture. No point arguing. Barber caught her eye for a moment.

"If we need more information, we'll call. You'll be a key witness at trial. Any contact between the two of you might prejudice our case."

Barber addressed the officers sitting at the nearby tables, scowling at one stuffing the last mouthful of a chocolate brownie into his face. "Back to base. Lots of work to do."

She waited while they filed out, looking at Debbie. "You were the best DI on the team, you know. Such a shame you threw it all away."

As she walked away, Debbie thought of Tom on his way to a cell. He wouldn't have an alibi for any of the crimes, and they could get their DNA evidence now. It was over. Barber was right. She'd thrown her career away for nothing.

CHAPTER EIGHT

THE MEWS HOUSE in Islington remained Douglas Penrose's secret, a bolt-hole away from work. He still owned the family home in Highgate, but, since Mary's suicide, spent little time there. He ran the drugs business from his property development offices in Hampstead. The business wasn't just a front. Some years, profits from buying and selling land in the city outpaced the heroin trade.

The doorbell rang as he was about to warm the brown powder on a square of foil in his office. He always warned new recruits in his organisation that if they started taking the product, they were out. And 'out' meant your body ending up in the foundations of one of Penrose Properties' sites. He inhaled his first nostrilful of heroin smoke the day of Mary's funeral. Since then, it had become more regular than he liked to admit.

A screen gave him a view of the street. A delivery guy, open-faced crash helmet, with a rectangular box in his hand.

"Yes?"

On-screen, the man—short, overweight, scruffy—jumped, then pressed the intercom. "Hello? Delivery. It needs signing for."

"Well, I'm in the bath. Leave it on the step."

"Um, I'm supposed to get a signature. You have to be over eighteen."

"Do I sound like a teenager to you, you half-witted pissant?"

"Er, well, no, but I'm supposed—"

"I don't give two shits what you're supposed to do, you brain-dead arsehole. Leave it on my sodding step or I'll have someone come round to your depot and stick your stupid fat face through a wall. And don't for one second think that I'm joking."

Even on the grainy screen, Penrose saw sweat on the courier's face. The man wiped his brow, left the box on the doorstep, and backed away.

"Jesus." Leaning over the screen, Penrose watched the courier ride off. His already low stock of patience was definitely running short of late.

He opened the door, took the box back to his desk. There was a card attached.

Our mutual problem is in police custody. Stand down.
Maisie Barber

Maisie? Penrose pictured the Detective Chief Inspector. Maisie? Like naming a Rottweiler Buttercup.

So they'd nabbed Lewis. Not too surprising. Maisie—he snorted to himself—had a reputation for getting results. He'd been forced to tighten his own procedures during her climb through the ranks. The smart money was on her becoming Commissioner. An un-bribable officer in charge of the Met could make life difficult. A problem for another day. In the meantime, Tom Lewis was in a cell. There would be a trial, then prison. And London's prisons held lots of very bad men who owed Douglas Penrose a favour.

He opened the box. Cognac—a good one, too. Before Penrose had developed a liking for H, cognac had been his only weakness.

He poured himself a decent measure. Cognac with a heroin chaser. Oblivion for a few hours. It sounded good.

Back in his office, he took a sip. Smooth, rich, almost buttery. Harry had never shared his taste for the finer things in life. His only son employed tequila and cocaine to maintain optimum obnoxiousness at all times. Penrose would never admit it to another living soul, but he didn't miss his son. In many ways, Harry's death was a relief.

Barber didn't pick up when he called. He left a message.

"It's Douglas Penrose. Well done. Never thought I'd say that to a copper, but there you go. Strange times. Thanks for the cognac. Didn't think that was your style. Or are you just showing off that you know where my second home is? Either way."

He had trouble enunciating the last couple of words. His lips were numb.

He sat at his desk, downed the rest of the glass, and poured another. It wasn't a great idea to mix H and alcohol. This second glass would be his last.

He spilled the third sip. His mouth tingled now, like anaesthetic wearing off after a trip to the dentist. He licked his lips, but couldn't feel his tongue. The warmth of the cognac in his throat became painful, as if he had swallowed boiling water.

When he tried to stand, Penrose gasped. If a blunt blade had begun peeling strips of flesh away from his thighs, he doubted it would have been more painful.

Poison.

Penrose became very still. He knew a little about poison. Any physical exertion would increase the speed it spread around his body. As counter-intuitive as it sounded, he had to relax. He allowed his body to slump back into the chair, tried to slow his breathing and ignore the flares of pain from his arms and legs. His throat was burning now, each breath dragged across raw flesh.

The phone. He reached for it, cradling the handset, not trusting his fingers to grip it. Penrose leaned forward a fraction to see the screen, grunting with pain.

His throat closed like a Venus flytrap on its prey. Each thin breath produced a horrible whistle. He moved his thumb over the phone, peering through a blur of involuntary tears.

9

The pressure of his thumb against the glass was sandpaper

rubbed on an open wound. Penrose didn't have the luxury of howling, but the whistle of his breath rose a few tones.

9

Snot ran from his nose to his lips. As it passed through his nasal passages, it burned like acid. Penrose pictured his nose peeling apart like rotten fruit. He wept with the pain.

9

Call

His finger hovered over the button. It wasn't that he couldn't feel his extremities, rather that they'd been doused in acid, crushed, and set on fire.

Call

He couldn't do it. He couldn't press the button. He *had* to. With every ounce of his will, Penrose forced his finger onto the glass screen.

The whistling stuttered and died away. His throat refused another breath, and his hands became claws as he clutched at his throat, scratching away the skin in blind panic, blood running down into his chest hair.

Penrose had watched people die, sometimes speculating about their last thoughts, and wondering what his own might be. He would never have guessed at this: no thought at all, no realisation, no regret, just a desperate need to cling to life as it receded beyond his reach.

"Emergency services, which service do you require? Hello? Hello?"

CHAPTER NINE

DEBBIE CAPELLI, if asked, described herself as a social drinker. She liked the blurring of inhibitions alcohol could induce in situations that might otherwise have been awkward. At heart an introvert, she found happiness with a good book and a cup of tea, but police work brought its fair share of unavoidable social occasions. A big glass of rosé could make the most tedious evening bearable.

Tonight was different. Tonight's approach to drinking might be described as *antisocial drinking*. Debbie sat outside an overpriced wine bar within sight of Olympia's great glass roof. The evening was warm, and she picked a table in a roped-off area separating this particular purveyor of indifferent Sauvignon Blanc from its neighbour. After the first couple of glasses, the enterprising waitress checked back regularly, ready for the next top-up.

For years, Debbie watched colleagues turn to alcohol as an escape route, its temporary comfort coming with a significant downside. Every officer had a point at which they couldn't cope. For some, it was seeing their first body, particularly a child. For others, it was being at the receiving end of an outburst of vitriol and hatred aimed at the uniform they wore. For most, though, it wasn't one incident; rather the rhythmic tide of stress crashing against their defences day after day, month after month, year after year, until they had all but worn away.

Debbie considered herself stronger than those who succumbed to binge drinking on days off. She had congratulated herself on having the kind of stolid, down to earth personality able to cope with the knocks without letting it get to her. Now she knew the truth.

She ordered another glass and toasted the philanthropists behind the police pension scheme. Without it, plus the income that now came in from letting her parents' old house, she wouldn't be able to live in London, let alone afford to get drunk.

When she'd arrived at the bar, she watched passers-by, making up stories to keep her mind busy. The man carrying an umbrella on a cloudless evening was a spy. The two women huddled together on the bench had been best friends since school. Married to men they met in their twenties, their children now grown up, they were only now acknowledging the fact that they belonged together. The group of loud twenty-somethings were rehearsing a show for the Edinburgh Fringe.

The attempt at distraction worked for a while. Ten, twenty minutes, perhaps. Debbie lost track of time. She looked away from the busy street when every third face became Tom Lewis, his open, trusting features twisted into an expression of hurt shock.

"Another." Debbie only realised she had shouted when the waitress gave her the unmistakable look restaurant and bar workers reserve for problem customers. Debbie held her hands up in apology. "Last one. I have to go soon." It was nearly dark.

The waitress brought the bill and a keypad with the glass, and Debbie was surprised she could hold the credit card steady long enough for the device to recognise it.

When she got to her feet, she did so carefully, ready to grab the back of the chair should her legs refuse to cooperate. To her surprise, she weaved between the tables and turned towards home without incident. She even remembered her jacket and bag. She walked with the exaggerated care of a drunk, already regretting the stupid attempt at a quick fix.

Why had Tom turned up today? Didn't he understand her warning? Was the other side of his personality separate, unable to respond? It made no sense. No sense at all. Her mind kept plucking the same few seconds and replaying them. Barber walking up to the table, that neutral expression on her face, so bloody professional, not gloating.

We got him.

And that was that. Twenty years of protecting Tom Lewis ended with those three words.

We got him.

How the hell would Tom cope with being locked up? What would happen if the judge made no allowances for his limited mental capacity and sent him to a standard prison? His fellow inmates would soon know who he was. Who he had killed. They would line up for the chance to execute Jimmy Blue.

Behind an industrial bin at the side of a restaurant, Debbie crouched and vomited, over and over, until nothing was left other than acidic bile. Shaking and sweating, she bought a litre of water at a news stand and drank half of it between big, gasping breaths, leaning against a traffic light, crying. Pedestrians swerved away from her. She watched their feet as they passed. She wasn't making up stories about them now.

It was just over a mile back to her flat. Debbie could have called an Uber, or found a taxi rank, but she walked it. It gave her body a chance to recover and pump some oxygen through her bloodstream. And it delayed the inevitable moment when she opened her front door, picked up the post, slumped on the sofa. Just like any other day. Except this was the day she had handed Tom Lewis to the police. He would spend the rest of his life in prison or a high-security mental hospital.

Her flat was on the top floor of a three-storey Victorian terrace converted during the eighties. She had to pause on the first floor landing to get her breath. The inevitable headache made its presence known with a gentle throb already threatening to become far less benign. There were paracetamol and ibuprofen in the kitchen. Two of each, another pint of water, and perhaps tomorrow morning wouldn't be the horror show she deserved.

Inside, she dropped her bag and jacket on the floor, kicking the door closed behind her. She didn't turn on the kitchen lights, instead using the spot over the hob to find a glass and pills. She swallowed them, drained the glass, then refilled it.

After a pee which seemed to last ten minutes, during which time she nearly dozed off, Debbie kicked off her trousers, didn't bother with her blouse, and shuffled into the bedroom in the dark. She placed the glass on the table, sat down, swung her legs onto the bed, and sank back onto the cool pillow.

From the deepest darkness in the corner of her room, a large shape moved forward.

She didn't scream, but made a kind of choking, gasping sound of fear and disbelief.

"Hello, Debbie."

CHAPTER TEN

BARBER SNAPPED AWAKE, as if someone had slapped her. She twisted sideways to look at the clock.

03:47.

She slipped out of bed, went to the bathroom, and splashed cold water onto her face before gargling mouthwash.

Back in the bedroom, she dressed, brushed her short hair, and grabbed her car keys. She rarely drove, only keeping a car for times like this, when she needed to get into New Scotland Yard fast and didn't want to wait for a patrol car.

Most colleagues would describe her actions as 'acting on a hunch'. While she slept, Barber's subconscious had turned over pieces of information, weighing one against the other, and reached a conclusion it had yet to share with her waking mind.

Barber drove without thinking. She knew the signs of an oncoming epiphany. Experience told her it was pointless to force it.

Tom Lewis had been in custody for over twelve hours and was yet to utter a word. He looked at people when they spoke to him, his expression neither sullen nor uncooperative. If he understood what was happening, he gave no sign. He checked the clock regularly and accepted cups of tea and coffee without comment.

He was, Barber had to admit, somewhat of a disappointment, considering the flamboyance and brutality of his crimes. Perhaps his silence was calculated to see him through the thirty-six hours before they had to charge him. Barber had applied for an extension to ninety-six hours, long enough to get the DNA report back, and compare it to what they'd taken from Robert Winter's house last Christmas.

She waved her pass at the New Scotland Yard's front desk fourteen minutes after leaving home. In the lift, she pressed the button for the basement.

Officially, New Scotland Yard boasted it had no cells. Prisoners were locked up in other police stations, Paddington mostly. Unofficially, the building housed a small suite of cells, enough for four prisoners. Useful when discretion was required. Barber interviewed a prominent member of parliament there a year ago after a fraud accusation which, if proved, might have brought down the government.

At basement level, she nodded at the officer on duty, whose eyes widened at seeing her back again. She pretended not to notice the game he had been playing on his phone.

"Prisoner asleep?"

"Yes, ma'am."

"Let's wake him up, shall we?"

The young officer—Ronson? Ransome?—slid the phone off the table and into his pocket. "Of course, ma'am." He called over his shoulder, and a second police officer joined them. Both men were six-footers and played rugby at weekends. The prisoner, other than his silence, may have been cooperative, but underestimating Jimmy Blue would be foolish.

The first officer led the way to a self-contained set of rooms. Each cell had a bed, desk and chair, television, radio, and an adjoining toilet and shower room. Another good reason for keeping them secret; Barber could imagine the newspaper headlines if they found out the Met kept suspects in humane, even comfortable, conditions.

As the only prisoner, Lewis had the first cell. A screen outside showed the interior. A touch of a button switched the view to the camera in the en suite. Comfortable, yes; private, no.

Barber flicked the light switch and watched the screen as it flicked between night vision and standard view. Lewis turned over, blinked, looked around him, then up at the clock above the door. Barber had seen him do the same thing through his interviews. She checked her own watch. Four-fifteen.

"Why keep looking at the time?" she murmured at the screen. "You got an appointment?"

The prisoner sat up and placed a hand on the scars that ridged his scalp. His ankles were cuffed. He would have to hold his hands through a slot in the door and allow them to be cuffed before being allowed out. Lewis looked at the door. Was he smiling?

"Bring him through."

In the interview room, Barber waited while the two officers secured Lewis's feet to the chair—screwed onto the floor—and his hands to the table.

"Hello again, Mr Lewis." He didn't respond. "For the benefit of the recording, this is Detective Chief Inspector Barber." She waited while her fellow officers followed her lead for the microphones and cameras.

The silence that followed the routine opening remarks stretched on for a minute. Lewis stared at the table. The two officers looked at the prisoner, occasionally shooting nervous glances towards the DCI.

Barber waited for her subconscious to supply the answer. It had woken her at this hour, brought her back here. She'd woken the suspect and had him brought to an interview room. The cameras were watching, the microphones listening. But she had nothing. The expected revelation remained hidden; unreachable.

Barber pulled out a chair and sat opposite the suspect. The minutes ticked by. The two officers said nothing. Lewis either looked down at the table or up at the clock. He didn't acknowledge Barber.

She, in contrast, stared at him openly. Stared, but didn't see the man in front of her. Not really. She free-associated paragraphs of reports, photographs of bodies, CCTV footage of Capelli walking Lewis to her car on Christmas Day. He had been barefoot. Then a series of snapshots from yesterday. The arrest itself, low-key, undramatic, a compliant Lewis allowing himself to be hurried away from the cafe door and into the back of a waiting patrol car. Back at base, Lewis with no personal possessions to hand over. No phone, no bank cards, no ID, nothing. Not even a watch. No cash to pay for his coffee. As if he knew he wouldn't need it. Fingerprints, DNA swab, then down to the cell. Lewis nodding or shaking his head, but saying nothing.

The prisoner yawned and folded his fingers together on the table.

"Ah," said Barber. It was the first word she'd spoken since giving her name eleven minutes ago, and Lewis looked up. She leaned forward and took his hand as if they'd just been introduced.

"Ma'am," warned one officer, but she waved him away. She turned the prisoner's hand over and looked at his palm, pressing the pads of his fingers between her own before examining his nails.

Barber sat back, put her face in her hands for a count of five, then swivelled to face the first officer.

"Notebook."

It was in his hand almost immediately, pencil poised.

"Put out an All Ports Warning for Tom Lewis. I want his description everywhere. He knows we're onto him, and he's proven to be resourceful, so I doubt he'll risk a commercial flight. Send the photograph we have on file from his last job."

The officer's eyes flicked from Barber to the prisoner. "But, ma'am,"

"Now. Go."

The man flinched. "Yes, ma'am. Um." He swallowed. "I'll need to get another officer down first to replace me."

"I know the regulations, constable. It's commendable that you don't want to leave your colleagues alone with such a dangerous prisoner. But did your brain engage, at any level, with what you just wrote?"

Judging by his blank expression, the officer seemed unlikely to be fast-tracked to detective.

Barber stood up, looked at the camera. "Tom Lewis is a manual labourer. His employment history shows he has frequently worked on building sites."

She pointed at Lewis. "The suspect's hands and fingers are soft. No cracks, no broken nails, no evidence of doing anything more taxing than filling out a form."

The prisoner was staring at her, as were both officers. The one with the notebook frowned.

"Oh, for God's sake." Barber walked round the table and stood next to the prisoner. The two guards blanched.

"Ma'am, you really shouldn't... please step away from the... oh."

Like peeling away a scab, Barber pulled at the edge of the mass of scarring on the bald man's head. For a horrible moment, she thought she was wrong. Then, with an obscene sucking sound, the whole piece lifted under her fingernails and came away.

The two onlookers swore at the same moment, inadvertently creating a new word.

"Shuckit."

She tossed the rubber scar onto the table and glared at the stupefied officer, his notebook held in front of him like a priest brandishing a crucifix at a vampire.

"Why are you still here?"

The man ran for the door.

"Wait." He half-turned, his hand on the doorknob. "Send a car to bring in Deborah Capelli. Her details are on file."

She turned back to the handcuffed man. "Start talking. If you don't, rest assured I will make sure you go to prison."

The man looked at the fake scar on the desk, at the clock on the wall, then back at Barber. He smiled.

"Hello." He pointed at himself. "My name am Mikail from Russia. I am apologise, no English."

It was Barber's turn to offer no response. The man tried again.

"Mikail. Russia. Mikail. Hello. Er... what are you?"

"Me?" Barber clenched her fists. "I'm an idiot."

CHAPTER ELEVEN

DEBBIE WAS on the M40 and ten miles out of the city before most commuters were eating breakfast.

She had a bottle of water in the cupholder, and took regular sips. As the sun rose, the balance of vehicles on the road shifted from lorries to cars. Thank God her little Fiat had air conditioning.

At Birmingham, everything slowed, and she didn't clear the city until ten past six.

Debbie felt remarkably well, considering seven hours earlier, she'd puked a Waitrose sandwich and a bottle of Sauvignon Blanc onto the pavement. Strictly speaking, she shouldn't be driving. By her estimation, she wouldn't be able to pass a breathalyser test until eight-thirty. Assuming, of course, that the police pulled her over. Which was exactly what she *did* assume, as Jimmy Blue had told her they would.

You'll never see Tom again, he'd said in the darkness of her bedroom. She didn't turn on the light. She'd looked into Tom Lewis's eyes and seen Jimmy Blue before. She had no desire to repeat the experience. She wanted to picture Tom as the damaged, gentle, kind boy who trusted her. Not this. Whether it was shock, the fact it was dark, or the after-effects of the alcohol, Debbie didn't get scared this time when confronted by the monster in her bedroom. She got angry.

—What the hell are you doing here? How the hell did you get out? Are you crazy?

—*I knew the police were closing in. But I wasn't finished.*

—Look, I understand you going after Winter's crew, but the rest? And Penrose?

—*It's not just Tom whose life has been ruined by unaccountable scum. There are others. Who helps them? Who avenges their dead?*

—The police. The legal system. And it's justice, not revenge.

—*The justice you're talking about can be bought. I can't be bought. I have talent, skills, knowledge. I have money. I can help.*

—No. No, you can't. If the justice system isn't working, our duty is to fix it. No one is above the law.

—*Where was the law for the people Robert Winter and John Strickland killed? Where was the law when Douglas Penrose got schoolchildren addicted to heroin? Or when Harry Penrose started harpooning people?*

—Don't lecture me. I saw you in action, remember? You enjoy killing. Don't imagine you're some kind of avenging angel. You're a thug, a killer, nothing else.

—*I'm far more than that. But you will never understand.*

—Oh, spare me the self-serving psychobabble. You belong behind bars.

—*Then why warn me? Why prevent my arrest?*

—Because of Tom.

The M6 remained slow until she passed Warrington. Debbie rubbed eyes heavy and red-rimmed with lack of sleep. Worrying she might nod off, she pulled into Charnock Richard services for a twenty minute nap to recharge. She pulled into a space at the edge of the car park and was asleep before the engine fan stopped whirring.

She dreamed of her parents' house in Suffolk, of walking into the guest bedroom to find Jimmy Blue wearing Tom's skin, his eyes burning with a horrible intelligence devoid of pity. And yet, Jimmy Blue saved her life that night. Even as Jimmy Blue, Tom must be

45

present. A wisp of the child-man watched the world from somewhere inside the predator. Debbie refused to abandon that belief.

If Jimmy Blue ran out of bad guys, would Tom come out of the shadows? Would Blue disappear?

"Step out of the car."

Grey and green. Debbie blinked the scene into focus. Tarmac and grass. The car park, trees at its edge, yellow patches between them where a thousand dogs a day, released from car boots, relieved their bladders. Sun, bright now, still low, sky clearing to a baby blue. Cobalt strobes across her windscreen, figures crouched behind open car doors. Weapons. The voice again, terse, tense, commanding.

"Hands where we can see them, Mrs Capelli. Step out of the car."

Ms Capelli, she mentally corrected. She kept her married name because she liked it, not the lying shit who shared it with her.

She looked around the interior of the Fiat in confusion. Half a bottle of lukewarm water and a gardening magazine on the passenger seat. Receipts and pay and display tickets stuffed into the door pocket. A faded cardboard Christmas tree that smelled of nothing dangling from the mirror.

"Do it now, Mrs Capelli."

Fully awake; half-afraid and half-annoyed. Debbie's dislike for being ordered around had been partially responsible for her choice of career. It stung to be on this side of a shouted command from a police officer.

She opened the door and pushed it ajar with her foot. The man giving the orders was mid-forties, good looking. Very serious. He wasn't pointing a gun, but four other officers were, crouching behind patrol car doors.

"I may not have had my first cup of coffee yet," she said as she stepped out of the Fiat, "but reports of how grouchy I am in the morning have been grossly exaggerated."

"Walk towards me."

She did so. Her lips were dry, and the inside of her mouth was dry muesli and cabbage.

"That's far enough."

She stopped, and three armed officers, two male, one female, approached the Fiat as if it might rear up on its back wheels and attack. The lead male reached the car first and pulled the keys out of the ignition, examining the electronic fob. He joined his colleagues and pointed the keys at the boot. They raised their guns. He pressed the button, and the boot popped open an inch. When nothing happened—what did he expect; a gang of armed pixies? It was a Fiat 500, not a Transit van—he leaned forward and flicked the boot up, leaping backwards.

Debbie smiled at the lead officer. Quite a looker. She wondered if he was attracted to older, hung-over, menopausal women.

"What were you hoping for?" she said.

The looker ignored her, speaking into his phone. "He's not here, ma'am."

Debbie looked at him. "DCI Barber?" She pointed at the Fiat's open boot. Big enough to hold her weekly shop. "What does she think I've got in there? Oh. Have you lost your prisoner?" She hoped Barber could hear this. The DCI cut her out as soon as they had Tom in custody. Debbie left messages for the rest of the day, none of which her old boss returned. She raised her voice.

"It's a Fiat 500, Maisie, not a bloody TARDIS."

The looker held out his phone. "She wants to talk to you."

Barber wasted no time on niceties. "Where is he?"

"If you mean Tom, as memory serves, he's in a cell. Have you misplaced him?"

"Don't play games, Capelli. Lewis is a very dangerous man."

"Barber, I'm too old for this. You asked for my help and I gave it. You wouldn't even let me see him. OK, that's your call. But I'm out. Clean up your own mess."

"Why are you running?"

"Running?" Debbie remembered her instructions from the voice in the darkness the previous night.

—*I'm ready to leave. Get away from here. Somewhere no one's trying to put me in a cage.*

—Somewhere you won't kill anyone?

47

—Yes, Debbie, that too. You can give me a head start.

"I'm not running anywhere, Barber. Hard as it may be to understand, life continues after a career in the police force. I'm on my way to Glasgow to collect a book I bought online. A first edition, rare, and quite valuable. I don't trust couriers with things like that."

"Hand me back to Carter."

Debbie returned the phone to the looker, who held a hand up for her to stay put before walking far enough away not to be overheard. When he came back, he didn't look happy.

"This book you're collecting."

Debbie took her phone out of her bag and opened the auction site page to prove she had been bidding on the item in question for four days before winning it. It seemed Jimmy Blue's IT skills were as impressive as his fighting ability.

"It checks out, ma'am. Yes, ma'am. Hold on. It's called *A Magician Among The Spirits.* Three thousand, two hundred and forty."

Debbie winced. It was a significant amount for someone living on a fixed income. Jimmy Blue told her to keep it for a few months, then sell it on. He said she'd make fifteen hundred profit on it, easy. She was trying very hard not to think of it as blood money.

"The author, ma'am? Hang on."

Debbie hadn't known whether to laugh or scream when she'd seen who'd written the book she was driving more than four hundred miles to pick up.

"Er, yes, ma'am, I've got it. Well. Yes, of course." The looker caught Debbie's eye, looking for a reaction. She gave him her best poker face. "It's by Harry Houdini."

CHAPTER TWELVE

ON THE SECOND day at sea, Tom left his cabin.

The ship's motion didn't make him sick, but fear and confusion kept him away from the crew.

He slept through the previous day, not knowing where he was or how he got there. On the few occasions he opened his eyes, he never fully woke up, allowing the distant hum of engines to lull him back to sleep.

He was awake now. For an hour, sitting on the end of his bed and watching the endless water outside, he waited for a little of Blue's purpose to percolate and inform his sense of self.

This slow return was nothing new. The ebb and flow of his personality, the drift in and out of a miasma of dreams, was part of the routine when he rejoined the world as Tom Lewis.

He waited for enough clarity to allow him to re-engage with reality.

The world never fully revealed itself to Tom, not in any comprehensible way. It appeared in pieces, challenging and tiring to deal with. Tom appreciated solitude, taking jobs where he could work without engaging much with others. He avoided conversation and the inevitable questions that followed. He liked the ache of his muscles on a building site when he carried bricks or broke hard concrete with a pickaxe. Work, food, sleep. Fragments of dreams he could never keep hold of, based on someone else's memories.

He summoned enough courage to check out the view, staring across the endless sea. Or, rather, the Atlantic Ocean. Whether this knowledge came from childhood memories or from Jimmy Blue, he didn't know, but he turned the fact around in his mind, a smooth stone plucked from the bed of consciousness.

The window disappointed him. It should be round, not square. And no hammock, just a narrow bed.

Once the view lost some of its fascination, he paced from the door to the window. Six paces long. Four-and-a-half widthways. Beside the bed, a desk, and chair: a separate shower, sink, and toilet. The cabin was no smaller than many rented rooms.

Hunger drove him out that afternoon. Tom stepped into a featureless corridor with white walls and painted orange arrows showing the nearest emergency exit. A few more cabins lined the corridor.

A heavy door led to the stairs, which were made of metal and painted yellow. Tom looked up and down. Above him were five decks, below just one. Tom followed the steps down and opened another heavy door, stepping out onto the deck.

The sun on his face warmed his skin. The breeze carried a salt tang. Tom looked up at the structure he'd stepped out of and counted seven decks. The uppermost jutted out and had lots of windows. The bridge. He knew its name, and that the captain ran the ship from there.

Tom couldn't remember learning any of this. The knowledge came from Blue, as did the conviction that he had escaped danger to be here. This unfamiliar environment shouldn't scare him. It represented the first step towards freedom. Tom walked to the rail. More information about his surroundings came into focus. The containers piled up on deck and below, out of sight, were being transported to America. There were thousands of them on board. Tom peered up at the stack towering above him. He's only seen them on the back of lorries before. One container should have been his, with the contents of his storage unit in Soho. But Blue had been rushed. The police had closed in too fast. Everything he owned stayed in London.

It hit him then. He had left Britain. Not for a holiday. Forever. He couldn't go back. Too dangerous. Confusion washed over him as two conflicting mental states competed for supremacy. One was home-sickness. Tom ached with the sadness and fear associated with leaving everything he knew, everyone he'd ever met. His parents' graves. His friend Debbie. He would never see her again. But the dominant emotion was excitement, the thrill of escape combined with the allure of the unknown. This came mostly from Blue, but not completely. Something deep inside Tom reacted positively to the thought of a new beginning, in fresh soil, somewhere no one knew him. Somewhere he could start again.

He walked the length of the ship. It was much bigger than he'd imagined, longer even than the warehouse he'd worked in last Christ-mas. The deck was grey, textured metal. Yellow numbers marked each row of containers. Ladders and door handles sported the same bright yellow. Unlike normal handles, Tom had to pull the end of a metal bar anticlockwise, reversing the action on the inside to seal the doors behind him.

At the front of the ship, the layout changed. Tom remembered a different word for 'front' when you were at sea. It had been in *David Copperfield*, which he had finished listening to on headphones weeks earlier, thrilled and horrified by the shipwreck at Yarmouth it described in the closing chapters. What was the word? *Prow* or *bow*?

Along the deck, patchwork skyscrapers towered above Tom, made up of different coloured containers stacked high. They might contain televisions, toasters, clothes, toys, furniture, phones; items made in one country then sent to another to be warehoused and sold on.

Gaps in the high walls revealed an uneven topography. In some places, the stacks were only four containers high, in others seven or eight.

The frontmost row boasted a single container, dwarfed by the edifice of its fellows that rose behind it. The grooves on the de where its neighbours would stand were marked by deep scratches. It looked odd, on its own like that. Even stranger was a line of bright red paint where the rear of the container touched the stack behind, extending across the walkway. Tom walked to the other side of the container and found the same line crossing the deck to the railing. The crimson line stood out against the grey.

At the very tip of the ship, accessed by a metal staircase, stood a platform. The white deck there held heavy equipment, metal protuberances shaped like giant cotton reels, their tops painted yellow. Tom sat on one and looked in awe at the anchor's giant chains coiled around a reel the size of a small car. At the foremost railing, he looked down at the deep blue water below. It frothed and bubbled like the water in a saucepan when he boiled an egg.

Tom's stomach rumbled at the thought. He retraced his steps and headed back towards the tall structure. Followed a corridor to a T-junction, taking the right fork without thinking about it. His quick familiarity with the ship's layout didn't surprise him. A gift from Blue.

The tall structure housing his cabin and other working areas of the ship had locks with numbers to open the doors, but the one Tom tried was unlocked.

Sailors called the dining room the mess. It had five tables and twenty chairs. It was an unremarkable room, bland and utilitarian in design. Tidy too, not a mess. Tom gave a mental shrug at the contradiction. The deck in here was a wood laminate, scuffed and worn. Irregularly spaced holes, deep slits about an inch long, scarred the flooring.

Tom went through to the kitchen—the galley—and filled a plate with sliced rye bread, cheese, a boiled egg, and an apple. He found a glass, but nothing to put in it.

When he returned to the mess, he wasn't alone. An Asian man in his thirties sat at the nearest table, a cup of coffee in his hand. He had what looked like a holster on his belt, but it held a large spanner rather than a gun. Tom put his plate on a nearby table. The man shot him a look but said nothing.

Tom ate in silence while the Asian man drank his coffee. Halfway through the rye bread, his dry throat protested, and he coughed, spraying crumbs onto the table. The man looked up as the coughing got worse.

"You OK?" He glanced at the empty glass. "Need a drink?"

Tom nodded. He broke off into another bout of spluttering. The small man took his glass over to a fridge and filled it with milk.

As soon as the man handed him the glass, Tom drained it, liquid running along his cheek. Not fresh milk, but long-life, which he hated. It tasted pretty good now, though. The coughs subsided, and he wiped away his tears.

He returned to his food, ignoring the bread, taking bites of the egg. When he took another sip of milk, he pulled a face.

A minute later, the other man brought him a glass of orange juice. Tom looked up in confusion.

"Sorry. You're better off with juice. The fresh milk runs out on the first day, then we drink this garbage. Tastes like shit, right?"

Tom didn't want to reply, just to be left alone. But the man had helped him. He nodded in agreement. He mustn't talk to anyone, he knew. The instruction came through loud and clear, left there by Blue. On board this ship, he must remain silent.

The orange juice was better than the milk. When he put the glass down, the helpful man handed him a napkin, and patted his own face to show his meaning.

"You spilled some." His tone was gentle.

Tom stared at the table while he wiped his face.

"Can you speak? Do you understand me?"

Tom looked up, then dropped his gaze back to the table. Shrugged. Picked up the apple. He'd go back to his cabin to eat it.

The Asian man glanced at the door, swallowed, then sat down opposite Tom, leaning forward. His words were no louder than a whisper, and he spoke so fast Tom struggled to keep up.

"Listen. Just listen. You're in danger. I'll get you through this if you trust me. I'll work something out, get a message to you. I—"

At the sound of footsteps, the man slid off his chair, left his coffee where it was, and jogged to the exit.

His progress was halted by the man filling the door frame

as Tom, wearing a sleeveless black weightlifting T-shirt designed to show off his muscles and Celtic tattoos, he put one big hand on the smaller man's head. For a second, Tom thought he would pick him up that way. Instead, he pushed him back into the room, grinning.

"Ronnie, you're so unsociable. Sometimes I don't think you're cut out for a career in hospitality."

The new arrival twisted the small man's head as if unscrewing a bottle.

"Come on. Let's say hello to our guest."

CHAPTER THIRTEEN

BARBER STOOD IN HER OFFICE, drinking water, looking at the brick wall opposite her window, waiting. It was six twenty-five. The delivery office in Hounslow opened at eight.

She closed her eyes, still seething about Debbie Capelli, convinced she must have warned Lewis somehow. Barber had rushed through a warrant to search Capelli's flat and go through her phone records, but she doubted they'd find much. The ex-DI had always been thorough. Careful. She wouldn't have left any evidence.

Capelli's treachery wasn't the worst of it. Douglas Penrose was dead. Poisoned in a house no one knew he owned, by a bottle of cognac with her name on the attached gift card.

Barber's professional reputation had taken a battering. The damage was done in one twenty-four-hour period, and the criminal behind it had vanished, leaving no clues.

Well, not quite. A Hounslow post office held their only sniff of a lead on Lewis. She knew it was unwise, unprofessional even, to hope for much, but she couldn't help it. She had been humiliated. Lewis needed to be brought to justice, but—just as importantly—she needed to get even.

———

The name of the man arrested three days earlier, the man posing as Tom Lewis, was Mikhail Plotnikov. He'd arrived in the country nine months ago. His sister and her British husband had lived in Hackney for a decade. Mikhail turned up in need of a bed. A few nights turned into months. The uncomfortable domestic situation didn't improve when Mikhail's contributions to the mortgage became unreliable. Other than cash in hand work on building sites, his daily routine involved an Xbox, cheap vodka, and the company of weed-smoking mates.

Barber knew this because Plotnikov's sister came to pick him up, and—when acting as his translator—took every opportunity to bemoan the day her brother left Russia to ruin her life. Plotnikov had been approached in a pub by a big, bearded man who spoke fair Russian. The big man wanted Mikhail to do something for him. A job, not entirely legal, but was easy. If Mikhail performed as instructed, he would receive a significant bonus on top of the two thousand pounds in cash he handed over.

The sister's eyes narrowed as she added her own comments. "He's lying. It was more than two grand, but he won't say because of the money he owes me."

Mikhail claimed the deal hinged on him remaining silent after he was arrested. If he made it through the night, he got his bonus.

The sister didn't translate his next few sentences. Her eyes went wide, and she started asking rapid-fire questions, which her brother answered, laughing. She shook her head in disbelief. He nodded. The sister took out her phone and walked to the door of the interview room.

"I have to make a call. OK? Then I carry on."

The guard at the door looked at Barber, who shrugged. The sister wasn't under arrest.

She was back within five minutes, transformed into a different woman. She hugged her brother across the table, laughed, and pounded the table with the flat of her hands.

Barber waited as patiently as she could throughout the surreal scene. The sister sat down and swivelled her chair to face the DCI.

"Detective Chief Inspector Barber. My brother is very sorry about what happened. He would like to go now. He has no more information. If he remembers anything else, he'll call you."

Barber explained the trouble Plotnikov was in, but the sister shook her head. "Mikhail doesn't speak English well. He doesn't understand your laws. And he tells me he's going back to Russia now. He does not have permission to stay, not really. You could arrest him, keep him here, but I will tell the papers how the police spent much time and money on an illegal immigrant with a rubber scar stuck on his head. You will be, what is the English phrase, a laughing stick."

Barber knew when she was beaten. After taking Plotnikov's statement, there was little more of value to be gained by holding him. She didn't need the press getting hold of the Jimmy Blue story. She could easily imagine the editorials of certain rags taking the side of a vigilante brutally removing violent criminals from their city.

"Let him go," she said.

The financial team followed up on Plotnikov, and the report that arrived four days later confirmed her suspicions. Not only had Mikhail become wealthy enough to return to the motherland, his sister became mortgage-free the day after his arrest. A big, untraceable, automated payment dropped into their account. No wonder the woman had been so bloody happy.

Barber was back to square one. Worse than that, she may have lost Lewis already. Capelli's little jaunt up the country was no more than him thumbing his nose at her.

They sent Tom Lewis's photograph to every police station, every train station, every port, and airport. Nothing. Either Jimmy Blue hadn't run, or he'd done it before they started looking, while they thought he was in custody. His passport hadn't passed through any checks. If he had fled the country, it was under a false identity, or via a clandestine form of transit.

Lewis could be anywhere in the world. She drained the water and checked the time. Six thirty-two. This new lead probably meant nothing, but it was all they had.

Barber walked out of her office and pointed at the first officer she saw. "Get a uniform to drive me to Hounslow. At the front in five minutes."

The officer snatched up the phone as Barber swept past.

In the lobby, Cunningham walked in. He was an obnoxious man, but his deductive skills and experience were solid, and Barber doubted her own judgement today.

"With me," she said.

Traffic was slow, even in a patrol car, but when they arrived, they still had ten minutes to wait until the delivery office opened. Barber spent it pacing; Cunningham peeled and ate an orange. Neither spoke.

As soon as the key rattled in the door, Barber was up the steps.

———

Dave Hillman had visited Hounslow police station as a witness to a hit-and-run. While there, he'd seen Tom Lewis's photograph on the wall. Barber could hardly bring herself to admit her stalled investigation now hung its hopes on this single piece of luck.

Now, mug of tea in hand, in the back room of the delivery office, Hillman looked at the photograph again.

"Yeah, definitely him. Big guy, but shy, y'know? Wouldn't say boo to a goose. Look, I told the constable everything yesterday."

"We're very grateful for your help, Mr Hillman."

"He some murderer or what?"

In her sleep-deprived early morning state, Barber had to run that sentence through her brain twice before it made sense.

Cunningham took up the slack. "We can't discuss what the suspect may or may not have done during an ongoing investigation. But, take it from me, the sooner he's behind bars, the sooner we can all sleep easy in our beds."

"Cripes. And to think he was as close to me as you are now. Don't bear thinking about, do it?"

Barber's turn. "You say this happened a couple of weeks ago. Do you recall the date? And do you have a record of what he sent? And where to?"

"Hold your horses." Hillman took a gulp of tea. His thin, greying brown hair was styled into a mullet. "Well. There won't be a record as such. Data protection and all that gubbins. The customer gets a receipt, but the info don't stay on the computer. But, like I say, I do remember the bloke."

He took another loud slurp of tea. Cunningham rolled his eyes at Barber.

When Hillman put his mug down, he was smiling. "It so 'appens that I can recall the exact day, and what he sent. How does that strike you?"

Barber and Cunningham both nodded. Hillman kept talking.

"It was the day my youngest got that vomiting bug. It's been going round all the schools. Y'see, some parents send their kids in ten minutes after they chuck up their breakfast. Then all the poor sods get it, don't they? Anyway, the school called my missus, but she were across town shopping with her sister, so she put them onto me, and it were nearly lunch anyway, so I had a word with the gaffer and took off to pick up the nipper. Course, I missed that afternoon, so I swapped shifts with Smithy. That meant giving the carvery a miss Saturday lunchtime, but it's my kid, right? You have to make sacrifices. Anyway, that bloke in the photo was the last customer I dealt with on Saturday and..."

He looked at the expressions on his guests' faces. "Right. I'll see what details I can bring to mind, shall I? Yeah. I'll do that. Won't take a lamb's shake."

He promptly sat back and closed his eyes, frowning.

Barber watched Cunningham fight the urge to throttle the man. She looked away, towards the wall, gaze unfocused. Their quarry had stayed ahead of them every step of the way. She'd never found herself in this position before. Criminals were predictable. Murderers made mistakes. They always left a trail of evidence. Gather it, get witness statements, let the facts build the case. Not this time. It was blind luck that this postal worker saw Tom Lewis's mugshot. He might not have remembered him at all if his son hadn't been ill. Barber hoped good luck really came in threes, and that Hillman might stop a killer slipping through her fingers.

Hillman opened his eyes. Barber and Cunningham leaned forward.

"Sorry, folks. Nothing useful. A few bits and bobs, that's all."

Barber had never counted fishing among her hobbies. She didn't really have any hobbies, unless reading old unsolved cases counted. But she sometimes thought of suspects, or witnesses, as fish that needed to be reeled in using specific techniques. Some required a direct approach. Hillman needed the leeway to wriggle on the hook, to find his own way to the information. She needed to release the pressure if she wanted to land him.

A simple lift of the finger while holding Cunningham's gaze was enough, albeit barely, to stop him grabbing Hillman and pinning him against a wall.

"Bits and bobs will be fine, Mr Hillman. We appreciate you taking the time to help us. Any detail might prove crucial in this murder investigation."

"Murder?" The post office worker raised his eyebrows, straightened his shoulders.

"Forget I said that," said Barber. It did the trick. Hillman compressed his lips and interlaced his fingers.

"Medium-sized parcel, weren't it? Yeah. Heavy. He said they was books. That's what he said, all right. Might have been lying, I s'pose, but they weighed the same as books. And he was sending them to this big book place in America. So I reckon it might have been books. What do you think? Books?"

"It does sound that way, Mr Hillman. Do you remember any details? Anything unusual? Anything at all?"

"As it happens, yeah. There was one thing, petal."

Barber didn't acknowledge Cunningham's smirk.

"He sent it by air. Cost a bloody fortune. Hundreds. Made me wonder if they were rare books. Or if he was an author, like, sending his books out to a bookshop. Do authors do that? I asked him, but like I say, he weren't much of a talker. I reckoned he were posting 'em for someone else, like, cos he didn't strike me as the sharpest tool in the box. Couldn't imagine him writing a note to the milkman, never mind a book, know what I mean?"

Hillman took his visitors' silence as confirmation that they did indeed know what he meant.

"And that's it, really. He buggered off, and the box went out for delivery that night. I already described what he was wearing to the first policewoman, didn't I?"

"You did." Cunningham was already standing, but Barber waved at him to be still.

"Now, I don't expect you remember every address on every parcel, Mr Hillman—"

He laughed. "Too bloomin' right!"

"But it would be a huge help to this investigation—crucial, in fact —if you could bring to mind any details."

"Tall order, flower, tall order."

"Picture yourself here that afternoon, Mr Hillman. Give it a try. Please."

He closed his eyes again. Opened them three seconds later.

"Blow me down. Would you believe it? I do remember. I was thinking about me kid, cos he made a bloody miraculous recovery from being ill once we got home, and then I found out he'd been taken ill at the start of double maths, so, well, I was thinking about the little sod while I were typing up the receipt. Had to do it over, cos I misread the address, like. Thought it said Bookbrat. Weird name for a shop, I thought. Then I took a closer look. Bookbart, not brat. Had a little chuckle to myself, din I? Well, bloody 'ell, there you go. Dunno how much use it'll be, but it's all I've got."

Barber stood up, too. "Do you remember where Bookbart was

located, Mr Hillman?"

"You know what? I do! Cos the address finished just like the song."

"What song is that?"

"A classic. Frank Sinatra. *New York, New York*."

They left before he could sing.

Barber was searching the net on her phone by the time Cunningham caught up at the patrol car.

"Bookbart, New York. It's an online business. Wholesaler of used books. Ships to bookstores all over the US."

Cunningham looked over her shoulder and chuckled. "That's your big lead? A second-hand bookshop?"

She ignored his taunts, presenting an impassive expression to the DI. "Your transfer came through, Cunningham. I'm delaying signing off on it until we're done with this case."

She watched him process the implications. His record was good. Not as good as Barber's, but showing enough competence to make him a decent candidate for promotion. Their current case, if left unresolved, would be a black mark. If she had to live with that, so would Cunningham. This way, he would do everything he could to help hunt down Lewis.

"Right you are, guv." He was getting better at concealing his emotions, Barber noticed. He was furious—the reddening at the tips of his ears was a giveaway—but at least Cunningham had learned to stop pressing his lips together and snorting through his nose when upset. Perhaps there was hope for him yet.

She looked up from her phone.

"If Lewis thought we were closing in, that parcel might be important. Why waste time and money sending books by airfreight when he needed to get out of London? Was he sending something on ahead?"

"You think he's heading for America?" said Cunningham.

Barber held up her phone. "There's a number for Bookbart."

She pressed the key, waited for the international connection.

"Hello?" Barber held up a finger to stop Cunningham talking, then swore. "Voicemail."

Cunningham tapped his watch. "New York is five hours behind us. Quarter to three in the morning. Maybe they haven't opened for the day."

Barber ignored the sarcasm, holding the phone so Cunningham could see the bookseller's website. "There's the business name and address. Call the office. I want the owner's home phone number. Now."

CHAPTER FOURTEEN

"HEY, FELLA, WHAT'S UP?"

Tom stared at the man in the weightlifting T-shirt. He was unshaven, with black bristles so thick he could have counted them individually. A pair of Ray-Bans pushed up his forehead. A tattoo of a snake curled around his right forearm and biceps, up to his shoulder, its mouth open as if to bite his neck. His accent was American. Another piece of information dropped into Tom's brain. The container ship was bound for New York.

Tom said nothing, Blue's instructions clear. Besides, he didn't understand the question the bristly crew member had asked. He settled for looking at the floor.

Each second that passed added to the awkwardness. The unshaven man lifted his T-shirt to scratch a sculpted stomach of which he was demonstrably proud. His feet were as big as Tom's.

"Hey, Ronnie," said the big man in the T-shirt.

The Asian crew member looked up at the newcomer. "Sean."

Sean bared his teeth in a grin. "You making new friends? That's nice."

He winked at Tom. "Ronnie here helps look after the engines. He's a frickin' genius with a can of oil and a wrench, but his people skills need work. Am I right, Ronnie?"

Ronnie looked like he wanted to be somewhere else.

"See you've met one of our passengers. Tom here—it is Tom, right?—"

Tom nodded.

"—has booked passage with us all the way to New York City, home of a second-rate baseball team, overpriced beer, and not much else of consequence."

He stuck his hand out. Tom shook it. Sean had a powerful grip. His brown arms rippled with muscles. A row of teeth appeared between the coarse black hairs around his mouth. It might have been a smile.

"Pleased to meet you, Tom. I'm Sean. Chief mate of the *Trevanian*. If the captain is Butch Cassidy, I'm the Sundance Kid."

Tom didn't like this man, although his tone seemed friendly enough.

"Shake the man's hand, Ronnie."

After he'd done as he was told, Ronnie spoke to Sean as if Tom wasn't there. "I thought we weren't taking any more passengers for a while. Brakesman said—"

"That's Captain Brakesman to you, Ronnie, my boy."

He gave the smaller man a playful punch on the shoulder that sent him crashing into the table.

"Our beloved captain has used the same small crew for years, Tom. We all rub along ok, I guess. But some of us don't like change, do we, Ronnie?"

Ronnie scowled at him. Sean smiled in return.

"I notice you didn't allow your anti-passenger principles to get in the way when you took your bonus last time."

Sean winked at Tom. "The captain pays extra when we take passengers. Ronnie gets a nice pay cheque out of it, even if he misses out on the big money."

He slapped the smaller man on the back. Ronnie got up, poured his coffee down the sink, upended the cup on a tray of dirty dishes, and left, darting a glance at Tom.

"Don't mind him," said Sean. "He's always been a miserable summabitch. Sit yourself down, Tom."

Tom saw no easy way out. He lowered himself into the nearest plastic chair. Sean took the seat opposite, turning it round and sitting astride it like a cowboy, something Tom had only seen in movies.

"Word is you can't talk. That right?"

He gave Tom a second to respond before laughing with a bark like a seal; more an assault on the senses than an expression of amusement.

"Guess you can't answer, am I right? Still, best kind of passenger, I'd say. No questions, no where-d'y'all-come-from bullshit. Suits me."

Sean picked up the half-full jug of coffee, waggling it. "Most important piece of equipment on the whole goddam ship, my friend."

Tom wasn't his friend.

Sean poured himself a cup.

"I don't know what brought you aboard. Don't care, either. But I know Brakesman. Sailed with him six years straight. He pays good. Better than most any other freighter gig. Know why?"

Tom didn't.

"I'll tell you why," continued Sean. Lack of response had no effect on his conversation. "Because Brakesman has business interests that aren't entirely... well... legitimate. He picks his crew carefully, and he looks after us. We look the other way, and we keep our mouths shut. Sometimes we carry cargo others might refuse."

The seal bark made a second appearance.

"That goes for our passengers, too. You'd know all about that, Tom, am I right?"

Sean drained his coffee and refilled it. "If you're on board, you've got something to hide."

He spread his arms wide. Shaved armpits to match his shaved chest. Yet he let his stubble grow. Tom couldn't work out why parts of his body warranted different treatment.

"Hey, that's fine with me, Tom. We all have our secrets, am I right? All done bad things. No problemo, amigo. "

Tom bit into his apple. The flesh yielded easily. He preferred hard apples. Sean talked a lot. Tom wasn't listening anymore.

"Glad we had this chance to get acquainted, Tom."

The chief mate stood up and pivoted the chair on one leg, spinning it round then sliding it back under the table.

"It's another seven days until we dock. Pretty sure we'll run into each other again."

At the door, Sean paused. "Meet-and-greet tonight. Ten p.m. You got the invite this morning."

Tom had seen an envelope slide under his door, recognising his first name on the front. The surname was new—it started with a different letter. It matched the name on the passport in his cabin drawer. Tom hadn't opened the envelope, as he wouldn't understand its contents.

His confusion must have shown.

"Twenty-two hundred hours, Tom. In here. Mandatory. That means you have to come. If you don't, we'll send someone down to get you. Don't be late. Safety briefing."

Sean's seal-bark laugh was still audible in the distance thirty seconds after he had left Tom alone in the mess.

CHAPTER FIFTEEN

THAT EVENING, Tom walked the length of the ship again. Halfway along the main deck, the sun warm on his arms, scalp sweating under the bandana, he stopped at the rail. He put his back against it, tilted his head to look at the stack of containers above him. They were all different colours, large stickers or painted words and numbers on their sides, slotted together like a giant wall of Lego.

He scanned the scene without thought, taking his time, looking left and right. He walked around the deck-level containers to examine them. The process took two hours. When complete, he blinked as if waking from a deep sleep.

After a turn around the deck, he found the only lifeboat. It looked more like a spaceship. Bright orange, enclosed, it perched on a steep launch ramp at the stern. Unlike a spaceship, the lifeboat's nose wasn't aiming at the sky, but at the churning sea. There were no ropes to lower it to the water. It looked designed to drop down the ramp, fall the height of the ship, and hit the waves. Tom shuddered at the thought. He hoped there would be no need to use it. Were there icebergs in the Atlantic? He scanned the empty swathe of water and saw nothing except a darker blue band of water on the horizon that traced the curve of the Earth.

A ladder took him below decks. The passageways here were narrow. He stopped in front of a schematic like the one on deck. This one showed the layout of the ship's insides. It looked complicated. Tom didn't understand any of it apart from the picture of a propeller at the back, but he stood gazing at it for ten minutes before heading back to his cabin.

He almost missed the message when he walked in. A square of paper, folded once, left on the desk. Someone had been in his cabin. Tom checked the bathroom and the single cupboard. Something was missing.

He unfolded the paper and examined the patterns of black ink on a white background. Tom recognised his own name at the top, but nothing else made sense. Without questioning why he did it, Tom ripped the paper up, flushing the tiny pieces down the toilet, which roared like a strange animal as it sucked them away.

His feet ached, so he took off his boots, positioned the chair in front of the porthole, and sat down.

He was still there, watching the ocean, mesmerised by the way the infinite waves reflected the changing light at dusk, when someone thumped on his door.

Sean held an open tin of beer. He handed a second tin to Tom. "Figured you didn't bring any of your own. My treat. Come on. Put some shoes on. Five minutes until the briefing."

Tom stared back at him, the beer cold in his hand. Stepped back into the cabin. His boots were in the middle of the room, but his feet still throbbed, so he opened drawers, looking for his trainers. They weren't where he'd left them.

Sean stood just inside, leaning against the door to stop it closing.

"So, before we go, help a buddy out, Tom. I know you can't say anything, but give me a nod if I'm right, because you're the dark horse of the group. My guess is you're the mastermind behind a bunch of daring bank heists. Is that why you skipped town?"

The explosive laugh bounced off the metal walls, making it sound even harsher.

Tom knew Sean was joking, but he'd asked himself the same

question. Why did he have to leave London? His life had changed over the past few months. No bedsits or rented rooms. Tom slept in squats, or in hostels where no one asked for ID. Twice, he woke up in unfamiliar, empty houses, letting himself out with no idea how he had got in.

Over the same period, Tom's dreams were often violent, full of dark alleyways, the flash of a street light on a blade, blood running into a gutter. Jimmy Blue had always looked after him, but it was months since he killed the people who'd murdered Tom's parents. Why did Tom still wake up with aches, scrapes, and cuts? Once, in the shower, he'd found every toe on his left foot covered with bruises. More days than not, his muscles burned with the after-effects of exertions he didn't remember.

He checked the bathroom for his trainers. They had gone.

"Two minutes, bud. Let's go."

In the corridor, Tom walked alongside the friendly man who wasn't his friend. Through the soles of his boots, he registered the throb of powerful engines pushing the massive vessel away from Britain. The excitement at having a fresh start faded as the fear of the unknown grew. He put a hand on the cold metal wall, breathing hard.

"You OK, Tom?"

With an effort, Tom pushed the fear down. Jimmy Blue took care of things. Jimmy Blue looked out for him. That hadn't changed. That wouldn't change.

As he followed Sean to the mess, he glanced out again at the darkening sea. A shadowy figure flitted past the porthole on the walkway outside.

Blue was never far away.

CHAPTER SIXTEEN

THE OWNER of Bookbart picked up on the twelfth ring. Barber checked her watch. Seven twenty-five in London. Nearly half past two in New York.

"This is Detective Chief Inspector Barber from the Metropolitan Police in London. Yes, that London. Correct. Is this James Cranstone, the proprietor of BookBart?"

She put it on speakerphone.

"It's the middle of the night, lady. Who the hell are you?"

Barber repeated her credentials and allowed him a few seconds to process it. When Cranstone next spoke, his tone was guarded, careful. Barber had interviewed enough suspects to recognise someone with no affection for the law. She would have put money on Cranstone being an ex-con. Maybe her luck had just run out.

"Whaddya want?"

"A package was sent to you from London on the third of June. We need to know its contents, plus any information regarding who sent it."

"Yeah, sure. Why not? I mean, sounds fair. Let me see. June third, you said?"

"Correct."

"Yeah, gotcha. Well, I guess we receive anywhere between five and twenty thousand books a day in the warehouse. But I take special care to make sure I examine every single one personally, because the people who send them are all my special friends. Chrissakes. I'm gonna go back to sleep now, and I'm turning the phone off."

The line went dead.

Cunningham yawned. "Now what?"

"I don't know. We won't get an international warrant to search an American business premises because a murder suspect sent them some books."

"Where do you think Lewis is?"

"No idea." Barber stared out of the window at the traffic. There was a stone in her gut. "We've lost him."

"What's your hunch, though?"

Barber spoke without turning. "I don't trust hunches."

"Don't bullshit me. Look. I don't like you, you don't like me. So what? You're good at your job. Me too. I would have been good at your job if they'd picked me."

Barber grunted. He might be right. She was hardly covering herself in glory.

"After this case, I'm out of your hair," continued Cunningham. "So don't give me any of your 'be thorough, examine every detail, build your case' bollocks. He's gone. By the time you've examined every detail, Tom Lewis will be settled down, married to a Peruvian, and raising alpacas."

Barber couldn't help smiling. She preferred Cunningham like this. Insubordinate, but engaged. Shame it had taken so long to show some backbone.

"What do you suggest?"

"I suggest we take every shortcut we can. Play our hunches. Where is he? Still in London?"

"No. If he's in Britain, we'll find him. And he knows that. His face is in every police station. A big bald guy with a scarred head will struggle to stay anonymous."

"I agree. What about this parcel of books?"

"As clues go, it's as tenuous as it gets."

"But it's all we have. We assume he's heading for the States, then."

Barber winced at the word *assume*. It had no place in police work. However, Cunningham had a point.

"We'll prioritise flights to America," she said. "Of course, he could fly to a European city before buying a second flight to the States."

"Nothing we can do about that."

"True." Barber sighed. "Christ. It's a needle in a haystack."

"Perhaps we'll get lucky."

"I don't believe in luck, Cunningham."

———

They got lucky. A weak bladder led them to Jimmy Blue.

Freddy Fullerton, a crane operator working at London Gateway, saw Tom Lewis's face in the Evening Standard. His son was nine months into a three-year stretch for burglary and Freddy played his hand well, dangling Tom Lewis in front of them in return for a deal. The paperwork for early release went through in record time and, an hour after his son walked out of Pentonville prison, the crane operator talked.

It was a gift. Barber let Cunningham conduct the interview. Keeping the smile off her face got harder and harder as she listened to the details.

The crane operator, Freddy, worked overtime the same night Barber exposed the Russian imposter in New Scotland Yard. The overtime was well paid, cash in hand, no questions. Not for the first time, either. The captain of the *Trevanian*—the container ship they were loading—often operated on the fringes of the law. At least one of the government employees checking passports and manifests at the port drove a surprisingly luxurious car, considering her salary.

There had always been rumours that Captain Brakesman took illegal passengers. He had been investigated a couple of years previously, the case dropped due to lack of evidence.

Freddy, with an early reunion with his errant son imminent,

proved keen to share his theory on how Brakesman smuggled people to America. Barber had seen this behaviour before. If someone had a few beans to spill, why not spill them all?

Freddy thought the *Trevanian*'s passengers boarded via shipping containers lowered onto the ship by crane. Since security at American ports was tight and no stowaways had ever been discovered in any container, he guessed the passengers must pose as crew members at the other end. Not a bad theory. Captain Brakesman needed to make his illegal passengers vanish before US border checks.

Barber was more interested in what happened after Freddy finished his extra shift that night. He'd made it halfway out of the building before heading back to the toilet.

"Bladder like a walnut," was how he put it. "Everything was dark, but I don't need the lights on to take a piss. Anyhow, the urinals are under a window. I heard voices. Then the forklifts started up. Had a look-see, didn't I?"

A man matching Tom Lewis's description had boarded the *MS Trevanian* at four that morning, walking between two forklift trucks, which concealed him from the security cameras.

Barber and Cunningham discussed options in her office over two mugs of coffee spiked with whisky from his hip flask.

"This is such a cliché," said Barber, as they toasted their minor success. "It's the twenty-first century, Cunningham, not nineteen seventy-three."

"Whatever. Cheers, Guv." They drank, Barber grimacing. As far as she could tell, adding whisky to coffee ruined two otherwise satisfactory drinks.

Cunningham looked through the window at the brick wall opposite. "Lovely view. And to think, all this could have been mine. How do you want to play this?"

"We're monitoring the *Trevanian,*" said Barber. "If it so much as swerves to avoid a porpoise, we'll know about it. I've put in a formal request to the New York Customs and Border Protection office for a joint operation. They get the crew, we get Lewis."

That night, Barber caught up on lost sleep before waking at six.

Lewis made a fool of them once, but now he had nowhere to go. Trapped on a hundred-thousand-ton floating prison, travelling at twenty-three miles an hour, in the middle of the Atlantic. And when he arrived in the land of the free, Barber would be waiting with the handcuffs.

CHAPTER SEVENTEEN

SIXTEEN PEOPLE WAITED in the brightly lit mess. They were divided into two groups: ten crew, six passengers. Sean gave Tom a light shove left before joining his shipmates.

Tom found a seat at the nearest table, next to a short white man with a grey complexion who shared Tom's aversion to eye contact.

At the neighbouring table, an attractive black couple in their twenties looked at him with frank curiosity before returning to their private murmured conversation.

Three passengers occupied the far table. One, a thin white man in his fifties, was whistling. A second man, twenty years younger, thickset with closely cropped ginger hair, watched the crew. Between them sat an Asian woman who looked like she occupied the middle ground, age-wise. The frown lines on her brow were so pronounced that, even at rest, she looked annoyed.

"Ah, good, that's everybody. Thank you for joining us, folks."

Captain Brakesman was American, like Sean, but his accent was different. He spoke slowly, almost chewing the words as he pronounced them. If he hadn't said he was the captain, Tom wouldn't have known, as no one wore a uniform. Shouldn't the man in charge of such a big ship wear a special hat? Blue jeans and a white polo shirt seemed inappropriate. Brakesman was in his early sixties, with a bald brown head and a bushy white moustache. Half egg, half walrus.

The captain sat behind a table flanked by four crew members, two on each side. Tom recognised the Asian man—Ronnie—who had warned him earlier. Sean stood on the other side, next to a flip chart. There were no women on the crew. The men closest to the captain carried short, stubby, automatic weapons. Tom frowned; he didn't like guns. Two more armed men covered the two exits: the door leading onto the deck, and the corridor back to the cabins.

The only crew member without a holstered gun or a rifle on his shoulder was a sandy-haired man in his forties drinking coffee, looking out of the window towards the stern. He had the broken-vein, mottled complexion of a drinker and his eyes, when he gave the passengers a brief scan, were red-rimmed. Maybe it wasn't just coffee in his cup.

Captain Brakesman held up a hand, and the murmurs stopped.

"Y'all don't look happy to be here. I understand your misgivings. When I granted you passage, I agreed on your right to anonymity. Regarding your desire to conceal your identities, you're all, if you'll excuse the pun, in the same boat."

No one laughed other than Sean, who broke the silence with three brisk yaps.

"Rest assured," continued the captain, "I have no wish to reveal your real names. In fact, I've indulged myself by giving you nick-names. It'll make things easier for everyone."

"Get to the point, will ya?" The interruption came from the young man at the next table. "Don't give us this bollocks about nicknames. I'm guessing I'm not the only one who doesn't want his time wasted. Safety briefing, yeah? Tell us about the fire exits, then wake me up when we reach New York. Right, babe?"

The woman alongside him laughed. "Right. Hurry it up, mate."

The captain treated them to what looked like a genuine smile. "Of course. I'm as keen to move this along as you are. But the introductions are crucial. I promise you'll be glad of them later."

"Whatever."

At a brisk tap on the deck-side door, the nearest crewman opened it and two more crew entered, rifles slung over their shoulders.

"All ready," said the older of the two. Tom wasn't good with accents, but he thought it might be German.

"Excellent," said Brakesman. "Just one item of business to attend to. Phones on the tables in front of you, please. Also, any weapons."

The outspoken young man bristled. "You what, mate? I don't think so."

Captain Brakesman's smile broadened. "It wasn't a request."

The two crew members with guns raised them at a nod from the captain.

The Indian woman complied and placed her mobile phone on the table, eyeing the armed men. "No signal out here, anyway."

Others followed suit. Tom mirrored their actions, placing his phone in front of him.

"Weapons too." No one moved. "Folks," said Brakesman. "We searched your luggage when you boarded, and you all submitted to a personal scan, but please don't pretend you're not armed. Metal isn't the only material used for weapons. Sean here is gonna search y'all anyhow, and I won't be happy if any of you hold out on me."

The couple at the table next to Tom exchanged a glance, then pulled matching knives from sheaths on their ankles, placing them alongside their phones.

The only other weapons came from the stocky ginger man. He pulled a long ceramic blade from behind his back, a shorter one from his ankle. The older man and woman at his table looked as if they wished they had sat somewhere else.

The first mate stepped forward and, one by one, they submitted to a body search, but there was nothing else to find.

Ronnie dropped the phones and knives into a canvas sack. He held up the ginger man's phone before placing it with the others.

"Satellite."

The captain took a small notebook from his pocket and opened it. "You are all leaving the country illegally. No paperwork, no checks, no trace. You have disappeared. You paid handsomely for this service."

"A bit too bloody handsomely," muttered the thin man at the far table.

The captain continued as if he hadn't heard. "Everyone we bring on board is a risk, so, as well as taking your money, I make sure I know as much about you as your own mothers. More, in most cases. I pay a team of techie kids in San Bernardino a fat retainer to squeeze the juice on every one of you. Partly to lower the risk of accidentally offering passage to any law enforcement agents. But mostly because the information makes the game more fun."

The pause following that last remark stretched out until the frowning woman asked the inevitable question.

"Game? What game?"

Captain Brakesman ignored the question, smiling instead at the couple with the matching knives, who scowled back.

"Our lovebirds. I'll start with you. No real names. Not to protect your anonymity. It's just that I find nicknames easier to remember."

He paused, looking around the room, making sure he had their attention. There was a touch of the theatrical about Brakesman.

"Let's call them Bonnie and Clyde, shall we? It's appropriate. As of last week—and please correct me if I'm mistaken—this charming couple has robbed fourteen gas stations and seven motels across Europe. At gunpoint. They've shot and killed three people. Not sure if they're planning on continuing their lethal road trip on our side of the pond. Well? Is that your intention?"

The young man was halfway out of his chair when a crew member raised his weapon.

"You dirty fucker," said the woman. "Shut your mouth."

"Ah," said Brakeman, once 'Clyde' had sat down. "I'm afraid I won't be able to promise that. Now then." He looked at the man sitting next to Tom.

"Folks, this is Hannibal. Named after a famous fictional killer. Unlike Doctor Lecter, our Hannibal doesn't eat his victims. He strangles them before applying make-up and lipstick to the corpse. He has killed twelve women in his native country. The authorities believe

Hannibal is dead, after finding a suicide note, along with his clothes, on a beach. As you can see for yourselves, they are mistaken."

Hannibal dipped his head in a little bow. The woman at the far table pointed.

"God. I knew I recognised him. He's the Antwerp Strangler. I saw a documentary." She turned back to Brakesman. "What the hell is this? Are you serious? He kills women. You guaranteed my safety."

"Ma'am, please. I did no such thing. I said you'd be safe from the authorities. Now, a little quiet."

"Jesus Christ," the frowning woman whispered. "Jesus Christ."

"You next, my dear. Your nickname is Miss Felicity."

"Why Miss Felicity? Who is she?" Tom watched the deep frown lines with interest. Even when scared, she looked like she had judged Brakesman and found him inadequate.

"Oh, no one famous. Just a teacher I once had. Never had a good word for anyone. Nobody liked her."

"I see."

"You're welcome. Folks, our very own Miss Felicity, until a couple weeks ago, held a senior position at the UK headquarters of one of the world's biggest investment banks. She joined the bank's management training program straight out of college—"

"University," corrected Miss Felicity.

"Of course. University. By the time she became the youngest vice president in the bank's history, Miss Felicity was bored. An over-achiever surrounded by dullards. She alleviated the boredom by stealing from her employers. After getting away with small amounts, she wrote an algorithm to syphon funds day and night. Even when the bank announced an internal audit, she continued the fraud, convinced her abilities were beyond those of any auditor."

Brakesman chuckled. Miss Felicity's frown deepened. She could have held a pound coin between the creases in her forehead.

"She was wrong. So she ran."

Miss Felicity had become very still. The captain smiled and turned his attention to the thin man next to her.

"Whereas Miss Felicity's crimes were cerebral, and confined to the virtual transfer of digital information between encrypted accounts, Buster here is old school. A thief, too, but hands-on. Named after a particularly poor movie I once endured on a long flight."

"Call me what you like, mate," said Buster. His voice was high and wheezy. "I'm only half-listening anyway, tell you the truth. I'm gasping for a smoke, though. Mind if I nip outside?"

Brakesman muttered something, and one of the crew placed a saucer in front of the thief.

"Don't mind if I do," said Buster, taking out a tin, opening it to reveal loose tobacco and papers. He rolled a cigarette without looking at it. Tom found the process entertaining, but Miss Felicity was unimpressed.

"It's illegal to smoke indoors," she said. When everyone ignored her, she coughed and waved her hand at the smoke.

Brakesman continued. "Buster can pick any lock, crack any safe. In these days of cybercrime, as Miss Felicity's ex-employer will tell you, cash-rich organisations are wary of keeping all their reserves online. Many have bought gold, keeping it in physical vaults safe from fifteen-year-olds with a laptop. Not safe from Buster, though. He wants to retire—"

"Too bloody right," added Buster, coughing wetly. Miss Felicity wrinkled her nose, adding a layer of disgust to her disapproval.

"However," said Brakesman, "Buster is a victim of his own success. His clients don't want him to retire, and they are used to getting what they want. When Buster found out he had eighteen months to live—"

"Cancer, innit." Buster laughed at the expression on Miss Felicity's face. "You never would have guessed, right? Anyway, what the Captain is trying to say is that, since I ain't got any family or whatnot, I thought it was about time I treated myself. Lived a little. Made the most of the time left."

He nodded at Brakesman. "I've got nothing to hide, mate. Whatever you're up to, I'm past caring. Fags, booze, and fanny, that's what I'm after. Sorry, love."

This last was addressed to Miss Felicity. "I should hope so," she said, stiffly. "I don't want to listen to such foul-mouthed—"

"Nah, poppet. I'm not sorry about that. I'm just letting you down gently. You're not my type. I like 'em a bit bloody happier. With some meat on their bones, too."

He laughed again, this time joined by the couple at the next table. Hannibal turned his dead eyes towards the noise.

"There are two of you left to discuss," said the captain. He pointed at the broad-shouldered ginger man. "Clint first."

He might as well have been addressing a statue for all the response he got.

"Here's what we know. Clint is military, almost certainly SAS, after being cherry-picked from his class at Sandhurst. According to his records, he has served with honour in various hotspots, but achieved nothing exceptional. There are gaps in his records. Odd gaps. I'm guessing Clint here has been serving his country in a more secretive capacity, and the records are a smokescreen. Which is all very exciting. How am I doing?"

Clint gave Brakesman the blank stare a lizard gives a scorpion, just before its tongue flicks out and it crunches it into pieces.

"I did think of calling you Bond, but I've never been a fan. So, Clint it is. In my estimation, folks, Clint is the most dangerous man on this ship. Not to be underestimated."

Miss Felicity had inched away from Buster, who was stubbing out his roll-up on the saucer. Now, she was thigh-to-thigh with Clint, who seemed unaware of her presence. As she listened to what the captain said next, she reversed the manoeuvre.

"Although his records were doctored, we found references in the records of commanding officers that told a sad story. For a man like Clint to end up here, there must have been a colossal fall from grace. A sudden attack of conscience, perhaps, when his country asked him to do something that clashed with his personal morality. If he has any personal morality. The information I paid for suggests the opposite. It suggests Clint went the other way, killing because he enjoyed it. A rogue assassin who loves what he does a little too much. Closer to the truth?"

Sean barked his laugh again, but cut it short when Brakesman shot him a look.

"Of course, I could be wrong about Clint being the most dangerous." Brakesman swivelled to face Tom, who saw a gold tooth at the edge of the captain's smile before he dropped his head.

"Because we have someone even more mysterious. A man who doesn't speak, who has no past. His ID is forged—beautiful job, by the way—and, due to lack of time, we have no useful information on him. Tom Thumb here—Tom's the name on the fake ID—could be anyone. His crimes might be more heinous than the rest of y'all put together. What do you say, Tom?"

Tom was aware of everyone looking his way. He kept his eyes down, waiting for the excruciating moment to pass. His cheeks reddened.

"How sweet. Little Tom Thumb is blushing. Now, we may not know much about Tom other than he—now, what's the politically correct expression?—suffers from learning difficulties, but we do know he wants out of England. A day before we sailed, an anonymous benefactor paid three times the going rate for Tom's passage to compensate for the short notice."

Bonnie whistled at that. "That's a shitload of money."

The Captain nodded at Sean, who turned over the cover of the flip chart. The page contained all of their nicknames, each with a figure opposite.

Bonnie22
    Clyde22
    Hannibal15
    Buster7
    Miss Felicity5

Clint3
    Tom Thumb1

. . .

Tom found his name on the flip chart. He couldn't read the rest, but he looked anyway. He knew his mind stored information, even if he didn't understand it. It was like taking photographs for Jimmy Blue.

Looking away, he glimpsed a face in a window. It was dark outside, and the face was a pixilated blur, swaying, coiling, watching. A crewman saw Tom look and followed his gaze to the window. After a second, he turned back. Blue remained Tom's secret for now. An uninvited guest.

"What are these numbers?" said the man next to Tom. Hannibal. Tom couldn't remember what Brakesman had said about him.

The crew exchanged smirks, apart from Ronnie.

Tom attempted to focus on the Captain's words.

"We may not have the glamour, glitz, and facilities of a cruise ship, but the *Trevanian* scores more highly than the most exclusive cruises in one area: entertainment."

"Yeah. We saw the table tennis table," deadpanned Bonnie.

"What I'm referring to, as hard as it is to believe, may be even more exciting than ping-pong."

Brakesman leaned forwards. "We arrive in New York Wednesday night, twenty-three hundred hours local time. Four nights from now. Between our current position and our destination is the body of water known as the Atlantic Ocean, upon which we are sailing at a speed of between fifteen and twenty knots.

"Our encrypted internet router is off-limits, and—now that we have Clint's phone—we control access to the only satellite communication devices onboard."

The silence in the room was complete. They didn't know what was coming next, but no one expected anything good.

Brakesman gave Ronnie a nod, and the engineer picked up the canvas bag containing their phones and knives. He left the mess, and —under the harsh floodlights outside—he took a run up to the railing, his right arm windmilling. He released the bag as he reached the side, and it shot out over the water, vanishing into darkness.

The Indian woman half-stood, then changed her mind.

Ronnie came back in and stood alongside his crew mates as

Brakesman spoke.

"Out here there are no countries, no police, no laws. The *Trevanian* is my domain. My country. My laws.

"There are no records of your passage. The only evidence you were on board *Trevanian* is your belongings, and your physical body.

"The contents of your cabins have been noted, plus the value represented by the containers each of you—apart from Tom— booked passage for."

Clyde's fists were clenched in front of him. "If you've been messing with our stuff..."

"Your stuff? Not anymore."

Clyde couldn't hide the murderous expression that crossed his features, but Bonnie's hand gripped his forearm, and he didn't move.

Brakesman appeared to be oblivious. "We have a rough total of the value you represent, as a group. Which stands at a little over seven million dollars."

A few members of the crew grinned. Tom looked at his fellow passengers. Hannibal was unmoved, Bonnie and Clyde still eyed the automatic weapons. Buster rolled another cigarette, and Miss Felicity went pale, making her frown lines even more prominent. Clint, almost imperceptibly, shifted his position to perch on the very edge of his chair.

"The numbers on the flip chart represent the percentage of the prize pool assigned to each of you."

"No, they don't."

The captain's brown, bald head jerked at the interruption. Miss Felicity's voice had lost all colour.

"And why is that, Miss Felicity?"

"It adds up to seventy-five, not a hundred."

"How astute. The twenty-five percent covers my expenses. Consider it a finder's fee."

Clyde spoke next. "Okay. Fine. So how do we win this money?"

Sean's seal bark was joined by a chorus of laughs from his side of the room. Even the captain chuckled.

"Oh, it's not for you. I'm afraid you won't be sharing the prize pool. That's not your role at all."

"What is our sodding role, then?"

"A very simple one. Your role is to run, to hide, and to die."

CHAPTER EIGHTEEN

PANDEMONIUM. Everyone got to their feet on the passenger side of the mess, apart from Tom and Clint. Tom looked across at the man Brakesman had called an assassin, whose eyes remained on the armed crew.

Brakesman raised his hands.

"Folks. Simmer down. Simmer down."

Sean produced a knife from behind his back, shaking his head at Clyde, who—yelling and pointing—was edging around the table towards the crew. When Clyde ignored him, Sean flicked his hand and caught the knife by its blade. The dark steel weapon had no handle.

One moment, Sean's fingers loosely gripped the flat of the blade. The next his hand was empty, and Clyde was stumbling backwards. An inch ahead of where he had been standing, the knife quivered in the floor.

Recovering his composure, Clyde darted forwards to snatch the knife. As he reached down for it, a second blade joined the first with a solid *thunk* that sent Clyde back again so abruptly he slipped and fell, landing on his backside.

Tom looked at Sean. He held a third knife now.

"Sit down. All of you."

They did as instructed. Sean retrieved his blades, which left their scars in the laminate flooring to add to the dozens already there.

When Sean returned to his post, he reached behind his back, re-sheathing the knives without taking his eyes off the passengers.

The captain waited for silence.

"Let me explain how this works. It's now almost twenty-three hundred hours. The game begins at midnight. You have from the end of this briefing until then to talk through strategies, alliances, what-ever. Discuss the weather if you like. Your cabins are now locked and off-limits. All access doors leading below decks are also locked. Once the clock strikes twelve, you will leave the mess. After midnight, everything from the superstructure to the stern is off-limits, and will be guarded. Come back and we shoot you.

"The game runs between midnight and oh-eight-hundred hours. Outside of that time, you are at liberty to get some rest, enjoy the view, consider your mortality.

"At the bow, you'll find a large unlocked container. It's not part of a stack, and there are air holes up top. Wouldn't want you suffocating and spoiling our fun. It contains mattresses for all of you, supplies of water, dried fruit, cheese, bread, and tinned goods. You'll need to keep your strength up. In the back is a bathroom. Of sorts.

"During the day, you are free to use the area between that container and the bow, including the forward mooring deck. This territory is clearly marked."

Tom thought of the painted red lines he'd seen by the solitary container at the prow.

"Stray out of bounds outside game hours and you'll be shot. I advise you not to test me on that. Someone is always watching from the bridge. We take turns on the sniper rifle."

Buster put his hand up. "Oi."

Brakesman acknowledged the interruption. "Yes?"

"Let me just check I've got this right. You bunch of bastards are going to try to kill us?"

"Correct."

"I've got months to live, pal, which I plan to spend drinking, gambling, and shagging, and you're seriously telling me you're going to hunt me down on this piece of shit boat and finish me off before I even get a chance to unhook the first bra?"

"I'm afraid so."

Buster gave Brakesman a look associated with finding something dog-related on the sole of a shoe.

"Wanker."

The captain chuckled again. With the laughter lines around his eyes, his white moustache and bald head, he looked like a benign grandpa, giving his words a surreal dissonance. It was more like watching television than reality. Which made what followed doubly shocking.

"Question for you, mate." Clyde was looking at the flip chart. "If you think Clint here is so dangerous, how come he's worth fuck all? If he's some super spy assassin, he'll make a crossbow out of his watch and a piece of string, and pick you off one by one. You're just a bunch of amateurs. I don't fancy your chances much."

Brakesman pointed at Clint, who still maintained his state of alert stillness, perched on the edge of his chair.

"Clyde makes a good point. Why *is* Clint's share of the bounty so low? Think of it like golf. What happens when amateurs play with the professionals? Stand up, Clint."

The wiry man ignored him until Sean produced one of his throwing knives. When he stood, Brakesman picked up a green first aid box from the wall behind and tossed it over. Clint caught it, his expression unreadable. He spoke for the first time. His accent belied the Bond comparison, being broad Welsh.

"And what do you expect me to do with th—"

The captain pulled out a handgun from his desk drawer and shot Clint an inch above his right knee. His leg gave way, and he fell. The heightened silence beforehand exacerbated the shock of the sudden sound.

Clint's dark blue canvas trousers shredded as he buckled, and the laminate floor became wet with blood and flecks of bone. His face, grey and shiny with sweat, tensed with pain, but he didn't make a sound. He opened the first aid box that had fallen alongside him, took out a small pair of scissors, and cut through his trousers. Once the wound was exposed, he examined it. He removed a roll of bandages and a pair of tweezers from the kit. Rather than unroll the bandages, he put them in his mouth and bit down, pushing the tweezers into the open wound, which seeped dark red blood.

"Oh, no," said Miss Felicity, turning away.

The bleeding man's hand stayed steady as he pushed into the wrecked, torn flesh with the tweezers. Clint didn't hesitate as he located the bullet, gripped it and pulled, dropping it, and the tweezers, onto the floor. He carried on biting the bandage roll while spraying antiseptic into the wound. He held a pad across the bullet hole, then used the bandage from his mouth, wrapping the fabric tight.

Once done, he looked back at Brakesman, his neutral expression replaced with something darker. There was a promise in that look, and the older man blanched, covering his reaction by applauding the impromptu first aid demonstration.

"Impressive. As I was saying, we're amateurs playing with a professional. Only fair to give him a handicap. Don't be offended, Clint. You're still worth a couple hundred thousand bucks. Not bad for a cripple."

The silence returned, heavy now with the knowledge that the captain's briefing had not been an attempt at black humour.

"Make sure you're out at midnight," said Brakesman, standing, "and the game will begin. We'll give you ten minutes' grace. Good luck."

He winked.

Most of the crew followed Brakesman out through the corridor leading to the cabins and the bridge above. Sean remained with two armed men.

"I have a question." The voice came from Hannibal. Sean turned.

The Dutchman, who looked more like a doctor or solicitor than a serial killer, rose to his feet.

"What happens afterwards? What happens to those who survive your game?"

Sean treated them to his percussive laugh. "Well, that's an interesting question. I'm gonna have to come clean and admit I don't know. We've played twelve, thirteen times now. No one has survived yet."

The last crew members left, locking the door behind them.

The seven passengers looked at each other. A silent man, a serial killer, a professional thief, two twenty-first century bandits, a fraudster, and—if Brakesman's guess was right—a secret agent with one working leg.

All sentenced to death.

CHAPTER NINETEEN

THE PASSENGERS SEARCHED the mess after trying the doors and finding them locked. The windows were designed to withstand the impact of storms at sea. Anything that could resist tons of seawater wouldn't provide a means of escape.

The cutlery drawer was empty of anything useful as a makeshift weapon.

The first aid box yielded two strips of paracetamol, and Clint dry-swallowed three tablets while the others searched for anything that might help.

They found nothing, returning to their tables, each lost in their thoughts. The clock's tick was the only sound audible above the constant hum of the ship's engines.

They talked to distract them from the second hand's constant reminder.

Buster became the de facto leader of the group. Everyone accepted this, perhaps because of the thief's impending death. He had nothing to prove, and his workmanlike attitude to the deadly situation they were in kept the atmosphere calmer than it might otherwise have become.

He spoke in short sentences, broken up by puffs on a roll-up.

"Way I see it, we need to cooperate to stand a chance. We split up, and they can take their own sweet time picking us off. Hunt us down. One by one. Was that the entire crew just then? Nine of 'em including the walrus?"

No one laughed at his description of Captain Brakesman.

The Dutchman coughed. Every head swivelled round to look at the serial killer. "I have travelled this way once before. On a ship this size, I would expect more crew. At least twelve. Perhaps Brakesman runs a skeleton crew. Less chance of someone betraying him, or talking too much when they're home."

No one responded to his speculation, other than to regard him with a variety of expressions ranging from horrified to murderous.

"What?" Hannibal's tone remained mild. "Am I mistaken?"

"You shitting me?" Clyde was on his feet, standing between Bonnie and Hannibal. "You're the fucking elephant in the room, pal. None of us are saints, we get that, but you? You stalk women, drug them, and kill them. I don't want to breathe the same air."

He appealed to the group. "I say we off him now, save them a job. There are two women here. You happy teaming up with this sicko? Sleeping in a shipping container with him? Laney?"

His partner stood up and stood alongside him. "I'm with you, babe. And call me Bonnie. I like it. I say put him out of his misery. Who's with us?"

Hannibal scanned the room without any outward sign of emotion as Miss Felicity raised her hand.

"That's three," said Clyde. "One more for a majority. Clint? Buster? What about you, Tom?"

Tom wasn't sure what Clyde was asking. He hadn't been paying attention. Blue was so close, he imagined he could hear him breathing. He looked blankly back at Clyde.

"Great. Just great. A sicko, a thicko, and,"—he waved at Clint, unable to think of a rhyme—"a lame secret agent. Plus a bloke who's dying, and a fraudster. We're all screwed. Well? Who's with us? Who else reckons we're better off with Hannibal dead? Come on."

Buster spoke without removing his cigarette. "Nah. Sit down. I've got a better idea."

"You're joking, right? I'm not teaming up with him."

"No one's asking you to. Sit down."

Clyde glared at Hannibal as he and Bonnie complied.

"Thank you." Buster stubbed out the roll-up with yellow-tipped fingers. "I agree with you on one point. He needs to die."

"Excuse me?" Hannibal's tone was as calm as if Buster had asked him for the time.

Buster ignored him, speaking to Clyde. "But he's more use to us alive right now. We know sod all about the crew. How they plan to hunt us, I mean. We can find out more if we give them Hannibal. We get out there, find somewhere we can hide. Somewhere we can defend. They're armed, we're not. So we pick a spot where they'd have to engage us at close quarters, right? Somewhere we might even ambush one or two of them. On the face of it, I admit, 'scuse language, we're fucked. They have guns, knives, who knows what else. They know this ship inside out. Me, I get lost on the bleedin' Isle of Wight ferry. Anyone know anything about container ships?"

No one answered.

"Right. So, the way I see it, there's one thing in our favour. It's a competition for the crew, innit? Everyone wants his share of the prize. Two of them might work together, split the cash. But we're not up against one big, coordinated team, are we? They're cocky because they hold every card. They might get sloppy."

Miss Felicity had regained a little colour. "They've done this twelve or thirteen times. Statistically, it's unlikely we'll try anything that hasn't been tried before."

"Statistically? If I trusted statistics, love, I would have spent half me life inside. As it is, I ain't even been arrested. You can keep your statistics. We beat these tossers by using what's up 'ere."

He tapped his head, then leaned forward to get a better view of Clint. The wounded man had listened impassively throughout.

"What do you think, mate? Brakesman said you were the biggest threat."

"I think we're all going to die."

"Fuck me. Glad I asked."

Clint's mouth twitched in amusement. "Doesn't mean we can't take some of them with us. Make them work for it. We do that, and we make room for the *deus*."

He grimaced with pain and shifted his leg to a more comfortable position.

"The what?"

Miss Felicity answered. "*Deus* means god in Latin."

"Great." Buster rolled another cigarette. "Didn't peg you for the religious type. No offence, but I'm not pinning my hopes on the big fella swooping down and helping us out."

"Not god. *Deus ex machina*. God from the machine. It's a literary term."

"Lawdy. An intellectual *and* an assassin. And how does your sex machine help, exactly?"

"Ex. *Ex machina*." Clint scooted backwards to the table and pulled himself up, lips compressed in pain. Bonnie stepped forward to help, but he waved her away. "No. Let me do it. I have to test my limits. See if I stand a chance of making it through the first ten minutes."

He hoisted himself into a standing position, putting all his weight on his left leg. When he transferred a little weight to his injured leg, he hissed with pain.

"I'm going to need a crutch. Tom?"

Tom responded sluggishly. Jimmy Blue remained hidden. Tom's mental faculties were clogging, becoming hard to access. He stood up when Clint spoke to him.

"The curtain rail. Probably the best we can do. Can you get it for me?"

It took Tom a few seconds to process the request. Clyde, who had been talking with Bonnie, stood up. "Jesus. What a plank. I'll get it myself."

He walked over to the window, Tom following. Clyde knelt on the counter top and got both hands onto the metal rail, pulling hard. It didn't shift. He examined the fixings.

"Anyone got a screwdriver? Swiss Army knife? Anything?"

"I didn't ask you, Clyde," said Clint. "Why don't you sit down?"

"Fine by me." Clyde slid off the counter, glaring at the wounded man. "Try to do some people a favour."

Clint didn't respond, his eyes on the silent passenger.

Tom reached up. He was a few inches taller than Clyde, and could wrap his fingers around the metal curtain rail. He gave it one brisk pull, and it came away from the wall, the screws holding it in place falling on the floor. He handed it to Clint. Clyde looked on with disbelief at the demonstration of physical strength.

Clint gave Tom the tiniest of nods. "Thank you."

Tom looked at the table where he had been sitting. Hannibal looked back. Tom sat down next to Clint, who wrapped a second bandage around one end of the curtain rail, securing it with medical tape. He tested it under his armpit, taking a few steps.

"Not bad at all. Maybe I'll survive the first night." He looked around the disparate group of passengers.

"*Deus ex machina.* God from the machine. Something happens at the last minute to save the good guy, or the bad guy's gun jams as he's about to kill the hero. It's a way writers cheat. Readers hate it because they see through it. They stop enjoying the story when they see the workings behind it. They think it never happens in real life."

"They think?" said Buster.

"Yes. But ask any writer, and they'll tell you about real life incidents they didn't put in a book because no one would believe it. Real life doesn't worry about surprising, or disappointing, readers. More often than you realise, sheer bloody luck wins the day. Coincidence. The unexpected. Serendipity. Without it, I'd be dead a few times over. That's what I mean by the *deus.*"

"Nope," said Bonnie. "Still don't get it."

"Here's how it works. We do everything we can to screw up this sick game. We make them sweat for it, every step of the way. We delay them if we can, we strike back if it's possible. However badly the odds are stacked against us, we fight until the very end. Because our only chance of surviving is if something happens that none of us anticipate."

"The *deus*," said Buster.

"The *deus*," echoed Clint.

Buster chuckled. "It'll take more than a bloody *deus* to save me. Still, now you know how it feels having a death sentence. Funny how precious life gets when you're about to lose it."

They all jumped when the ship's horn sounded three long blasts.

A face appeared at the window. Moments later, the outside door opened, and Sean walked in, one of his throwing knives in his right hand. Two other crew members followed, guns held ready.

Sean grinned and pointed his knife at the door leading to the deck.

"It's eleven-fifty," said Sean. "Ten minutes before the game begins. Good luck, and thank you. This trip will buy me a new pickup and a few weeks in Hawaii."

He left laughing, followed by his gun-toting colleagues.

Clint looked down the dark corridor after the chief mate. "I don't know about you, but just the way that arsehole laughs makes me want to kill him."

CHAPTER TWENTY

THERE WAS little wind on deck. Early June, and the air was cool rather than cold. The passengers stayed together, knowing they had only minutes before they became prey.

"Come on," said Buster. "Let's put some distance between us and the bridge. Find somewhere we can defend. Oh."

The others followed Buster's gaze. Now they knew what the final two crewmen had been doing outside. Coils of barbed wire covered the deck between the superstructure and the railings, held in place by sandbags. A check on the port side revealed an identical barrier.

"Guess they don't want us going that way," said Buster, shrugging. At the port railing, he turned towards the bow.

Clint leaned out over the railing and stared up at the sky before limping behind Buster, makeshift crutch under his armpit. The rest followed.

"Good news," he said. "Cloudy. If they plan on sniping, the weather will make their job harder. Not that sniping will be easy on a ship like this."

Buster slowed to join the limping man. At intervals along the covered walkway, ladders led to the containers. Climbing to that level would expose them to anyone watching from the bridge. "Won't they have night vision, mate? That's real, right? You're the spy. You know this stuff."

"Not a spy. But yes, it's real. And we have to assume they have it."

"So how does the weather help?"

"Wouldn't help much on some ships. But this is one of the bigger container vessels. Three hundred metres long. Even the best night vision scope is only accurate for about two hundred metres. That's assuming no external motion, no wind, a tripod, and an expert marksman. Where's the best spot for a sniper?"

Miss Felicity was standing at Buster's shoulder. She pointed behind them. "On top of the superstructure. Great view from there."

"Correct." Clint winced as he shifted his weight to look up. "The flying bridge. A half-decent shooter with a telescopic sight stands a fair chance of hitting us during the day. Still tough, though, having to factor in the ship's motion. If they break their own rules about leaving us alone during the day, we're dead."

"Lovely." Buster lit up again. "Quite the morale booster, mate."

Clint plucked the cigarette from Buster's lips and flicked it over the railing towards the water. "This might be a good time to break a habit that involves waving a tiny flame around at night."

Buster glared at him for a few seconds before winking at the younger man.

"Fair point."

The group moved on in silence. Clint pulled at one of the metal hatches leading below to the cargo hold below. A heavy-duty padlock prevented access.

At intervals, painted signs indicated life rafts, but in each case, the allotted space stood empty. The lights that should have lit their progress were dark.

Halfway to the bow, Buster stopped to address his fellow passengers. In the shadow of the containers towering above, it was so dark he couldn't make out their faces.

"Hannibal?"

No one moved. Then the Dutchman stumbled forward, pushed from behind.

"This is where we say goodbye. You're on your own. Stay with us, and you'll be fish food by morning."

"Too right," said Bonnie.

"What do you expect me to do?" Hannibal's tone was neutral. The evidence of the past few hours suggested he was a stranger to extreme emotions. "Where should I go?"

"I think I speak for all of us," said Buster, taking out his tobacco tin, before remembering Clint's warning, and replacing it in his pocket, "when I say I don't give a shit. Just get out of our bloody sight, and stay out of it."

The serial killer looked into the dying man's eyes. Without a word, he turned and walked back towards the stern. Clyde unleashed a punch at the side of his head that sent him reeling into a container. He spat blood. They heard his footsteps fade into the darkness.

No one spoke for a while. They'd sent a man to his death.

Near the bow, alongside a ladder, Clint nudged Buster to stop.

"Pretty sure we're out of range now. If we climb the containers, it'd be a thousand-to-one shot for a sniper."

Buster stood at the bottom of the ladder and eyed the dark cargo towers. "Well, it's a million-to-one I could climb a single box, mate, so no worries on that score. You fancy your chances?"

Clint smiled grimly. "With two legs, it'd be a different story. As it is, unless one of us is a mountaineer?"

The others were catching up, lighter shapes in the blackness. No one volunteered to attempt the climb. Clint sighed.

"Any of these corridors between the containers might give us a spot to hide, but we'll have to post scouts, and be prepared to move quickly. There's a passage between the containers from the bow to the bridge. Like a central road, with narrower corridors every so often linking port and starboard. Like a spine with ribs. In theory, if we knew where the crew members were, we could avoid them by using those corridors, staying one step ahead."

Miss Felicity stepped closer.

"That's a big if. How would we know where they were?"

Clint leaned heavily against the nearest container. "That's a problem. Even if we post scouts, how do we communicate without drawing any attention?"

Bonnie and Clyde whispered to each other.

"You two got any good ideas?" said Buster. "The ten minutes are nearly up."

Bonnie nodded. "Yeah, actually. Just the one good idea."

"We're all ears."

"This ain't working. The whole group thing. Not for us. Hannibal's out there somewhere, looking for a hole to crawl into. Hopefully, the crew finds him first, and he keeps them busy before they kill him. But sticking together doesn't sound smart to us. They find one of us, they find all of us. No thanks. Me and Clyde are splitting."

Buster offered no rebuttal. His eyes dropped to the deck for a moment before he responded.

"I think you're making a mistake, but it's your decision."

Clyde took Bonnie's hand, scanned the faces of the others. "Good luck."

With that, they were gone, climbing the short ladder to the container corridor and jogging away, their silhouettes quickly blending into the greater darkness and disappearing.

The ship's horn marked their departure with three long blasts. The period of grace was over. The hunters were coming.

Clint looked at the others, then stumped a few feet back towards the bridge before stopping, his crutch tapping on the metal deck.

Miss Felicity stayed with Buster, but hissed after the limping man, "What are you doing?"

Clint took a long look back along the passageway, into the shadows.

"When was the last time anyone saw Tom?"

———

Tom followed the others out of the mess, hanging back as they passed the first ladder.

A darkness deeper than night called him, and he went towards it gladly. It was time. Time for Jimmy Blue to take charge.

It happened as he walked, and it happened faster than any previous occasion Tom could remember. The darkness came to meet him in a rush, filling his lungs, his blood, and his mind; a maelstrom of energy and wicked, violent mischief.

He was heading away from land, out into the middle of the Atlantic, trapped on-board with a ruthless crew who intended to murder every passenger before tossing their bodies overboard, where they'd be lost forever.

He started smiling as his posture altered, holding a latent energy that made him appear bigger, more solid. More dangerous.

Jimmy Blue jogged lightly along the corridor that spanned the width of the ship between the high container stacks. The height of the stacks varied above him, but Tom's tour that day had allowed him to build a mental map of the entire ship. The containers offered a maze to move around in once he located the lowest point to begin his climb.

Not yet, though. The stacks were for later. He had an appointment to keep.

He reached the end of the corridor and out to the port side walkway. Instead of turning right towards the bow, he headed left, back to the bridge and its murderous crew.

Jimmy checked his watch. Three minutes until the passengers became prey. Or until the crew became prey.

He grinned and broke into a run.

CHAPTER TWENTY-ONE

LEUNG KNEW SEAN DESPISED HIM, having done so ever since he joined the *Trevanian* eighteen months earlier. The chief mate referred to Ronnie as too small, too quiet, and too Korean. The bulked-up, show-off American trusted no one who didn't eat burgers or play poker.

Ronnie endured Sean's loud, frequent expressions of distaste concerning his looks, manner, nationality, and assumed sexual persuasion. Even on a vast ship, the communal areas were small, and often there was no avoiding the big American. One thing Ronnie wouldn't do, though, was respond. His calm demeanour proved a continual source of frustration and irritation to his tattooed crew mate. A minor victory, but satisfying nonetheless.

Perhaps because of the tension between the two men, Captain Brakesman teamed them up. Ronnie responded to the unwanted pairing with stoic silence. Sean sulked.

Their partnership had not yet achieved glory. Sean favoured displays of aggression and dominance, killing with his throwing knives if possible, using a handgun only if there was no alternative. Putting bullets into unarmed men and women jarred with his self-image as a pure warrior. A knife in the back was fine, though.

Ronnie, as Sean often pointed out, despite expressing distaste at

Brakesman's murderous game, was not so outraged to refuse his bonuses. He had responsibilities back in Busan and Ronnie's expanding property portfolio in the Philippines provided passive income ready for when he gave up the sea.

But Ronnie would need more than a letter of notice to the captain to leave this job. He had new ID papers waiting in New York, where he intended, at the end of this trip, to disappear. He just had to get through the next few nights. And, as much as he despised the thought of what would happen to the passengers, this time would be different. Since meeting Tom, Ronnie had decided to act. Nothing could make up for his prior involvement in the games, but he was going to try. Ronnie intended to save a life.

In the mess, as the echo of the ship's horn faded, Sean and Ronnie didn't rush to join their shipmates, who were keen to pick off the weakest of the passengers. As usual, they hung back, waiting.

The main lights in the mess were turned off when the passengers left. Desk lamps and the glow of screens now illuminated every room in the superstructure. Combined with the exterior floodlights, which lit the first twenty yards of the deck like a stage, the effect rendered the interior of the superstructure invisible to anyone outside.

The Binaries left first, touting semi-automatic weapons, night vision goggles pushed up on army surplus helmets. Both named Steve, and both fit, young Midwest Americans, the captain teamed them up so he only had to yell one name. The Steve who had been on the crew longest usually answered to Stevo. When his namesake turned up, some wit differentiated them by referring to the newcomer as Steve-one. Gary, the *Trevanian*'s navigator and the closest thing to a medical officer, collectively named Stevo and Steve-one the Binaries. It stuck.

"That's it, go pick the low-hanging fruit, why don't you?" Sean teased, throwing his knives over and over into the floor of the mess.

The Goodfellas were next. Mike and Tony were Italian-American New Yorkers. Mike was in his fifties, an ex-Marine with a dishonourable discharge on his record. A once brawny, muscled frame had given way to a paunchy heaviness, folds of fat rolling over the collars of his polo shirts. He shaved his head, and long exposure to the sun gave his scalp a leathery quality.

Tony was Mike's junior by a quarter of a century, his brown eyes and lustrous hair a shortcut to beds in ports all over the world. He dropped out of college after a scandal involving the Dean's wife, a bottle of baby oil, and a Facebook livestream. After his family disowned him. he found a father figure in Mike: permanently angry and explosively violent.

As they left, bristling with weapons, Sean looked up at the sound of a distant whine above them, rising and falling in pitch. He flicked his wrist to send a knife next to its fellows quivering in the floor.

"Captain's giving the new toy a quick test flight."

Brakesman's new toy was a drone as expensive as a small car. It had six cameras mounted on its chassis, a mix of regular, night vision, and infrared. He ran it from the bridge, watching on tablet screens, as it flew its pre-mapped course, sending pin-sharp images back. If his hunting obsession hadn't already been obvious from the animal heads adorning the stateroom, his long stories of tracking a pride of lions or a stray buck elephant in the African veldt would have made it tediously clear. Sean, the most technologically adept crewman, helped his boss familiarise himself with the drone's controls, even suggesting Brakesman could adapt it to hold a weapon. Brakesman drew the line at this unsportsmanlike application of technology.

"It's not pure unless it's man against beast, or man against man. It has to be pure, son." Sean didn't point out it was usually man with sophisticated sniper rifle and telescopic sight against terrified unarmed man or woman a hundred yards away. He liked his job too much. Especially the bonuses.

The final team were the ones most likely to win the big money on the leader board, but they were taking first shift in the mess tonight, so wouldn't be hunting until four a.m. Cashman and Hicks were both in their forties, both experienced sailors and, Sean suspected, both veterans of organised crime in their home country, Germany. After Sean, they were the longest-serving crew members, joining the *Trevanian* five years earlier. They used their surnames, which Sean found hard to pronounce, so he'd rechristened them. Nicknames were common among sailors, and Cashman and Hicks accepted theirs without complaint.

Both men wore dark, lightweight clothes. Shoulder holsters held handguns, and their belts hunting knives and spare ammunition. Weapons designed to be used at a greater distance, such as those the Binaries and Goodfellas carried, risked only injuring, rather than killing, their victims. A wounded passenger wouldn't trigger a bounty, plus their injuries made them easier pickings for whichever crew member found them next. But a handgun shot from twelve feet would put anyone down. A follow-up to the head ended them. Cashman and Hicks perpetuated the myth of Teutonic efficiency, and their record of kills stood as testament to their methodical approach.

The Germans nodded at Sean and Ronnie. Cashman left for the bridge, leaving Hicks to lock up behind the last team.

Sean and Ronnie's pairing had generated no nickname. Not yet.

Sean embraced the management principle of delegation to a degree previously unheard of. He barely worked, spending his days in the gym, watching movies, or playing poker with those who accepted losing a little money to him as a price worth paying to stay on his good side. He was volatile, unprofessional, and lazy. Whatever dirt he had on the captain, mused his shipmates in private, it must be pretty damn good.

Ronnie checked the names on the flip chart as Sean's knives *thunked* rhythmically into the deck behind him. Brakesman assured them this was the richest group of passengers they had ever welcomed on board. Given that previous Atlantic crossings featured well-funded crime families and the gang behind a notorious Paris bank heist, this meant a fat purse.

Ronnie thought about Tom. Had the silent man understood the attempt to warn him? Impossible to tell. There had been no sign of comprehension. If his attempt to communicate had failed, the big, dumb idiot wouldn't make it through the first hour.

He tapped his finger against the last name on the list.

Tom Thumb

"Okay, Ronnie, my little Korean friend." Sean tucked the knives back into their sheath behind his back. "Time to go."

Ronnie turned away from the chart. If Tom had run with the others, he was a dead man.

Sean held open the door with his foot to let Ronnie through.

He'd know in the next few minutes.

———

Out on deck, Sean and Ronnie fell into the patterns they had established on their first hunt together. Which meant Sean telling Ronnie what to do, and Ronnie doing it.

The Binaries and Goodfellas, representing the heavy artillery, checked obvious hiding places and sprayed automatic fire at anyone they found there. The crew's knowledge of the ship gave them a huge advantage, and they used it without mercy. For such a massive vessel, there were surprisingly few places to hide unless you scaled the maze of containers, and it took a talented, strong climber to do that. Which meant the next few hours involved picking off easy targets, those lowest on the bounty list.

Although they occasionally survived the night, some passengers —more used to being the hunter, not the hunted—made the error of trying to out-think the crew in the first couple of hours. They'd double back, get close to the bridge, try to overwhelm the guards.

It never worked. An array of CCTV cameras covered the surface of the superstructure. The floodlights meant no one got near without being seen.

But it gave Sean and Ronnie an opportunity for a decent bounty on their first sortie. With luck on their side. They stayed close to the stern and the bridge, ready to move on any overconfident, high-bounty passengers who couldn't stop themselves being proactive.

All the crew used shortwave radios. There were two channels: one general, the other private to each team. Ronnie and Sean split up. They made for their regular positions alongside the superstructure, which afforded a good view of anyone approaching. Sean covered the starboard, Ronnie the port.

Ronnie moved with a little less fear, and a little more confidence, than in previous games. For once, he held some power of his own. If Tom had read his note, he wouldn't need luck.

Instead of hunkering down behind a sandbag, he hurried to the container he had prepared that afternoon.

CHAPTER TWENTY-TWO

JIMMY BLUE WAITED in the darkness, his pulse slowing. He listened intently, paying attention to each individual sound. His body first, the blood, the breath, the slow thump of his heart. He moved his attention outwards to the permanent, ever-changing melody of the Atlantic. No, not a melody, a symphony, simultaneously dissonant and harmonically pleasing, a million individual sounds heard as a single, shifting song. The engine came next: a crude instrumental in a metre that ignored the main theme, instead providing a sloppily rhythmic counterpoint to the ocean. It made itself known through the soles of the feet as much as the ears, a vibration sailors continue to feel days after they disembark. The wind came next, more capricious than the ocean. A darting, probing breath, exploring gaps in walkways, between containers, and along the heavy anchor chains.

Human sounds provided the topmost layer, and they varied from the subtle to the obvious. The crew made little attempt at stealth as the first teams exited the superstructure and began their sweep of the deck. They were armed and prepared, with no need to skulk. The hunted passengers were harder to detect and—with the noise of the engine covering much of their movement—Blue couldn't be confident about what he heard. First, one sound signature moved away from the rest and into the stacks. Hannibal, most likely. No one wanted him anywhere near. Minutes later, the group split again. The obvious splinter group was Bonnie and Clyde, a ready-made partnership, meaning Clint, Buster, and Miss Felicity made up the larger team.

Jimmy held himself in relaxed readiness, allowing no internal distractions to interfere with his heightened awareness. Blue's mind was a powerhouse. With time, physical gifts would diminish, but his intellect, given the correct conditions, stimuli, and care, would continue to flourish. Snapped bones could be fixed, muscles and ligaments would heal, but attrition could only be delayed, not halted. His body might be broken over and over, but his will remained indomitable. Or so he assumed until the morning a sixty-eight-year-old Taoist slapped his face before he knew she had moved. Letting go of thought meant moving beyond time. She taught Tom to release his illusory will. Later, Blue tried to apply the same lesson, adapting the technique to suit his needs. In his practice, a shred of will remained, diamond-hard and unbreakable. His teacher would have considered that shred a flaw, but without it, he was nothing.

He used the method now, drawing himself into the darkness he wore like a cloak. Thoughts still sparked into existence, but lost coherence and vanished like curls of smoke when faced with his disinterest. Thinking became a tool, no more, no less. He didn't need it now, so Jimmy let his thoughts drift free of his attention.

Before stilling his mind, he pictured the words on the letter slipped under Tom's door.

Tom

Please trust me. I want to help you. You are in danger. Tonight, after the captain speaks to everyone, go to the spot I have marked with an X. The container there looks locked, but it isn't. Go inside. I will meet you. It's your only chance of surviving. You must destroy this note.

Ronnie

The container marked in the diagram was two rows away from where Blue waited.

When the Korean engineer rounded the corner and looked into the shadows where Blue crouched, he saw nothing, sensed nothing, because there was no one to see, no one to sense.

When Ronnie passed his hiding place, Jimmy Blue unfurled himself from the darkness and followed in silence.

CHAPTER TWENTY-THREE

IN THE MESS, the shortwave radio squelched, followed by the chief mate's voice.

"Sean and Ronnie coming in."

Hicks peered through the biggest window, which offered a view towards the prow, the first twenty yards of which were spotlit. Sean appeared from the darkness, the smaller Korean trudging behind him, carrying something. Hicks waited until they reached the door before unlocking it and stepping back, semi-automatic held ready. He didn't relax until both crew members were inside, the door locked behind them.

"Tell the captain to sound the horn." Sean had a big grin on his face. He walked over to the flip chart and picked up a Sharpie.

"Already?"

"Not me, Hicksy, not me. It's all down to my gook—sorry, *good*—buddy here."

Sean's sour expression belied his words of congratulation. Hicks folded his arms in mute disapproval. Sean's opinion, offered loudly, and often, was that the first few hours shouldn't be about killing, but about fun. Yes, the occasional passenger rushed them and got what they deserved, but he preferred chasing the hunted around the ship for a few hours, firing bursts of automatic fire to keep them terrified. Sean liked the passengers psychologically ragged and desperate.

"He had no choice, apparently," said Sean. "Says it was him or the other guy. Come on. You're impressed, right? None of us thought he had it in him."

Ronnie didn't look triumphant, but he smiled at the German and nodded. "He rushed me. Came out of nowhere on the port walkway. Guess he'd been hiding out, hoping we'd miss him. And he tried to take me by surprise."

Sean didn't even let Ronnie finish his own story. "But he got the surprise. Asshole runs at Ronnie while he's at the rail. All our friend here needed to do was to help him over. Momentum did the rest."

The chief mate pantomimed the scenario: Ronnie at the rail, the approaching passenger; his shipmate's instinctive drop to the deck, gripping his assailant's jacket as he fell, pistoning his legs to push him up and over, followed by a long drop to the water below.

Hicks gave his Korean crew mate a brief, semi-ironic, round of applause, and radioed the captain. Seconds later, the ship's horn announced the first scalp of the game.

"Shame we'll never know exactly how he died," said Sean. "It's a long way to fall. Drowned, probably. But he might have survived long enough to be dragged into the propeller." He barked out a laugh.

Ronnie put his prize on the nearest table. A pair of boots, size twelve, the laces knotted together. "Had them around his neck. They fell off when he went over. Guess he thought it would help him sneak up on me."

Sean grinned. "Nice try, Tom, you bozo."

He looked at the flip chart, talking around the Sharpie cap between his lips. "One percent. It ain't gonna make us rich, my young gook friend, but it's a start. It's a start."

He drew a line through Tom's name, wrote *Ronnie* next to it. "One down. Six to go."

CHAPTER TWENTY-FOUR

Twenty minutes earlier

———

Jimmy Blue followed the Korean towards the container he'd marked with an X on his note. In the shadows, he closed up behind Ronnie, his hand closing over his mouth to prevent the scream.

"Don't," said Blue. Ronnie's eyes registered shock, either at hearing the supposedly dumb passenger speak, or because the huge man had sneaked up without him noticing.

Once Ronnie had indicated his compliance, Jimmy Blue released him.

"Talk."

The Korean swallowed hard. It was rare for anyone to meet Tom Lewis *and* Jimmy Blue, particularly so close together, so Blue gave him a few seconds to gather his thoughts. The darkness helped. If Ronnie had examined the cast of Blue's face, the piercing intelligence behind eyes previously dull and witless, he might have run. As it was, he decided to continue as if nothing had changed.

"I... I want to help you, Tom. Look."

He backed away, took a small metal torch from his pocket, shielding it with one hand. The light revealed the door of the faded brown container behind them. It was sealed with a substantial red bolt. Jimmy Blue's research told him this was a bullet seal; an effective way to prevent tampering with containers. Each bullet seal had a unique serial number, documented onboard and in port. Once clicked into place, it could only be removed with bolt cutters.

Ronnie ignored the metal locking handles, opening the door as if the bolt didn't exist. It looked like magic.

Ronnie kept his voice low. "Made it in the shop today. I cut through the bolt. Glued it in place. Looks perfect unless you get close."

The Korean ducked inside. Blue listened, then followed, leaving the door open. He would hear anyone approach before they got close enough to see anything unusual.

Ronnie pulled the door shut, the metal scraping the floor. He pointed the torch back at the doors. "Can't be locked from the outside. I fixed it." He tapped the monkey wrench in the pouch on his belt.

Inside, large, stacked cardboard boxes took up two-thirds of the space.

"Washing machines," said Ronnie. "I checked the manifest for a container that wasn't full. Made it as comfortable as I could."

Comfortable was a generous description. The torch beam moved from the washing machines to the door, revealing two folded grey blankets, a bigger torch, a case of bottled water, a cardboard box, and a sealed plastic tub.

"Some fresh fruit," said Ronnie. "Dry food and tins in the other box. Enough to keep you going until New York. You'll have to stay out of sight until then."

Two items remained. The first was a sealed bucket.

"Toilet," said Ronnie. "Sorry."

The second item was a pair of trainers. Tom's trainers. "I broke into your cabin. I need your boots, see? To convince the others that you went overboard."

He pointed at Tom's feet. "Please."

Blue sat on the shiny floor and unlaced his boots. The Korean, voice low, spoke slowly and clearly, making sure to be understood.

"You'll hear gunshots, screams, shouting. It's going to be scary, but you're safe here. If they come close, if anyone searches nearby, you must stay still. Don't make a sound. Understand?"

Jimmy Blue nodded, intrigued. Why would Ronnie endanger himself for a stranger? This evening's briefing suggested the crew would have no compunction in tossing a traitor overboard. Unless this was some elaborate bluff, and the Korean intended keeping him here until he came to kill him. Unlikely.

"The game will be over by tomorrow night, Tom."

Blue looked up.

"Brakesman lied," said Ronnie. "The game never goes on past the first night. He can't risk anyone surviving. He tells you no one will attack during the day. It's a crock."

Jimmy Blue remained silent. Waited for Ronnie to finish.

"If anyone survives tonight, Sean and the Germans go to the container at the bow. Shoot you while you sleep."

Blue handed Ronnie his boots and squatted to put on his trainers. "Why help me?" he said.

Ronnie opened his mouth to answer. Then he shook his head, picked up the bigger torch and turned it on, handing it to Blue.

"Batteries are fresh, but try not to use it much. I drilled air holes on the side of the container, so not much chance of the light being seen, but it's still a risk."

He moved back to the door, tying the laces of Tom's boots together. "In a little while, we'll sound the ship's horn, Tom. One big blast. It'll mean everyone will think you're dead. So it's very important you stay here until I come get you. I know it's a long time. It's Wednesday today. We get to New York on Monday. Five days, Tom. And I won't be able to come before then. I'm sorry. But you'll be alive."

He opened the door, stopping when Blue gripped his shoulder.

"Tom, please. I know it's hard, but I'm the only friend you have now, understand?"

The hand released Ronnie's shoulder, moved to his belt, and plucked the monkey wrench out of its holder.

"I don't think that's a good..." began Ronnie, then stopped. Took a breath. "OK. OK. Keep it, if it makes you feel safer. It's yours."

He stepped outside, shutting the door behind him. Blue stood with one shoulder against the metal, listening, ready to barge out if Ronnie planned to lock him in somehow. The footsteps receded.

Jimmy Blue clicked off the torch, and the container became dark. Much better.

CHAPTER TWENTY-FIVE

WHILE JIMMY BLUE waited for the ship's horn, he ate the fresh cheese rolls, apple, and chocolate left from the plastic tub.

As soon as the loud, mournful scream—a prehistoric creature calling for its mate—echoed across the ship, he left the container, shouldering the door shut behind him.

He waited in the dark after the horn's note faded. Plenty of sounds of human movement, but none of them close to his hiding place.

The trainers made it easier to achieve near-silence. Blue put every fresh pair through a breaking-in process, flexing the rubber soles in every direction for hours, eliminating telltale creaks.

Jimmy stuck to the shadows until reaching the port walkway. Tom's evening explorations had revealed the best route up to the higher levels. His first destination was the next port-to-starboard corridor between containers.

He visualised his mental schematic, a map of the ship's deck as detailed as the most experienced crew member. More so. The sailors couldn't navigate the shifting landscape made up of tens of thousands of stacked containers. Blue had all the information he could glean from deck level; now he needed to make the mental map complete.

Every container on the ship was eight feet wide and eight-and-a-half feet tall. The majority were forty feet long, each container designed to sit on the trailer bed of an articulated lorry or truck. The remaining containers were half that length, these smaller boxes stacked nearest to the bow.

A forty-footer waited for Jimmy Blue, providing his entrance to the Tetris-style maze of containers. At a sprint, he could reach it in under ten seconds. Slowing his speed to avoid noise meant adding another five seconds to that estimate.

Fifteen seconds where, if someone looked, they would see him. Fifteen seconds during which he couldn't control the variables. Fifteen seconds as a moving target, easy enough for any half-decent shooter with an automatic weapon to hit. A risk. But a calculated one.

He broke from cover. Accelerated into the modified sprint, landing on the balls of his feet, rolling forward, only an inch or two of footwear in contact with the deck. Powered forwards, always looking ahead, choosing where each foot fell a few paces before it did so, identifying any uneven surface or piece of debris. Reached the gap in the containers and stopped, bouncing onto his toes, knees bending, holding his breath to listen for hostiles around the blind corner ahead. No sound. Safe.

He rounded the corner, dropping into a crouch to present the smallest target possible. He was alone. In the darkness, he exhaled through his mouth, allowing enough time for his breathing to return to normal before moving on.

The night was still and dry. The *Trevanian* rolled through the waves, a giant iron whale, dirty black smoke puffing from its blow-hole instead of water.

Jimmy Blue stepped between two containers and listened again. The sailors, probably unaware they did so, moved distinctively, their gaits adapted to the subtle roll and yaw of the ship. The difference between them and the passengers was subtle; a wider stance, the outside of the shoe making contact first, an almost imperceptible tilt of the shoulders as they matched the slow surge of the waves far beneath their feet.

No one saw him as Jimmy Blue pulled on the thin gloves Tom kept in his jacket, dropped Ronnie's wrench into an inside pocket, and took a three step run-up. He used the container's locking handles as footholds, pulling himself onto its flat roof.

The next section was more challenging; three containers to scale. The locking handles again made good holds, but the gap between the top handle of one container and the bottom handle of the next meant a jump each time, in total darkness, his fingers reaching for the narrow metal ledge above.

Once onto the roof, he took a break of ten seconds. Each leap from one container to the next meant making noise. It was unavoidable.

No one approached. The crew were looking for easier prey tonight, and they would find it.

Jimmy Blue's task for the next hour was simple enough. Simple, but not easy. The topography of the stacked containers revealed itself as he climbed through the semi-darkness. He intended to explore and memorise the entire layout. The *Trevanian* was about to become Blue's territory.

His hunting ground.

CHAPTER TWENTY-SIX

AFTER TWENTY MINUTES of whispered conversation and paranoia, the deafening blast of the ship's horn made the trio of passengers on the upper starboard walkway flinch. Miss Felicity clamped a hand over her mouth to prevent an involuntary shout.

Clint crawled over to join her and Buster, who rolled onto one side.

"They trying to scare us to death now?" said the old thief.

Climbing to the higher walkway was the wounded man's idea. With faces pressed against the metal, the vibrations of any approaching footsteps became discernible from the engine's vibrations. They took turns placing one ear flat to the deck. Clint assured them the technique would grant them a twenty to thirty-second window to move.

The mournful scream of the horn echoed through the containers. Miss Felicity, the two creases on her brow more furrowed than ever, sat up and hugged herself, shivering despite the warm night.

"I don't like it," she said. "You understand what it means, right? The horn?"

Buster shrugged. Clint offered no answers. The investment banker raised her eyebrows. "Hunger Games?"

Clint's turn to frown.

"Seriously?" Miss Felicity appealed to Buster, but he looked equally bemused. "You guys need to get out more. The games, in the books, when someone died?"

The older man leaned on his elbow. "I thought they were films. For kiddies."

Miss Felicity looked disgusted. "Philistine. The books were much better. In the games, when someone died, the horn let the other players know about it."

"It's hardly bloody Disney, is it?" said Buster, scratching at his stubbled chin.

Clint nodded. "Makes sense. A psychological tool against us. One blast, so one death."

"Shit." Buster stopped scratching. "I hope it's Hannibal."

No one mentioned the alternative.

CHAPTER TWENTY-SEVEN

THE DUTCH SERIAL KILLER, alone on the deck of a huge container ship in the middle of the Atlantic, was not afraid to die. A little disappointed that his plan to continue his hobby in a new land had been thwarted. A touch upset that the last woman he'd killed was too skinny and young to provide a satisfying release. Had she been closer to his ideal, it might have been many months before he needed a fresh candidate. As it was, the dull ache in his groin began its insistent pulsing within days of him leaving her body in the forest.

He found a piece of tarpaulin folded alongside a container. He sat down, pulled the heavy material across his chest, then shuffled under it. It might conceal him tonight. What then, though? His fellow passengers had threatened to kill him.

Although not afraid to die, he was afraid of pain. And he knew death could be painful. Mother had died in pain, despite the medicine he faithfully prepared every day. He didn't like to think of her face when she coughed out her final breaths, the distortion of her once beautiful features; the sparkling eyes dull and clouded, the generous mouth a wrinkled line of agony.

Despite his fear, he could still draw upon the qualities that provided his few moments of genuine happiness: logic, clarity, preparation. He was a methodical man, praised at the bank for his perfectionism. Chided for his lack of ambition. His manager lacked the imagination to perceive that his ambition, his pure and fierce ambition, lay elsewhere. Sometimes, surrounded by fatuous fools who thought him boring, he considered sharing his vocation, but he never did. He was an artist pursuing an ideal of feminine perfection. His mother proved such a state could exist, and he dedicated himself to finding it again after her death.

Hannibal's real name was Gert. Forty-five years old, he'd enjoyed a quiet, contented existence until Mother passed away six years ago.

Consumed with grief, he left her bedroom untouched after she had gone. He made the bed, but didn't touch the pillow that bore the imprint of her sleeping head.

When his mother's solicitor contacted him, Gert discovered Mother's estate was far greater than her humble lifestyle suggested. If he budgeted carefully, he could live off his inheritance.

He left the bank and the small town where he grew up. He didn't sell the apartment, intending to return one day with a bride his mother would have been proud to call her daughter-in-law.

But his quest had proved horribly difficult. In the city, he used dating apps to meet women, using a fake name and profile. Not for any sinister reason, but to protect himself. He knew the search might take months, maybe longer, and he didn't want the women he rejected coming after him, desperate to win back his affection. That wouldn't do. It wouldn't do at all.

Gert treated a date the same way as he treated everything else. He planned the evening, dressed appropriately, prepared a list of questions on moral issues, attitudes to traditional family values, that sort of thing. He even asked his dates about the television programmes they enjoyed. This was a trick, of course. Television was the Devil's instrument, and women who watched it were ineligible for consideration. Mother had been very clear about that.

Unfortunately, this single question disqualified every woman he met. Gert was forced to move to another dating app when negative reviews on his profile meant no one wanted to meet him.

The first date on the new app changed his life.

Dora was South American, a mature student attached to a nearby teaching hospital. She specialised in radiology, and, at thirty-one, was only five years younger than the age Gert used on his dating profile. His first reaction on meeting her for a walk in a park was disappointment. A little too heavy, pale from lack of sun, Dora's brown hair hung lacklustre around a forgettable face. She made little attempt to make conversation and avoided eye contact. But when Gert asked her back to his rented house on the outskirts of the city, she agreed.

After a brief period of sexual intercourse, he strangled her. Afterwards, he brought a bowl into the bedroom and washed her hair, combing it out as he had for Mother. He opened his make-up bag—containing items his mother loved—and worked on Dora's face until she looked beautiful.

All the outfits he had bought were too small for her, but cutting the back of a yellow dress enabled him to pull it over her sagging belly.

They left the city before dawn, Dora sitting beside him. He kept up a steady flow of conversation as he drove. She really was wonderful company.

He left her propped against a tree as if resting, hands folded in her lap. Mother's favourite place was the forest. Picnics under the trees. Fresh strawberries. Always in a summer dress.

Gert had almost taken a photograph. Dora looked beautiful. But it was too risky. He stared at her instead, determined to remember the scene. For weeks afterwards, he could conjure up the image of Dora whenever he needed release.

One day, the picture he called to mind refused to sharpen. He would have to try again. For a few weeks he fought it, succumbing to waves of guilt and self-hatred. He even considered handing himself in to the police. But the urge that began in his groin, then warmed his whole body and mind... the impulse, the compulsion to create beauty, became impossible to deny.

He stopped used dating apps, instead imitating the shallow,

empty men who picked up women at concerts, in museums, at the library. Sometimes even in bars or nightclubs.

He kept his small rented house, but drove many hours to find suitable candidates. He killed them in their homes, dressing them and making them beautiful before leaving. Occasionally, his suggestion of a walk in the forest led to near-perfect situations where the sexual act didn't leave him riven with disgust. One woman—Inge— even had pale blue eyes the same shade as Mother's.

During these golden years, Gert scoffed at newspaper headlines calling him a serial killer, a pervert, a monster. Ordinary people's opinions held no interest for him. What did they know about art? The authorities floundered in their attempts to track him down.

His confidence took an unexpected knock when the police interviewed him as a suspect.

Although they asked many questions, they didn't arrest him. This meant they weren't sure. Gert assumed they were interviewing all men whose cars were photographed by traffic cameras near one of the bodies. He had registered himself as a small business owner for this eventuality, filling his boot with paper samples he tried to sell to independent stationers.

But they didn't ask him about that. They asked about dating apps, and about fake profiles. Before they let him leave, a detective showed him a photograph of Dora.

Dora. His first. Before he had refined his methods. Before he had learned to control his more shameful urges and leave no physical evidence.

Gert knew it was over. Tomorrow, the next day, a week perhaps, but they would have him.

He had planned for this.

By the time a dog walker found his folded clothes on the beach, Gert was on a ferry to Harwich, England, with a new identity. It bought him enough time to organise his ticket to America, wiping out all of his savings. Still, resuming his passion in a new country was a very appealing thought. Very appealing indeed.

But now it was truly over.

He crouched under the tarpaulin for hours. Footsteps passed on three occasions, but did not pause. Gert used the time to think. To plan. To prepare.

At two-forty-two a.m., he heard bursts of gunfire and a scream. More gunfire followed.

Eleven minutes later, the ship's horn sounded twice.

Gert folded back the tarpaulin and got to his feet. His legs tingled and cramped, so he rubbed some life back into his calves and thighs. He looked up. Clouds obscured the stars.

It was too long since meeting someone special, and his memory of their faces had faded, so when Gert walked to the rail, hoisted himself over it, and looked down at the churning water, none of the women he had immortalised came to mind. He gripped the rail and tried to conjure a clear picture.

When he released his grip and tumbled towards the cold embrace of the ocean, it wasn't Dora, or any of the others, who smiled back at him, coral lips wet and shining, dark lashes framing blue eyes.

It was Mother.

CHAPTER TWENTY-EIGHT

THE BINARIES—STEVO and Steve-one—had rarely troubled the top of the leader board during the captain's games. They lacked the criminal experience of some of their older crew mates. Other than taking potshots at rats on their respective childhood farms, the closest either of them had come to firing weapons in anger before the *Trevanian* were paintball tournaments. Stevo's father farmed three thousand acres of soybeans in the Corn Belt. Steve-one's family in the northern Midwest turned cabbages into pre-packaged sauerkraut. Both men abandoned their roots, lured by the most exotic life they could imagine; lured by the sea.

Steve-one tightened the straps of his backpack and dropped the night vision goggles over his eyes.

"A hundred bucks says the Dutch guy is in the trap."

Stevo pulled his own night goggles into place. "Nope. Bonnie and Clyde."

"It's your money you're throwing away."

They shook hands on it. Before reaching the first corridor between stacks, they stopped talking, communicating instead with hand gestures. When they turned the corner Steve-one kept going, taking care to keep his footsteps quiet, rifle held ready.

Both men—and most of the crew—favoured AR-15s, modified to become fully automatic, capable of spitting out ten rounds a second. A human being was a bigger target than a soy-fat farm rat, but far more dangerous. Stevo was the better shot, so he hung back, climbing a container opposite. Steve-one's approach to shooting favoured efficiency over style, sweeping the barrel left to right as if hosing down a soapy tractor.

When Steve-one reached the trap, he checked over his shoulder before braving the narrow aperture ahead between containers. He spotted his teammate lying on top of a single container behind, rifle held steady, eye to the scope.

The aperture, eighty feet long, ended at an access hatch to the hold. A tempting proposition for any passengers looking for somewhere to lie low. The downside was obvious—once you descended the ladder to the platform below, you ran out of options.

Belowdecks, the hold was a cathedral of containers. A dark city of steel boxes. The massive doors above stayed shut for the voyage, all remaining containers stacked above deck. Corridors bisected the ship widthways, and narrow metal steps little better than ladders led to the bowels below. The area of the hold underneath Steve-one had been sabotaged by the Binaries, leaving only one ladder from one hatch as access. It led to a platform with no other exit, unless you counted the long, fatal drop to the iron hull below. There was a reason they called it the trap.

So far, the trap had netted the Binaries over fifty thousand dollars in bounty. The crew complained it strayed from the spirit of the game, but the two Steves were practical farm boys at heart, and fifty grand was a useful chunk of change. The trap only annoyed the others because they hadn't thought of it first.

Before each game, the Binaries made the route to the hatch obvious. The clever bit was the sand. Along the narrow corridor—wide enough for two people side by side—the Binaries spread a sackful of the stuff before the *Trevanian* sailed.

Night vision goggles in place, Steve-one saw clear footprints in the sand he had swept flat before the captain's briefing. He grinned, gave the thumbs up without turning. His grin faded when he looked closer, distinguishing two sets of footprints, one smaller than the other. Shit. As well as the hundred bucks he'd lost, Stevo would brag about his victory for the rest of the trip. On the plus side—and it was a huge plus—Bonnie and Clyde meant two bounties. The top two names on Brakeman's list this trip. Not a bad result. Not bad at all. Even that crazy asshole Sean would be impressed when they bagged Bonnie and Clyde.

He took a step forward and stopped. Examined the footprints again. They didn't tell a consistent story. Instead of moving to the hatch, the green and white prints Steve-one followed through his night vision changed course more than once, moving up and down the narrow corridor. Arguing? Discussing whether to risk the hiding place?

Steve-one turned back to his teammate, who responded with a hurry-up gesture before returning his hand to the rifle's stock.

Fine. Steve-one reminded himself that he was the one with the automatic weapon, a hunting knife in his belt, and the ability to see in the dark. So much easier than picking off rats in a barn.

He walked forward into the green-white scene, rifle pushed into his shoulder, safety off, finger resting on the trigger guard.

Night vision goggles, while conferring an obvious advantage, also have drawbacks. The major problem is a loss of peripheral vision. In close combat, the limited field of view puts the wearer at a disadvantage, as anyone who's ever played a single player POV shoot 'em up can testify.

When Clyde dropped from the top of the container alongside the aperture, landing on Steve's shoulders, pushing him into the deck, all the Midwest farm boy saw—when he turned his head to avoid smacking his face into the metal—was an out of focus white and green blob.

Time slowed, became sticky.

Steve-one fell face-forward. Not winded, but close to it. His ribs hurt where they pressed against the AR-15, pinning the rifle to the deck.

He didn't stay there long. Strong hands grabbed his jacket, rolled him over, gripped the gun. Stunned, but recovering quickly, Steve resisted. Clyde pulled harder.

Steve sagged backwards, then whipped his head forward, simultaneously pulling on the gun. The top of the helmet made contact hard enough to hurt Steve-one's head. He knew it must have done serious damage to Clyde, and, sure enough, the passenger's grip loosened.

The night vision display flickered and died. Steve-one tore the goggles away. The helmet came with them, rolling into the darkness. He blinked to get used to the dark. Wondered why Stevo wasn't taking the shot. Then an arm snaked around his neck. Whether by luck or design, Clyde had got behind him. Stevo couldn't risk shooting while Steve-one's body obscured Clyde's.

It was down to him, then. A brawl. Fine. He could handle himself, and Clyde had already taken a significant blow to the head.

The grip on his throat stayed tight enough to cut off the air, but Steve-one didn't panic. Entertainment in the Corn Belt had been scarce, so he spent his early adolescence learning how to box. His later teenage years added a portfolio of fighting moves not covered by the Queensbury rules, after his first fight outside a ring ended with him flat on his ass in fifteen seconds. He learned to fight dirty, and fight to win. Some Brit asshole wasn't gonna take him. Not today, not ever.

Dropping his hands from the arm at his throat, he put all his strength into three backward jabs of the elbow, hard and fast, the first knocking some wind out of Clyde's diaphragm, the second finding a rib, the third cracking it.

Clyde's grip loosened enough for Steve-one to slide free, turn on his knees, and deliver a right hook that snapped the man's head back. Not as effective as he'd hoped, because Clyde proved a canny fighter, riding the punch rather than avoiding it. Shit, he was fast. Too fast.

Steve-one didn't register the blow, but, when Clyde's sweating, bloodied face disappeared, replaced by wisps of clouds above the containers, an uppercut was the only explanation that made sense.

The time gap worried him. The hole in his memory, between Clyde's face and the clouds. Half a second? A second? Five seconds?

With a cold, sharp shock of panic, he reached for his gun. It wasn't there. He lifted himself up on his elbows.

"Guess what?"

London accent, more nasal than in the briefing. The head butt must have broken Clyde's nose. Good.

Clyde held the missing rifle. The Brit, squatting on his haunches, had scooted back six feet or so.

Clyde smiled. "You're fucked," he said. And, had he lifted the weapon and pulled the trigger, his prediction would have been accurate.

Instead, the Brit stood up. Maybe it was the dramatic tableau that appealed to him: the bloodied, defiant warrior standing over the defeated enemy cowering at his feet. Maybe he just preferred shooting standing up.

Whichever it was, Steve-one didn't care. What mattered was that, once Clyde was on his feet, he made a clear, unobstructed target for Stevo.

For one horrible moment, nothing happened. Steve-one had a vision of Bonnie hiding back in the walkway, up on the container, creeping towards the oblivious Stevo, sliding his own knife from its sheath before slitting his throat.

Then the vision disintegrated along with the left side of Clyde's face.

Steve-one's first inclination was to puke. Not because of the damage the first four rounds made of Clyde's head before his body collapsed on the deck. No, the nausea came from how close the farm boy had come to buying the farm. He swallowed acid bile.

Adrenaline flooded his system in a torrent that made his hands shake, his teeth chatter. He crawled forward to collect the rifle. If he stood up, his legs might give way. Couldn't let Stevo see that.

The scream confused him. It didn't sound human. It started quiet and low, like a siren winding up. More of a moan, rising in pitch and volume. Close, too, and getting closer.

Before Steve-one reached the AR-15, bullets pinged off the metal deck, ricocheted off the sides of the containers, a deadly drum roll.

Stevo was shooting at someone. Stevo missed.

The scream continued. A shape threw itself across Clyde's body towards him.

Steve-one looked up.

He had a weight advantage of forty pounds, much of it muscle, over the woman who hurled herself at him, but what Bonnie lacked in bulk she made up for in ferocity. It was clear she intended to kill Steve-one, and no physical disadvantage would stand in her way.

It was too dark, Bonnie moved too fast, and Steve-one was too focused on avoiding the flurry of blows to see his assailant's eyes. Had he been able to, he would have found no sanity there. No fear, either. Just pure, primal rage. She scratched, punched, kicked, smashed her head repeatedly into his. The combination of blows combined with their speed and his recent concussion took their toll, and Steve-one fell backwards.

This time, no burst of gunfire saved him. Everything happened too fast, and Bonnie stayed too close for his crew mate to get a clear shot.

As they rolled in the thin layer of sand, Steve-one's compromised brain shut down every unnecessary synapse, sending only the most urgent messages to his body. That meant protecting his face with both hands as the grief-crazed passenger, wailing like a sackful of cats set on fire, went for his eyes. Her nails raked every inch of his face she could reach, blood welling to mark the parallel lines she drew down his cheeks.

Had Steve-one considered the consequences of the message his brain sent next, he would never have acted on it. But all higher intellectual functions had shut down to prioritise life and death decisions.

He dropped his right hand to the knife in his belt. His fingers closed around the handle at the same moment Bonnie's nails punctured his right eyeball.

Steve-one kept his blade sharp. There was little resistance as he punched six inches of serrated steel through clothing, skin, and muscle, into the screaming woman's spleen. There was no pain from his ruined eye. Not immediately. It started a second later and provided an agonising counterpoint to the struggle between the two of them.

Bonnie didn't slow down, but her scream became a prolonged *huff* of air. She went for his neck next, strong fingers searching for his windpipe as if intending to rip it out.

He pulled the knife out and stabbed her again, then a third time. Still her fingers closed on his throat. He kept repeating the action, over and over, her warm blood on his hand.

The sound stopped all at once. The two of them ended up lying sideways, facing each other. All the ferocity had drained from Bonnie's empty eyes, and her features were slack. Steve-one gasped in pain and relief, staring at his would-be killer. Death made her ugly.

"Fuck. How many times did you stab her?"

Stevo's attempt at casual bravado was betrayed by a shaking voice that jumped an octave mid-sentence.

Steve-one rolled onto his back. His backpack was still there. He hadn't told Stevo about the pipe bombs he'd built in his cabin, devices with five second fuses that would spray bolts, screws, nails, and metal shrapnel in every direction when detonated. He wanted to surprise his partner, but now he flushed hot with panic at how easily he might have lost the backpack during the fight. He'd hardly be up for employee of the month if the passengers got hold of two pipe bombs.

Then his teammate saw his face.

"Jesus, Steve."

"Yeah. I know. Come on. Gary can patch me up."

"He's an alcoholic with a first aid kit, not a plastic surgeon."

Steve-one got to his feet, took some deep breaths. Retrieved his broken night vision goggles and AR-15. Wiped his wet knife on Clyde's shirt.

They walked back to the superstructure, pace slow, Stevo talking the whole time, making jokes, never looking at his crew mate's face.

"Let's go sound the horn, compadre. What do you think? You're supposed to say, 'aye, aye'. Sorry, bad joke. Still, this bounty will get you the best glass eye money can buy. Bionic. Can they do bionic eyes yet? They must be able to. It'll have night vision built in. Probably connect to the internet, too. You'll be able to surf porn any time. I'm jealous. Oh, or you could go for an eyepatch. A sailor with an eyepatch. The ladies will love it."

As they emerged onto the starboard walkway and headed towards the bridge, they passed within four feet of a shadowed recess. After they passed, a darker shadow detached itself from the inky blackness, approaching them with a liquid silence neither man registered.

It was a two minute walk back to the bridge. Only one of the Steves made it.

CHAPTER TWENTY-NINE

IT WASN'T that Stevo had never learned about morality, rather that he had examined the concept and found it wanting. A moral code, baked into law, stopped society descending into the dog-eat-dog mentality that had once made America's Midwest a dangerous, lawless land. Mrs Bergin, his history teacher in junior high, had relayed this information as a caution. Stevo had been appalled by the notion that anyone would ruin a perfect system by making restrictive laws. He had never heard of Charles Darwin—his parents insisted the planet was only six thousand years old—but he would have approved of one aspect of evolution: the survival of the fittest.

Walking alongside his namesake, who moaned and complained now the adrenaline had worn off and the missing eye was smarting a little, Stevo was struck by a thought. A thought Mrs Bergin would have described as a moral conundrum, a concept which would have sailed clear over the young Stevo's sandy-haired, freckly head.

I could upend Steve-one before he knows what's happening. Tip him over the rail. Captain says this is the biggest bounty pool yet. The prize for Bonnie and Clyde is gonna be big. Real big.

He looked over at his teammate. The cuts on Steve-one's face would heal, but he wouldn't be the ladies' first choice at the barn dance anymore. And having only one working eye made him a second-rate wingman. And if his injuries prevented Steve-one from participating in the games, what then? Would he leave the ship? The bounty they had just earned, added to what he'd already banked, might buy him that hacienda in Mexico he talked about.

Yeah. That's what he'll do. Leave me here working while he sits in the sun drinking cold beer, with enough American dollars to buy any woman he wants.

His resentment at this prospect was so real Stevo clean forgot it was a product of his imagination.

One big shove'll do it. It's not like he'll suffer.

He thought of the photographs from home Steve-one kept on the walls of his cabin. Two older brothers. One older sister. One younger sister. Her nickname was Peaches, because when she was small, it was her favourite fruit. When Stevo thought of the way she filled out her blouse, he reckoned he would owe it to Steve-one—his best friend, after all—to head over to Nebraska and offer some comfort to the grieving family. Especially poor little Peaches. He could imagine plenty of ways to comfort that plump little beauty.

Okay. I'm gonna do it.

As easy as that. Like at McDonald's when they ask if you wanna go large. Yeah. Sure. Why not? Wanna push Steve-one over the rail to drown? Yeah. Sure. Why not?

It had to be now. Before they reached the superstructure and the bridge. Eighty feet.

Now.

He turned to his crew mate as if to pat him on the shoulder. A concerned friend, making sure he was gonna be ok.

He braced himself for the push when something flashed in the darkness. For the second time that night, Steve-one crashed to the deck.

"Hey!" Stevo reacted, blood pumping hard. He swung round to face Steve-one's attacker, bringing up the AR-15 to fire.

The deck was empty. He had a clear line of sight along the walkway. No hiding places, nowhere to go. The next corridor between stacks was twenty yards away. No one could cover that distance in the second it took him to react.

Which meant?

Stevo kept the barrel of the gun pointing towards the bow, finger on the trigger. Held his breath. Listened intently. Just the ship's usual rumble, the distant wash of waves against the hull. Nothing unusual.

Maybe something fell off a plane and hit him. Things fall out of planes, right? Some guy on the news said his house got crushed by an engine off a 737. Smaller bits must fall off too.

Despite the odds against this explanation, Stevo accepted it. The alternative—that a passenger came up behind him, whacked Steve-one, then melted into the darkness without a trace—was unthinkable.

Unless...

Unless he's behind me.

He couldn't accept that possibility either, because no one was that fast.

No. Something fell off a plane, is all. When I turn around, there won't be a psycho killing machine behind me.

Stevo decided to do it quickly. Like pulling a Band-Aid off.

He swung around, AR-15 held ready.

There was a psycho killing machine behind him.

His impression of the man who grabbed his rifle with one hand and his throat with the other only had a short time to form. A broad forehead smashed the bridge of his nose, and everything went black for a second.

He staggered back but didn't fall.

Scars. Scars on the head. He was bald. None of the passengers were bald. But one of them always wore a bandana or a cap.

The dumb guy.

Stevo brought his hands up to his face, exposing two serious problems. One was a broken nose, its blood mixing with more blood and spit from a split lip and loose teeth. The other issue was the fact that his hands were empty. His rifle was missing.

The world, blurred with tears, revealed no trace of the scarred man as Stevo blinked to clear his vision.

He still had a handgun and a knife.

He pulled the gun from its shoulder holster, dropping it immediately when the stock of his AR-15 smacked into the side of his head. The gun slid away, hitting the side of a container as he spun, staggered, and fell.

When he opened his eyes, he was drowning in blood, coughing, sucking air through nostrils clogged with liquid and cartilage. He swallowed blood and...

My knife.

Stevo's fingers reached for the handle, found nothing.

Where's my knife?

As if in answer to his question, a jolt shifted his whole body six inches forwards on the deck, mashing his nose again, causing him to cry out. The renewed agony faded into the background when a sensation of intense heat radiated from the base of his spine, accompanied by a terrible sensation as he lost control of his body. A nanosecond of indescribable pain. Then his brain shut down every receptor.

Big hands lifted his head, removed his helmet and night vision scope, then dropped it again.

Stevo's vision remained blurred. He could smell and taste nothing but blood, but his hearing worked perfectly. Stevo heard drumming. His brain latched onto the sound, so alien yet so familiar. Like someone practising snare rolls, but not getting it quite right.

Dabba dabba dabba dabba dabba dabba dabba dabba.

Not fast enough for a drum roll. Unmusical. Annoying.

He saw something; a blurred something. Getting closer. Sneakers. From Stevo's recumbent position, the shoe near his face was as big as a house, the monster wearing it the size of Godzilla.

The scarred man stood astride him. Bent down. Moved something in Stevo's back. The sailor pictured a metal key in his spine. Maybe the monster would wind it up. Would he be able to move again then?

Instead of winding the key, the scarred man pulled it out. The drumming stopped, and Stevo had an awful moment of clarity he really could have done without. It wasn't a key, it was his knife. The drumming was his own feet, spasming on the deck after the monster stabbed him in the spine.

Stevo's body floated away from the deck, his bloody face peeling off the metal like paper from wet bubblegum.

The world tilted, then tilted again. The third time, release. Stevo flew over the rail and began his descent to the waiting ocean.

His last emotion was a childish outrage at the injustice of it all.

It's not fair. I shouldn't be thrown overboard. You got the wrong Steve.

CHAPTER THIRTY

Ronnie and Sean found Steve-one.

For forty-five minutes after crossing Tom's name off the bounty list, they watched from the wings of the bridge, Sean on the starboard, Ronnie on the port.

The wings jutted from superstructure like ears. During the game, they provided a superb vantage point from which to survey the Tetris-sphere, a term Gary had coined for the stacks.

The top layer of the containers stayed dark, tonight's clouded sky not offering much illumination. The night vision binoculars revealed nothing amiss during the hourly sweep of the Tetris-sphere. Although theoretically possible, no passenger had ever scaled the stacks. Three had tried, failed, fallen, and died, and that had been on brighter nights. You'd be insane to risk it tonight.

Ronnie caught the occasional glimpse of his fellow crew members as they headed for their favourite hunting grounds. The odd burst of gunfire punctured the quiet. The radio squawked when Brakesman checked in. With their automatic weapons, night vision devices and the captain's drone, they looked prepared, organised, slick. But there were no drills, no protocols, no real discipline. They relied on their advantage of being heavily armed on their home turf, so the lack of discipline had never told against them. Besides, Brakesman had shot the only passenger he thought might give them any trouble.

Ronnie shifted his weight from foot to foot. He squinted towards the corridor leading to Tom's container. He prayed the man would stay hidden, otherwise it could be both their lives at stake.

Ronnie couldn't stop thinking about the change in Tom. The fact he could talk, after all. The way the big man sought the shadows. The stillness of him. Ronnie thought of Chul, his brother. In the mess that day, Tom reminded him of Chul. Slow of mind, nervous, vulnerable. But the man who met Ronnie tonight wasn't vulnerable. Not gentle, not lost, not scared. Not much like Chul at all.

He wished he hadn't let Tom take the wrench.

The occasional shots fired around the ship meant little. The crew liked to fire off a few rounds to keep the passengers running, keep them scared.

A sustained burst followed by screaming meant another bounty was about to be claimed. A woman's scream, full of rage. It sounded like she'd lost her mind. The abrupt way it stopped could only mean one thing. Ronnie bowed his head.

A burst of static from the radio made him jump. It was Sean. "Something's wrong. Get to the mess."

Downstairs, Sean bobbed on his toes, always in motion. The Germans on duty were as laid back as Sean was wired; Cashman slicing an apple, Hicks filling in a newspaper crossword.

Sean loved the game, Ronnie knew. The knowledge that the chief mate got off on killing made Ronnie sick to his stomach. He never openly showed his disgust, but he suspected Sean knew and enjoyed it.

"Saw the Binaries on the walkway," said Sean, a knife pinched between finger and thumb. "Coming this way. They should have been back by now. Looked like one of them is injured. Let's go get them."

Hicks looked up from his puzzle. "Want me to radio the Good-fellas for you?"

Sean picked up an automatic rifle from the table, slid a handgun over to Ronnie. "I think we can take care of it."

The Germans drew their weapons and covered the door as Sean and Ronnie left.

————

They found Steve-one's night vision goggles first, dropped on the deck.

"Broken," said Sean, flicking the switch.

A dark shape lay in the pool of darkness between the lights on the starboard walkway.

Ronnie saw the shape, stopped dead, hissed, "Sean," grabbing the bigger man's forearm.

"I see it."

The sole of one foot, a steel-capped boot. Splayed legs, the angle of the feet clearly wrong. Closer, and they could see why. Both ankles broken, badly broken, shattered. In Hong Kong eight years ago, Ronnie witnessed the aftermath of an over-speed generator explosion, where flying engine parts hit some of the crew. Their limbs weren't so much broken as crushed. This looked the same.

Closer still, and any theory this might be an accident became untenable. Whoever had smashed Steve-one's ankles had done the same to his wrists.

Ronnie's face flushed, his skin prickling with cold sweat. He made it to the rail before sending semi-digested ramen into the Atlantic.

Sean didn't throw up, but the swagger vanished, and he gripped his rifle, eyes darting all over the deck. He offered no comment, no easy quip. He waited for Ronnie to wipe his mouth, then pointed at the unconscious Binary.

"Check his pulse. I'll cover you."

No use arguing or pointing out that Sean could have done it while Ronnie was ejecting his supper. The Korean knelt next to Steve-one's head, placed his fingers on his neck, found the reassuring thrum of blood pumping through veins.

"He's alive."

"Flashlight. Quick."

"Why?" Ronnie unhooked the flashlight from his belt and tossed it over to Sean, who clasped the flashlight to the side of the rifle, playing its beam across the stacks above, then along the nearest corridor.

"What are you doing?"

Sean pointed at blobs of blood on the deck. "They came this way. Let's check."

Ronnie hated the way the chief mate vacillated between cowardice and macho bravado. He didn't have to be a psychologist to suspect the latter was compensation for the former. He left the injured man and jogged to catch up with Sean.

"Stay here and cover me."

Ronnie did as he was told, watching his teammate move between the stacks, keeping the flashlight and gun barrel moving as he checked every shadow.

Halfway down, Sean turned, pointed the flashlight down a narrow aperture between containers, then stepped inside and disappeared.

Five seconds went by, then ten.

"Sean," called Ronnie, his voice low. No answer, so he called as loudly as he dared. "Sean. Are you ok?"

The chief mate reappeared, the light beam bobbing as he jogged back to the walkway.

"Don't be a pussy, Ronnie. I was only gone a few seconds. No need to wet your panties."

"What were you doing?"

"I found Bonnie and Clyde. Both dead. The pretty one's full of holes. It's a mess."

"So who attacked the Binaries?"

"Your guess is as good as mine. No. That's not true. My guess is gonna be better than yours, right? Right?"

He punched Ronnie on the shoulder. The Korean knew the signs. The bully needed to convince himself and others that he wasn't afraid. Pathetic, really. Didn't stop his shoulder from hurting.

"Yeah, right, Sean. You're right."

"I know I am."

Steve-one was face down. Ronnie turned the man's head, made sure his airways were clear. His stomach spasmed.

"His eye," he croaked. "It's gone."

"Jesus shit." When stressed, Sean's range of curses narrowed to random combinations of a religious provenance, often with a scatological twist. It was the closest Ronnie ever heard the chief mate come to a profession of faith. "Christ on a turd."

"We need the stretcher," said Ronnie, thinking about the poor level of medical help available to the injured man.

A regular ship would put out a call for help to Maritime Rescue so they could helicopter the victim to shore. The *Trevanian* wasn't a regular ship. Medical problems were Gary's responsibility, a man who dropped out of veterinarian school thirty years ago to join the navy and further explore his commitment to alcohol abuse.

Maybe the injuries weren't as bad as they appeared, thought Ronnie, but he didn't look at Steve-one as he thought it.

Then the stricken man regained consciousness, groaned, and—as if his various injuries were, one by one, making their presence felt—the groan became a moan, a strangled cry, then a full-throated scream.

"God, god, shit, Jesus, shit." Sean's unimaginative contributions were barely audible under the man's screams. He stepped closer, waving the gun around. "Shut him up, will you?"

Ronnie ignored him. "The stretcher," he repeated when Steve-one took a breath.

"No. No time. Whoever did this is out here somewhere. Grab his arm."

Ronnie didn't bother to protest. Sean, for once, was right. He didn't want to spend any more time than necessary out here. When the screamer paused for another breath, he leaned closer.

"This is gonna hurt. I'm sorry, Steve. I really am."

Bracing the rifle against his hip, Sean leaned down and took hold of Steve-one's jacket, gripping it and the T-shirt beneath. Ronnie did the same.

Their first manoeuvre involved turning the man a hundred and eighty degrees, so his head faced the stern and the superstructure.

The expected scream never came. Stevo's shattered wrists and ankles moved for the first time since being broken, splintered ends of bones rubbing, prodding tendons and muscles from within. He fainted.

CHAPTER THIRTY-ONE

SEAN AND RONNIE dragged the unconscious man back to the super-structure. Cashman and Hicks pointed submachine guns into the darkness behind as the pair dragged their burden inside.

"Gary!" barked Hicks into his radio. "Get down here."

When Hicks saw the way Stevo's booted feet hung from his legs as if attached with string, he picked up the radio again.

"You too, Captain. You will want to see this."

Cashman locked the door and backed away.

"The other Steve? Where is he?"

Sean held a throwing knife between finger and thumb, the colour returning to his face, along with some of his confidence.

"We didn't see him. Probably dead."

"The Binaries left here with AR-15s, handguns, knives. Where are their weapons?"

Sean had no answer.

Captain Brakesman appeared first. Gary wasn't far behind. Ronnie was relieved to see the navigator didn't seem too drunk.

Brakesman stood over Steve-one, shook his head.

"His weapons?"

Sean was ready with his answer this time. "Gone when we found him, sir. And no sign of Stevo."

"Goddammit."

He lifted the radio from his belt, used the common channel.

"Mike. Tony. Back to the mess. Now."

The gentle crackle of static that followed his message seemed to last minutes. In reality, only a few seconds passed before Mike's New York bass came buzzing through.

"We ain't barely got started, boss."

"We've got trouble. I want both of you back here now. That's an order."

Brakesman's recruitment criteria targeted those with a healthy disrespect for authority. He rarely gave orders, but when he did, god help anyone who didn't toe the line. Mike knew the captain wouldn't pull rank without an excellent reason.

"On our way."

Sean and Ronnie fetched the stretcher, carried the still-unconscious Steve-one to sickbay, where Gary pulled bottles, packets of needles, and bandages from cupboards. He opened a medical app on a tablet and looked between it and the poster of the human body on the wall. While Sean and Ronnie settled the patient on the bed, Gary tore open a packet containing a sterilised scalpel, dropping the blade twice before gripping it between shaking fingers.

Ronnie hung back after Sean left, opening a drawer under the cupboard, pulling out a pint bottle of vodka. He emptied half and handed the bottle to Gary.

"You can't operate on him like that. Drink this."

When he left, the bottle was at Gary's lips.

Back at the mess, no one spoke. The Goodfellas hadn't returned. Ronnie joined the captain, Sean, and the Germans, all five of them staring out at the point beyond the floodlights, willing their crew mates to appear.

When the two men jogged out of the darkness, the atmosphere broke. Cashman stepped forward to open the door, locking it again as soon as they were inside.

Mike and Tony looked around at their grim-faced crew mates.

Mike took off his baseball cap, smoothed his leathery brown scalp. "What's up?"

"The game is over," said Brakesman to the silent gathering. "Stevo is missing. Steve-one is injured."

Mike and Tony exchanged a glance. "What happened?" said Tony. "How bad is he hurt?"

With perfect timing, a scream of pure agony emerged from the sickbay at the end of the corridor.

"Pretty bad," said the captain.

The screams continued. Gary must have got a needle into him, because they didn't stop all at once, but subsided in waves.

Brakesman surveyed the crew. "One or more of the passengers is now armed with Steve-one's weapons. Stevo's too, maybe."

No screams broke the silence that followed this statement.

"Like I said, it's over. No more teams. We decide a strategy here and now, then we all put it into action."

Brakesman caught Sean shooting a look at the flip chart.

"You say one word about bonuses and I'll shoot you myself. Shit."

The captain paced, stroking his oversized moustache. "We got complacent, is all. Either the passengers organised themselves better, or they're more capable than my information suggested. That's for later. Let's deal with the here and now."

He shouted through to the sickbay. "Gary? I'm gonna need to talk to that boy, find out who got the jump on them. How long you gonna be patching him up?"

Instead of shouting back, Gary walked down the corridor, stood in the doorway. Surgical mask, latex gloves splattered with blood. Pale. Hands not shaking anymore, Ronnie noted. Guess the slug of vodka did the job.

"Too much damage for me to fix. It's way beyond my capabilities. The eye is gone. Looks like it was scratched out. The rest was done by someone with good aim and a blunt instrument. Something heavy."

Ronnie thought of his wrench.

"I'll splint his feet and hands, but he won't be walking any time soon. He'll need everything re-broken and re-set if he ever wants to use his hands and feet. There's no way he could hold a gun, let alone fire one. Not sure how we're gonna explain those injuries back on shore."

"There are doctors I trust in New York," said Brakesman. "You let me worry about that. When can I talk to him?"

"A half hour at least. But he's pumped full of everything I could find for the pain. He might not make a whole lot of sense."

"Come get me when he's awake."

"Sir."

After Gary had left, Brakesman went back to stroking his moustache.

"Here's what we're gonna do. We don't know which passengers did this. But we still have a massive firepower advantage. What's the worst-case scenario? Hicks?"

Hicks had a cool head and a logical mind. He hesitated, then nodded to himself as if conceding a well-made point during an internal discussion.

"Worst case is someone stepped up as leader. Took charge, organised them, and targeted the Binaries. We heard gunfire from their position, yes? More than one burst."

Sean and Ronnie both nodded.

"Gunfire suggests the passengers also took casualties. So. Here's what we know. Ronnie eliminated Tom."

The Goodfellas saw Ronnie's name next to Tom's on the flip chart. Gave him a respectful tilt of the head. He didn't trust himself to acknowledge their approval.

"Clint is the natural leader, but not in the way of foot soldiers. Buster is old, Miss Felicity a fraudster with no history of violence. Bonnie and Clyde are already an established team. I don't think they would easily take orders."

"They're dead," said Sean, interrupting the German.

"Who are?"

"Bonnie and Clyde."

Brakesman frowned. "And you didn't consider that fact worth sharing?"

Sean shrugged. He didn't do apologies. "Found their bodies near the Binaries' trap. One shot, one stabbed."

"OK. Good news. Very good news. Hicks?"

"Sir. That accounts for the gunfire. So, that leaves us with a woman whose crime was financial, a dying safe-cracker, and an ex-soldier with one working leg. As for Hannibal..."

Sean completed his thought. "We saw their faces when they found out who he is. Any one of them would happily strangle the sick fuck."

"Yes. Quite. But it is theoretically possible they included him to boost their chances of success. We should not discount this."

"That's our worst-case scenario, folks," said Brakesman. "Four passengers, organised and armed. Two rifles, two handguns, two knives. Limited ammo."

"We're assuming Stevo is dead?" said Cashman.

"For now, yes. If he escaped, it's a point in our favour, but no radio, no more gunfire... I don't think he made it."

They accepted the probability in silence.

"But that's only the worst case. More likely they have no leader. These people aren't team players. Clint, maybe, but not the others. They're all strong personalities, criminals, outsiders. Used to working alone. I think they got lucky."

Hicks nodded. "This hypothesis is, I think, most likely. Now we must think like they do. The passengers' goal is survival. They don't need to kill us, they only have to survive until New York. Even if we deviate from our route, we have to dock somewhere, and that will be their chance to escape, or alert the authorities. If they are smart, they will take the food from the sleeping container, and find somewhere easy to defend. A place where they can pick us off if we attack."

He picked up Steve-one's broken night vision goggles. "They share one night vision device between them. We still have the advantage at night."

"Three hours until dawn," said Brakesman. The captain took a cigar from his jacket pocket, rolled it between his fingers. "We have two long-barrelled guns with telescopic sights, four sub-machine guns, six AR-15s. All of us own handguns. And plenty of ammo. Here's how we play this. We kill all the lights, use the drone to locate them, then we finish them. It's a cloudy night, folks, and that's in our favour. Only one set of goggles means all but one of them will be firing blind. Steve-one's radio was still on his belt, but let's assume they took Stevo's. Use the backup channel."

The captain had abandoned his trademark drawl and relaxed delivery. Brakesman usually circled a point a few times before landing on it, but he was wasting few words now.

"Let's give them long enough to think we're not coming. An hour. If Steve is awake by then, I'll find out what he knows. One hour. We send out the drone, find their positions, and kill them."

Brakesman clipped off the end of his cigar. "Goddamnit. They ruined my game. Next time, I'll shoot all of them in the leg before we start. Ok. Get some rest. We leave at four."

The crew obeyed their orders. Brakesman sat down, a sub-machine gun on the table beside him. He lit his cigar and stared out at his vessel.

"Clock's ticking, suckers."

CHAPTER THIRTY-TWO

AFTER BONNIE and Clyde split off from the main group, Clint, Buster, and Miss Felicity kept moving, obeying a primal instinct to put distance between them and the hunters.

Buster shot regular glances at the wiry military-looking type beside him. The pace was a sight quicker than he was used to, and he needed a smoke, but he didn't want to ask the guy who'd been shot to slow down.

"We'll find the container where they expect us to sleep," said Clint. "Take what we need, then pick a spot to rest. Take shifts keeping watch, ready to move if we have to."

Miss Felicity regarded the ex-soldier—if that's what he was—as if he had farted at a dinner party.

"No. The container is the only safe place during the day. You heard the captain."

Clint kept walking, taking the weight on his crutch. He didn't answer for a while. Buster did his best to keep up.

"Look, no one's in charge. You don't have to take orders from me. But I know more than you about Brakesman and his crew. The kind of people they are. Don't ask how, because I won't tell you. But I'm not spending tomorrow in a forty-foot container with one door, waiting for a bunch of thugs with sub-machine guns to pay a visit."

Miss Felicity thought about saying something, but Clint's expression changed her mind.

"It's a big ship," he continued. "They have a crew of ten. They won't leave the bridge unattended. I'd guess at least two of them will protect it at all times. That leaves eight men to search the ship, probably in pairs, in radio contact. Our best bet is to climb a container. One that can't be seen from the bridge. We'll rest there tonight."

Buster wanted to add something, but it took most of his strength to keep up.

"What then?" he managed.

Clint looked at him, raised a questioning eyebrow. Great. He wanted Buster to elaborate. The old thief did so, choosing short words, punctuated by a few panting breaths.

"Say we... survive... what then? Tomorrow... We're still up... shit creek, ain't we?... Still... no... paddle."

When they heard gunfire from the far end of the ship, Clint halted. Buster sucked in a few lungfuls of oxygen, then coughed for thirty seconds, his lungs rattling like bags of marbles.

Miss Felicity put a hand on his shoulder. Was she human, after all?

"Can't you cough more quietly?" Maybe not.

After the coughing fit subsided to his usual wheeze, Buster listened with the others to the terrible sounds coming from somewhere between their position and the superstructure.

A scream like all the cats in hell followed the gunfire. It could only be Bonnie. When it cut off suddenly, all three of them exchanged glances. No one spoke.

Clint limped away, the others scurrying after him. Buster waited for the ship's horn to announce Bonnie's death—Clyde's, too, possibly—but it didn't come.

Clint noticed it, too. "They didn't blow the horn. Either the Hunger Games idea is off base, or something's changed."

"Like what?" said Buster. Clint's only answer was a shrug.

With the bow of the ship in sight, when they had reached the last corridor between the container stacks, he stopped suddenly, held up his hand, whispered, "Wait."

"Why have we stopped?" said Miss Felicity, matching Clint's low volume.

"A shortwave radio. Someone is close." He pointed. "Port side."

Miss Felicity froze. Buster concentrated on not coughing. Naturally, a tickle in his throat threatened to develop into a full-blown hacking fit. He swallowed, breathed through his nose.

Clint leaned in. "If they come towards us, we double back, take the next corridor."

The three of them listened. Buster heard the crackle of a radio, but nothing else. Oh, for a younger man's hearing. Clint tilted his head like a hungry dog who smells a treat in someone's pocket, his head tracking the progress of the unseen hunters.

He waved them into the corridor. They crept in, Clint bringing up the rear, walking backwards, watching and listening.

When the radio burst into life again, they all froze. Much closer this time. Too far away to pick out individual words, but close enough to detect the urgency in the voice.

When the radio fell silent, the sound that followed was far scarier. Footsteps. Not walking, jogging. Towards them.

Buster, never much of an athlete even when his lungs weren't full of nicotine or his body terminally ill, braced himself to run. Clint's heavy hand on his collar brought him up short.

"No. Against the wall."

The old thief flattened himself against the nearest crate. The unlit corridor wouldn't offer any cover if anyone took more than a cursory glance their way.

The footsteps came closer. Just before they reached the entrance to their corridor, Buster closed his eyes. For some reason, he thought it would help.

When the footsteps continued without pausing, running past and continuing back towards the stern, Buster broke into a grin, slapped Clint on the arm.

"Bugger me sideways. How did you know they weren't coming for us?"

"I didn't."

Miss Felicity looked at him in horror.

"Best guess," he explained. "They reacted to the radio message, not us. If we had run, they would have seen us."

"You guessed?" The financial whizz was obviously horrified that someone would take decisions without weighing all the options.

"Bloody good guess, pal," said Buster. "What now?"

"Food and water. Wherever they're heading, it's a break for us. We take advantage of it."

The food and water waited alongside rolled-up bedding in the container at the bow. Sandwiches and fruit. Not enough fuel for seven passengers to get through twenty-four hours. Brakesman preferred any survivors to be weakened by hunger.

Buster picked up three blankets. After he left the container, Clint blocked the doorway. Miss Felicity glared at him, arms crossed unnaturally in front of her.

"Do you mind?"

He didn't move. Buster watched the two of them square off. "Put them back," said Clint.

"What on earth are you talking about?"

"The extra sandwiches. Put them back."

She paled, but stood her ground. "Now you listen to me. We don't know who's dead and who's alive. This might be the only food we get. You'd be crazy to leave it to rot."

"Then I'm crazy. But there may be other survivors, and I won't take their food. Neither will you. Are we clear?"

The glare didn't subside, but Miss Felicity dropped her arms to her sides, allowing four cling-filmed packages to fall to the floor. When Clint stood aside, she stepped over the sandwiches and walked out, head high, eyes looking straight ahead.

It took forty minutes to find a container matching Clint's requirements. Some stacks were nine or ten containers high. Stacks of two or three were rare. Rarer still was a single container.

They found something even better than Clint had suggested: a single container alongside a double, meaning an easy climb.

Clint went first. For a man with a bullet in his leg, the soldier made short work of shinning up the eight-foot-high door. Once he'd pulled himself over the lip, he lay on his front and offered Miss Felicity a hand up.

When it was his turn, Buster got his right foot onto the first handle and—with Clint's help—slid his fingers over the lip at the top. But when he reached for the next handle, his arm twitched, his fingers spasmed, and he slipped and fell. Clint took his weight without complaint, and leaned back, enabling the old burglar to walk up the container.

They repeated the procedure to reach the top of the second container, Buster letting Clint pull him up rather than risk another fall.

"Bloody hell. Work out a bit, do ya?"

"Free solo."

"Who's that?"

"It's a climbing technique. On your own. No ropes, no harness."

"No brains."

Clint smiled at that. Buster grinned in return. He had a rule of thumb when working with others: trust no one without a sense of humour. It had saved his skin more than once.

Clint eyes him. "What happened with your hand back there? Looked like a spasm."

Buster shrugged. "The pills, innit. Take 'em to stop the nausea, but they have side effects." He rolled a cigarette. "Before you say anything, it's just the one. I'll blow the smoke straight up, all right? Had me first drag on a ciggie when I was nine. I can't just go cold turkey. Besides, it'll settle the cough."

Clint nodded his consent. Miss Felicity huffed and moved as far away as she could, which was thirty-six feet.

Buster lit the cigarette and took a long, satisfying drag. Why was it that the things that make life worth living shorten it in the process? "Didn't answer my question, did ya?"

Clint adjusted his sitting position, wincing.

"Which question was that?"

"You know perfectly well, pal."

"Ah. The one involving creeks. And paddles."

"And shit. Yeah. That's the one."

Clint unwrapped a sandwich while Buster talked, eating fast, barely chewing. He repeated the procedure with a second, washing down a handful of medkit ibuprofen and paracetamol with bottled water.

"I mean, top job, pal," continued Buster. "You kept us alive. We might make it through the night. That's down to you. Smart fella. But the question stands. Daylight comes, and it all starts again. You're the one who said they've probably got night vision gear. It's not a question of if they find us, it's a question of when."

"You're right." Clint unrolled a blanket, draped it over his body. Stretched out, hands behind his head. Buster envied his ability to relax. The man looked ready for a little snooze. He pressed his point.

"So you've bought us some time. What are we gonna do with it?"

Clint smiled, his eyes half-closed. He called Miss Felicity over. Handed her a blanket and told her to lie next to him. She gave him the look. Buster knew that look. His ex-wife had given him the look when he asked if she wanted to give things another go after she caught him with his hand up her sister's blouse.

Clint didn't notice. "It's your decision, but the nights are cold out here. And once you're asleep, your internal temperature will drop. You'll burn precious calories just trying to stay warm, and it will make you weaker."

She scowled, wrapped the blanket around herself, and lay down in the far corner, turning her back on the two men. Within a minute, her breathing deepened as fear-induced exhaustion dragged her into sleep.

Buster waited for his answer. Clint sighed, kept his voice low, so he didn't disturb the sleeping woman.

"I've lost some blood, and I've put weight on this leg when I should have been resting it. I need to build my strength back up. Can you stay awake for the next hour? Take first shift?"

The days when Buster could sleep for more than an hour before pain woke him were long gone. Besides, he was looking forward to taking a long piss up the side of the neighbouring container as soon as this pair were asleep.

"No bother."

"Good. If either of us snores, kick us."

"My pleasure."

"I have a plan, but it's a long shot. You're not going to like it."

Clint told him his plan, closed his eyes, and was asleep in seconds. He was right. Buster didn't like his plan. He didn't like it at all.

CHAPTER THIRTY-THREE

WHEN GARY CALLED through to say Steve-one was conscious, Ronnie waited ten seconds, then followed Captain Brakesman to the sick bay, standing just outside the door.

If he hadn't known it was Steve-one speaking, he would never have guessed the thin, querulous voice belonged to the muscly, tanned, Midwest farm boy.

At first he couldn't make out any words, so he stood as close as he dared, leaning his head against the door frame.

"You're gonna be OK, son," lied the captain. "Gary has patched you up for now. When we get to New York, I'll get you the best doctor money can buy. You'll be back doing laps of the deck in a couple of months."

Ronnie pictured Steve-one's ankles. No doctor could repair that kind of damage, however much they charged.

"Now listen, whoever attacked you is still out there. We're gonna go get them. Nobody does this to my crew. Did you see what happened to Stevo?"

"No." A voice like static between radio stations. "Something hit my head. I passed out. Is he OK?"

"He's fine." Brakesman was keen to keep the conversation on point.

"We'll get the son of a bitch. He'll regret laying a finger on you, I swear. Now who was it?"

Ronnie held his breath. Waited for his drugged-up crew mate to reply. Offered a prayer to any deity that might be listening.

"We killed Bonnie and Clyde. They jumped us."

"And you'll get the bounty, son, the whole thing. Now who attacked you?"

"My eye... that crazy bitch scratched it out. Afterwards, someone hit me. I didn't see who it was, Mrs Hughes. I'm sorry."

Mrs Hughes? What drugs had Gary given him?

"That's OK, Steve. Rest up. We'll take care of things. You just get yourself better."

No response. Ronnie guessed the injured man had passed out again.

Brakesman's tone was all business now.

"Gary. No more drinking tonight. I'm serious. I need every man. Where's your stash?"

The next sound was a bottle being unscrewed, its contents tipped down the sink. Ronnie didn't need to see Gary's face to know the horrified expression on it.

"Take this, Gary. Just make sure you don't shoot one of us."

He'd given Gary a gun? Things really were bad.

"With me," said Brakesman.

Shit. With no time to get back down the corridor, Ronnie ducked into the room opposite—a storage cupboard for cleaning products.

The captain paused in the corridor on the other side of the cupboard door. Gary spoke first.

"One foot is badly smashed up. I think he'll lose it. But I'll keep him stable until we dock."

"No."

"I'm sorry?"

"I said no. I can't trust him not to run his mouth off when he's home. He's a liability. Some folk have bad reactions to anaesthetic, right? Never regain consciousness."

"Wait. Do you expect me..."

"I do."

"But—"

"But nothing, Gary. You're a two-bit drunk who got lucky. You want me to believe you've grown a conscience? You want to cross me? You're only here so long as you do as I say. We clear?"

Silence. Hicks had once said something about the captain running his crew through greed or fear. Now he knew which one it was with Gary. He wondered what Brakesman's hold was over the navigator.

"OK. OK."

"Good. If he's still alive at dawn, you and I will be having a conversation. You got that?"

"Yes. I got it."

"Then get it done. Oh, and Gary? I'm serious about giving the sauce a rest. I need you thinking straight until the passengers are dead."

"Sir."

When both men had gone, Ronnie eased the door open and stepped back into the empty corridor, only to jump three feet when Sean shouted from the mess.

"Captain!"

A scuffling of chair legs, tables being pushed back, guns being picked up. Ronnie sidled into the room hoping the captain wouldn't notice him enter, but he needn't have worried. All eyes were on the floodlit section of deck directly in front of the mess, where a figure stood, hands up, facing them.

"What the hell is this?" said Sean.

The woman. What had Brakesman called her? Miss Felicity.

"Open the door," said the captain. "Looks like she wants to talk."

CHAPTER THIRTY-FOUR

MISS FELICITY DIDN'T COME to talk, she came to deal.

From their positions on the bridge wings, Cashman and Hicks pointed sub-machine guns down at the woman pinned by the flood-lights below. In the mess, four more weapons were aimed in her direction.

Hicks opened the door, keeping it between him and any shooter waiting in the dark. Miss Felicity walked forwards.

Ronnie hung back while powerful hands grabbed the woman, pulled her inside, and shoved her into a plastic chair. Hicks locked the door.

She looked terrified.

Ronnie empathised, biting down on his own fear. If Tom had been Steve-one's attacker, at least the injured man hadn't identified him. But what about Miss Felicity? Did she know Tom was still alive? Ronnie stayed near the corridor, ready to bolt. His only hope for escape was the free-fall lifeboat at the stern. A last resort, but one he now considered for the first time. If he launched it without being shot, he'd take his chances heading out across the shipping lanes, hoping to encounter another vessel before the *Trevanian* caught up and sent him to the bottom of the ocean. But that would mean abandoning Tom. The man in the container might be different to the silent, vulnerable Tom in the mess, but he didn't think he could leave him behind to die.

"You're either very brave or very stupid," said Brakesman, standing in front of the shaking passenger. "The game began at midnight, and I made the rules quite clear. No passenger survives. No exceptions."

"And yet you let me in here."

Her voice trembled, but she met his eye. Brakesman grunted.

"Don't try my patience. If you have something to say before I have you shot and your body tossed overboard, say it now."

Miss Felicity swallowed, but didn't drop her gaze. "I have something you want. And I have a proposition."

Ronnie didn't find it hard to imagine this woman in a business meeting, holding the attention of everyone present. Her voice settled as she spoke, despite her audience comprising armed men who wanted her dead.

"This ain't a negotiation, lady." Mike, the older of the Goodfellas, unwrapped a stick of gum, his other hand tapping the barrel of his sub-machine gun.

"Actually, that's exactly what this is. I can tell you where Clint and Buster are hiding."

The captain thumbed the safety off of his handgun. "Not good enough. We can find them without you."

"True." Ronnie was impressed by her control. She looked at the captain, but she was addressing the entire room.

"I can save you time. They're sleeping now, but they'll be on the move again as soon as they realise I've gone. Oh, and there are fifty million additional reasons not to kill me."

That got their attention. Even Sean stopped spinning his throwing knife between thumb and finger.

"Your little bounty chart probably adds up to—what—a few million? Ten? That's a nice bonus. But did you think the diamonds you found in my cabin represent my entire worth? Think about it. I nearly brought down the third biggest investment bank in Europe. And they're still in financial trouble. Why? Because they didn't recover all the money. I diverted it to various accounts. The real money—the money they don't even know I stole—is in accounts they'll never find. I can access those funds once I'm in America. I'm offering fifty million dollars. It's yours, to be split between your crew however you see fit."

The crew looked at Brakesman. He stroked his moustache.

Oh, she was smart. Really smart. Brakesman kept an office near the port in New York. Ronnie knew he could smuggle her through the same way as the big-ticket single passengers they took a couple of times a year. Get her to the office. Give her broadband access and a couple of hours to prove she wasn't lying. He guessed she'd done enough to delay her execution.

Brakesman lowered his gun. "Nice speech."

She closed her eyes for a second. Brakesman slapped her, hard.

"Where are Clint and Buster?"

She told them. Brakesman didn't miss the way the Goodfellas looked at their prisoner. Like hungry men being offered free pizza.

"You two. Go relieve Cashman and Hicks. Use night scopes, cover the rest of the crew when they leave. Tell the Germans to bring two more long-range rifles and scopes from the armoury."

They didn't look pleased, but the Goodfellas left without argument.

Ronnie eyed the rest of the men. Brakesman ran the *Trevanian* pretty tight and chose his crew carefully. Paid well, with crazy bonuses some trips. But fifty million dollars was a lot of money. If she was telling the truth, Miss Felicity might survive the game. Until the money changed hands.

Brakesman grabbed her by the chin. She flinched.

"What weapons do they have?"

Miss Felicity looked surprised at Brakesman's question. Genuinely surprised.

"Where on earth would we get weapons? You searched all of us, remember?"

Sean grunted. "So it's Hannibal. He turned out to be more dangerous than he looks, the psycho sonofabitch."

Miss Felicity's composure cracked a little at the news that Hannibal was still alive. She looked over her shoulder at the flip chart, saw Tom's name crossed out. Showed no emotion, but her permanent frown deepened a little.

"Ronnie." The Korean, lost in his own thoughts, jumped at the sound of Brakesman's voice. "Lock her in the Hole."

The captain unhooked a keyring from his belt, tossed it over.

She stood up as Ronnie approached. The Korean kept his gun by his side, nodded towards the corridor. Followed her out.

"It's not as bad as it sounds," he said as they walked.

The Hole was the first cabin on the passenger corridor. It had two padlocked bolts on the outside. He unlocked them, drew them back, and opened the door for her to step inside.

The only light came from the tiny window. A bare mattress in one corner constituted the only furniture. In the bathroom, toilet roll, a thin towel, soap and a plastic cup.

Ronnie closed and bolted the door. She had just bartered for her life, in the process betraying two of her fellow passengers. They weren't her friends, but still... Ronnie wondered how someone could be so cold. Or was she just wired differently? Maybe she saw no moral dilemma in saving her own skin, whatever the price.

He stood in the corridor for a minute, taking long, slow breaths. Twice now he had been close to being exposed. The risk in helping Tom could yet turn out to be a big mistake. But, rightly or wrongly, when he met Tom, he didn't see a violent criminal fleeing justice. He saw Chul. His own brother. Big, gentle, confused. Afraid. At school, waiting in the playground for Ronnie, two years younger and half-a-foot shorter, to look after him. Make sure the bullies didn't steal his lunch. If Ronnie wasn't around when someone shoved Chul, punched him, called him names, left him sobbing, he'd find them later.

Ronnie hadn't been a fighter until he arrived at Chul's school. When he saw the way the other kids treated his sibling, heard the nicknames, and took a few punches for protecting his sibling, he'd learned to handle himself. He'd begged his parents for martial arts lessons, applying himself with a resolute determination that surprised everyone. After months of practise, spending every spare hour at the gym or in the yard, repeating his *hapkido* moves over and over, Ronnie worked his way through every student who had hurt his brother, administering beatings with a calm efficiency. Word spread fast, and they left Chul alone.

His brother never really left school. Chul's first job brought him straight back to mop the floors and clean graffiti off the walls of the same institution.

Their parents were poor, and, when their father developed Parkinson's disease, he stopped working. His small pension only just fed the family. The pressure to help fell to Ronnie. He took up the challenge with the same focus he'd brought to his martial arts practice, leaving school, working in a car factory, pulling double shifts whenever he could, spending nights putting in the hours on a long-distance engineering degree.

Ronnie never got to finish the degree. He'd been out for a rare drink with friends one night and they ended up in a busy bar near Busan Port, where some European sailors had taken an interest in Ronnie's small group. Lewd comments about the girls were followed by the drunk men trying to sit at their table. Ronnie asked politely for them to leave. When they responded by throwing punches, he put the loudest of them flat on his back.

As he and his friends left, he'd seen an older American with a long white moustache watching him.

Three weeks later, the same man stood outside the factory when Ronnie finished his shift.

"How'd you like to own one of those cars rather than screwing them together?"

Ronnie had shrugged. The man introduced himself as captain of a container ship.

"Someone told me you study engineering," he'd said. "I can use a man like you."

He named a monthly figure, and Ronnie knew he couldn't refuse. A salary like that would pay off his parents' mortgage in less than a year. They could move somewhere nicer, and not have to worry about Chul.

Since then, Ronnie's conscience had taken an extended vacation while his savings mounted up.

Then he had seen Tom in the mess. And the vacation ended. His tenure on Brakeman's crew was over.

He just had to survive the next four days.

————

No one acknowledged Ronnie when he walked in and sat down. Cashman and Hicks, back from the bridge, were checking their rifles. Gary nursed a cup of coffee. Brakesman rolled a fat cigar between his fingers, a clear signal he was thinking.

Sean looked wired. Scared. Excited. Typical. Sean reminded Ronnie of the kids who'd bullied Chul. The cliché about not picking on someone your own size fitted Sean perfectly. A big man, quick too. A talented fighter, possibly, but it was hard to tell as he'd never been tested. If his opponent was unarmed, Sean pulled out his knives. If they had a knife, Sean used a gun.

"We'll talk about Miss Felicity later," said the captain. "We know where Clint and Buster are holed up. I'm sending two teams. One port, one starboard. Watch for Hannibal."

"Let me at 'em," said Sean.

"Uh-uh. You and Ronnie stay with me."

"But—"

"But nothing. You're the best shot onboard. I need you upstairs with me. We're going to kill all the lights. I want it pitch black out there. Night scope, sniper rifle.

"Ronnie, Gary, stay in the mess. Shoot anyone you see who isn't us. Mike, Tony, take the starboard. Here's how you play it. Maintain ten yards between the front and rear man at all times. The second follows the first at a distance, covering the angles. Rear gunner, keep your eyes on the stack—Hannibal might be a climber."

Ronnie doubted it. The Dutchman was middle-aged, in average

condition. Tom, although his bulk was far from that of a natural climber, looked strong. Very strong.

"I'll run the drone from the bridge," said Brakesman. "I'll stay high. Don't want to spook them. I'll check for Hannibal. Once you reach the others, hit them hard and fast. Leave the bodies. We'll clean up tomorrow. Radios on backup channel. Get ready."

The captain left for the bridge. Three minutes passed by Ronnie's watch before Brakesman's voice crackled through the radio.

"Launching drone now. Go."

Every light on the ship died. The hundred-and-fifty thousand ton vessel, loaded with fifteen thousand steel containers, motored invisibly through the dark night, five miles above the bottom of the Atlantic.

The Germans and the Goodfellas left, Cashman leading Hicks, Tony following Mike. They parted ways and headed for opposite sides of the ship.

Gary was a talker when the drinks flowed, but since the captain turned off the tap, he'd fallen silent. That suited Ronnie. He didn't want to talk. He picked up the shortwave radio on the table, running his thumb along the buttons. Licked his lips. Couldn't stop blinking, the after image of the brightly lit deck still scrolling across his retinae.

Ronnie couldn't see the drone, but he heard the rise and fall of his high-pitched whine. It was a top of the range device with powerful motors and flight time of fifty minutes. He had enlisted Ronnie and Sean's help to cover the machine—the size of a Korean barbecue hot plate—with night vision and infrared cameras. Six ten-inch tablets gave the captain a three hundred and sixty degree view of everything the drone saw through its cameras. If Tom wasn't safely hidden inside the container, things were about to get ugly.

CHAPTER THIRTY-FIVE

BUSTER PRESSED his head against the safe and moved the stethoscope across the metal door, close to the dial, until he found the sweet spot. Every safe had one; the point when the fence fell into the notches before the door swung open.

Buster wore oversized ear protectors of the kind pneumatic drill operators wear. After one of his clients had referred to him as Cyberman, he had painted them silver, mostly for his own amusement. Also to claim the nickname. A good nickname goes a long way in the burglary business. The ear protectors were his secret weapon, but none of his peers fancied copying him. They gave him close to total isolation during a high-tension robbery, but the downside meant trusting others to alert him if things went sideways.

There was something odd about this job. Buster never returned to the same location twice, but he recognised this luxuriously furnished office, thirty floors up in a Docklands bank. Out of hundreds of burglaries, it stuck in his mind because of the painting hanging above the safe. An original, in oils, of the CEO's wife. Stark naked, she was. Bloody off-putting, and no mistake. Buster remembered wondering how visitors to this office reacted to the portrait. Hard not to look. Hard not to stare, actually. The woman's eyes were closed, but her nipples followed you around the room. Every time he glanced up, Buster found them looking back disapprovingly.

Disapproving nipples? Buster shook his head, reapplied himself to the task, the final *clunk* of the cylinders a sweet note in his ears. He grinned, turned around to make sure his colleagues were paying attention.

Funny. He was alone. That wasn't right.

He opened the safe anyway, desperate to see what was inside. Professional courtesy meant standing aside, allowing the client to check the contents first, but since no one else was there...

Inside the safe, a man's face glared at him. An angry man's face. An angry ginger man's face. It hissed.

"Wake up! Wake up!"

Buster woke up. The angry ginger man shook him by the shoulders. He remembered where he was.

"Oh, bollocks."

Buster blinked rapidly, scanned his surroundings, adjusting to the lack of light. Other than Clint, now standing and flexing his injured leg, they were alone. The woman had gone.

"Shit. I'm sorry. My medication. Sometimes I can't keep my eyes open. No excuse. Sorry."

Clint was all business.

"It happens. But it changes things. We have to move. Now."

The soldier rolled off the side of the container, hung from his fingertips, and dropped to the container below.

"Come on," he whispered. "I'll help you down."

Buster did as instructed, keen to make up for his unintended kip.

"What's the hurry?"

Clint grabbed Buster's hips as he lowered himself over the side, helping him to the top of the adjoining container.

"Judging from her behaviour so far, I'm guessing Miss Felicity doesn't intend to go it alone. Most likely case scenario, she's hoping to cut a deal with the captain. We know her crime is financial. She may have enough money stashed away to convince them to spare her. And she has something else to trade."

"What's that?" Buster asked as they repeated the procedure and reached the deck of the ship.

"Us."

"Ah. Shit. Sorry."

"Don't waste time apologising. It doesn't change much. The bad news is, I have to try my plan now. I could have done with more of a rest."

"So... what's the good news?"

"Mm?"

"The good news? That's how the expression usually works, innit? You know. The bad news is blah blah blah. Then you give me the good news."

Clint shook his head.

"Oh," said Buster.

The soldier gripped his shoulder. "Quiet."

Those magic ears weren't what they used to be. Buster had looked after his hearing with all the care of a world-class music producer, but there was no preventing the deterioration that started in his late fifties. Three seconds later, he clocked it too. A high-pitched whine, rising and falling. Buster used to lie awake in his bought-and-paid-for council house in Hounslow, listening to kids racing up and down the A4 on Japanese bikes. Sounded the same as this. But who rode a motorbike on a container ship?

"Drone," said Clint.

As it got closer, the drone sounded like a swarm of bees having a heated argument with a battalion of wasps, cheered on by a crowd of mosquitoes.

Clint looked around them, tried the doors of the two nearest containers. He pulled Buster to the side, and they both flattened themselves against the metal side as the buzzing got closer.

"If it's only equipped with night vision, we might be ok. But if it has thermal imaging..."

The drone passed high above them. Buster looked, but saw nothing. A dark shape against dark clouds in the early hours wouldn't stand out. The device paused, hanging above them.

Clint tensed as if about to make a break for it. Then the drone zipped away. The whine got quieter then abruptly stopped.

"Let's go," said Clint, and Buster once again struggled to keep up with the injured man stumping ahead with his makeshift crutch.

Knackered old ears or not, Buster heard the next sound just fine, and they both froze, thirty yards from their hiding place.

Shouts, the hiss of shortwave radio.

Footsteps running their way.

Buster turned in the opposite direction, but Clint grabbed a handful of his collar and dragged him over to another single container.

"They'll come from both sides," he said. "Our only chance is to climb. Come on."

Clint dropped his crutch and threw himself at the door of the container, scaling it like a spider. But as soon as he put weight on his right leg, it gave way and he dropped. Buster, acting on instinct, stepped forward to break his fall, and both men went down heavily, the crash of the impact echoing along the corridor.

Buster saw a figure out of a nightmare. The clouds parted to reveal a helmeted man, night vision goggles across his face, raising a sub-machine gun, and firing.

Bullets smacked on the metal deck, followed by ricochets like metallic echoes. Getting closer.

It's over, he thought, closing his eyes.

It's over.

CHAPTER THIRTY-SIX

WITH ALL THE LIGHTS OFF, the only illumination on the bridge came from instrument panels and Brakesman's drone screens, which displayed the deck in shades of blue, yellow, and orange. The brightest oranges belonged to the *Trevanian's* crew and passengers. Impossible to identify individuals from a thermal image, but—when Brakesman piloted the drone over the starboard side—the two pulsing blobs moving from stern to bow could only be the Germans.

The captain flew the drone using a dedicated controller. He pulled back on one of the dual joysticks, and the device gained altitude before sweeping over the containers.

Ronnie stood behind his boss. Brakesman wanted another pair of eyes on the screens, looking for Clint, Buster, and Hannibal. He watched the surreal images with mounting dread. The thermal cameras weren't high-definition, showing every figure as human-shaped blobs. But the night vision camera gave an accurate representation of what it saw. Which meant they would find out he'd lied about Tom. If the night vision camera picked him out, no one could mistake Tom for Hannibal. And if the thermal cameras revealed four surviving passengers instead of three, Ronnie's treachery would be exposed.

Sean crouched outside, eye to the scope of a long-barrelled rifle, waiting for instructions from Brakesman. Ronnie put a hand on the butt of his handgun. If it came to it, could he do it? If they found out Tom was alive, could he take two lives to protect a man he hardly knew? Two evil lives, yes, but who was he to judge?

But Ronnie wouldn't be much help to Tom, or anyone else, if he was dead.

Actually, that wasn't quite true. Ronnie's life insurance would ensure his family got by. The thought made his flesh prickle with goosebumps. He didn't think he'd inherited his mother's superstitious nature, but thinking about his life insurance half-convinced Ronnie it was about to be cashed in.

"There you are." Brakesman's walrus moustache lifted in a smile.

Two human blobs appeared halfway down the corridor Miss Felicity had specified, trying to flatten themselves up against a container.

"Unarmed, just like she said." The captain sounded delighted. Tonight's game was the closest they'd ever come to disaster, but order would soon be restored.

Perhaps Brakesman would lay off the game for a while, or restrict passengers to the secretive individuals who joined them a few times a year. They boarded in baseball caps, heads down, never emerging from their cabins during the crossing. Brakesman took them their meals personally. Ronnie guessed these passengers explained the high wages on the *Trevanian*, three times that of any other ship. He didn't know who they were. He didn't want to know.

The captain lifted his radio. "Boys, we have them. They've left the container, but they're still in the corridor, unarmed. Kill them and get back here."

He manipulated the controls, and the drone lifted back over the stacks.

"Let's see if we can't find our serial killer friend, shall we?"

Ronnie tensed. Watched the screens as the drone flew a few feet above the top level of containers, the captain looking down into the gaps, the stacks like metal foothills.

Ronnie saw the heat signature first, although he nearly missed it. It appeared on a rear-facing camera, and it was moving. Fast.

"Captain." He said the word as Brakesman reacted to the same image, hunching over the controls.

"What?" said Brakesman, reacting to the sprinting figure, now only yards away from the drone. "Shit!"

He yanked at the joystick to take evasive action, and the view on the screens tilted as the device banked hard. Three screens showed an orange and red figure, then a fourth screen bloomed with colour as the man leaped, one hand pulled back over his head as if about to strike with a weapon.

A wrench, possibly.

The screens went crazy as the drone flipped over and over. When it settled, its displays showed a fixed, blue image of the top of a container. Brakesman pressed buttons and pulled the joysticks. The drone spasmed and fell still.

"There's someone on top of the stacks," yelled Brakesman into the radio. "Near your position. He may be armed."

He swivelled in his seat, facing the open door to the wing. "Sean!"

Ronnie watched his crew mate raise the rifle, track the end of the barrel over the top of the container.

"I see him," shouted Sean. "Mother*fucker.*"

He lowered the gun, looked back into the bridge. "There's a container blocking my line of sight. Sonofabitch is behind it. But the Germans are heading right towards him."

"Shit," repeated Brakesman, raising the radio. As he held it to his lips, automatic gunfire echoed from the far end of the ship. Sub-machine guns. The firing pattern was too rapid to be an AR-15.

"Captain." Sean had his eye at the scope again. "I can't be accurate at this distance, but I'll try to plug him if he comes out from behind there."

The captain stood up, tossing the controller onto the table.

"I'll make you pay for breaking my drone, you piece of shit."

Given that Brakesman had passed death sentences on every

passenger just hours earlier, Ronnie thought it an empty threat. He fought the urge to smile. His own chances of surviving, with the drone destroyed, had just gone up considerably.

CHAPTER THIRTY-SEVEN

Jᴊᴍᴍʏ Bʟᴜᴇ ʟᴇꜰᴛ the stricken drone upended and dashed across the stacks, dropping a level to block the line of sight between him and any sniper on the bridge. Not much risk at this distance, but there was always the possibility of a lucky shot.

He pulled on the night vision goggles, kneeling on the last container before the corridor. Blue hated losing his natural connection with the night, but he couldn't see in the dark, although some of his enemies believed otherwise.

He had found Clint and Buster's hiding place earlier, watching Miss Felicity lower herself over the edge of the container and creep away towards the superstructure. Rather than go after her, he stayed close, listening to the night.

The approaching drone bore out the suspicion she'd sold out the others. A bullet might have brought it down, but would reveal his position. Instead, he chose his moment, raced towards the device and put it out of commission with one accurate swing of the wrench.

Back above Clint and Busters' corridor, Blue stilled his breathing, relaxed his body, brought the rifle up to focus on the port side, and tracked a crewman with a sub-machine gun rounding the corner towards the pinned passengers.

Blue aimed as the first bullets spat from the crewman's weapon, sending sparks flying from the deck.

He squeezed the trigger twice. Two in the chest, an inch apart. The gun below fell silent, and he swung his barrel starboard.

A second crewman experienced a sudden change of heart, skidding to a stop as his colleague dropped at the far end of the corridor.

The man reacted fast, and with intelligence. He didn't turn tail and run, guaranteeing a bullet between his shoulders. Instead, he jogged backwards, zigzagging, making it as difficult as possible for the unseen shooter to hit him. As he moved, he raised his gun, looking for the threat.

Blue didn't want to waste bullets, so waited until the moment the crewman's night vision goggles locked onto his own, his gun barrel rising.

"Yes," Jimmy Blue whispered. "Here I am."

His shot sent a round into the goggles, through the left eye, and out of the back of the man's skull.

Blue kept count of the shots he'd fired. The AR-15s were fitted with thirty-round chambers, and the one he carried had twenty-seven remaining.

Time to use some of those bullets.

Climbing the container to the top level, he rolled over the top, pointed the weapon towards the bridge, and started firing. The sniper on the wing returned fire, squeezing off a round so wide it didn't even ricochet off anything in earshot. Blue's onslaught sprayed bullets uncomfortably close. The sniper threw himself into the bridge.

Blue slung the rifle over his shoulder, pushed the night vision goggles up onto his forehead, and sprinted across the steel roofscape, moving towards the stern. He welcomed the darkness, kept his footsteps near silent, followed a memorised route.

Two enemies were on the move below. They'd reconsidered their strategy, dropping a level to put two inches of steel between them and the attacker above. Retreating to the superstructure.

He outran them, descending as he went, counting the containers that made up his maze-like route to the stern.

Six forward, two left, keep running. Two forward, drop one level, then another. Across two containers widthways, jump the corridor below, one forward, climb back one level, across four more, jump the second corridor. Drop a level.

Now the sprint to the final container that offered any cover. Jimmy Blue unclipped the rifle strap and let it fall beside him. He brought the weapon to his shoulder.

He intended to give Brakesman and his crew something new to worry about.

CHAPTER THIRTY-EIGHT

"Fuck me sideways, that was close."

Buster crawled back from his second trip, dumping another sub-machine gun next to Clint, leaning against the container. He rolled a cigarette and lit it. Clint didn't protest.

From the far end of the ship, a series of shots broke the silence, each echoing report accompanied by breaking glass.

Buster's forehead creased in confusion.

"The floodlights," said Clint. "Our guardian angel is giving them plenty to think about."

"Who is it, then? Ain't gonna be Hannibal after we sent him packing."

Clint shook his head. He flexed his leg, wincing, then stretched it out.

"Bonnie and Clyde then," continued Buster, taking a long, satis-fying drag on his roll-up. "Funny. Didn't think they were the heroic type. Acted like they only cared about themselves. Just goes to show, dunnit? Shouldn't judge people on first impressions."

Clint nodded at that sage observation. "Not that it changes much."

"What are you banging' on about? We're alive, ain't we? And we're armed now. I'd say things have changed."

"Ok. Maybe I'm being a little bit pessimistic."

"A little bit?"

"Hear me out. Yes, we have weapons, plus a spare clip for each gun. But they have an armoury and, I assume, plenty of ammo. They have working night vision devices. And a drone."

"Dunno about that, mate. It went quiet suddenly just before the shooting started. Reckon it's fucked."

Clint accepted Buster's diagnosis of the drone's condition with another slow nod.

"Maybe so. But they have food and shelter. We've got to survive four more nights. Possibly more. What's to stop them slowing the ship, adding an extra night or two to the crossing? Even if we ration our water, we'll either be dead or too weak to fight when they come to finish us."

"Well," said Buster, rolling another cigarette before tucking it behind his ear, "I bet you were popular with your army buddies, what with that sunny disposition and 'go get 'em' attitude, eh?"

Clint ignored the probe into his background. "I prefer to work alone. When people work with me, they tend to get killed."

"Oh. Grand."

The injured man stood up, tried to put weight on his bad leg. Grunted with frustration and pain.

Buster got to his feet too. Patted the younger man on the shoulder. "So, to sum up, you wish I wasn't here, and I'm gonna get killed. Thanks for the pep talk. When this is all over, you should consider a career in motivational speaking."

To Buster's surprise, a snigger from Clint turned into a burst of laughter. Buster looked at the usually grim-faced redhead and joined in.

If anyone could see us, he thought. *Probably the last night of our lives. Pair of bloody idiots.*

They were still smiling when Clint picked up the weapons one by one, handed Buster a sub-machine gun, and gave him a quick lesson on how to use it.

"Never touch the bloody things," said Buster, holding the gun like it might explode. "I'm as likely to shoot myself as anyone else, mate."

"You'll be fine. Heckler and Koch MP5. Fixed stock. A child could use one. Trust me, I've seen them do it."

Buster didn't ask. Clint twisted a switch on the side with four diagrams, the first a white bullet with a cross through it. "Safe," said Clint. A click clockwise showed a red bullet.

"Fires once each time you pull the trigger."

Another twist to a box with three red bullets.

"Semi-automatic. Each pull of the trigger fires three shots in a burst."

The last diagram showed seven red bullets in a row.

"This is the one you want. Fully automatic."

Buster twisted the knob back to the safe setting.

"I hope I don't have to use this bloody thing."

"Make sure to push the stock firmly into your shoulder. Aim for the midriff. Most beginners let the barrel drift up because they're not used to the recoil. It keeps firing until you empty the chamber. If your target isn't dead by that time, you will be."

"Marvellous."

The two men looked at each other. Buster put out his hand, and Clint shook it.

"This plan of yours. Think it'll work?"

Clint gave the question a couple of seconds of consideration. "If it doesn't, we're both dead."

He saw Buster's expression and smiled. "So, yes, I think it'll work."

"That's better, mate, much better. We'll have you booked for keynote speeches at vacuum cleaner sales conventions in no time."

They walked to the end of the corridor. Buster didn't look at the body of the crewman they passed, but stepped over the spreading pool of blood. At the intersection with the port walkway, Clint turned left and Buster turned right.

After a few steps, Buster stopped. The other man looked back. There was just enough light to make out each other's faces.

"My name's Roy," said Buster.

"Dafydd. My friends call me Daffy."

Buster took the cigarette from behind his ear, stuck it in his mouth, but didn't light it yet.

"Good luck, Dafydd."

Clint smiled. "You too, Roy."

He limped into the darkness and vanished.

When Buster reached the forecastle, he climbed the metal steps to the off-limits area, where reels the size of a telephone box held coiled ropes as thick as his thighs.

He sat behind the one nearest the port side, keeping it between him and the rest of the ship. He didn't know if he had it in him to shoot a man, but if anyone came up those steps, he supposed he would find out.

He checked his watch. Three-forty. It didn't seem possible under four hours had passed since Captain Brakesman's sick game began.

Clint had said to give him an hour. If Buster didn't hear what Clint had told him to listen for by then, he really was on his own.

CHAPTER THIRTY-NINE

THE CAPTAIN TURNED the floodlights back on as soon as the surviving German radioed in the news about Cashman and Mike.

The rest of the crew stared out of the mess window. No one spoke. Steve-one, ankles and wrists crushed, slept off the anaesthetic. Stevo was missing, Mike and Cashman dead. The game didn't seem much fun now.

Ronnie stood with his fellow crew members as they looked across the expanse of brightly lit deck and waited for Hicks and Tony to return.

Twelve huge lights hung on the superstructure. When the first one exploded, everyone jumped. Sean, back on the bridge wing, got off a shot. Before he could fire again, three more lights went dark.

Glass fell like hail onto the deck.

Brakesman stood by a table, shouted his orders. "Find out where he's shooting from. Look for muzzle flashes."

Two more lights shattered, then another three, accompanied by shots as fast as a thrash metal drum solo.

"There!" Gary pointed his coffee cup instead of his gun, the contents splashing unnoticed over his wrist. "Port side. Up top."

"Sean," barked Brakesman into the radio. "The top of the stacks. Shoot him."

The next shot from the attacker wasn't aimed at the lights. No one needed a radio to hear Sean's reaction above.

"Shitting Christ shit! I'm coming in."

Three more explosions.

Darkness.

"Down!" screamed Gary. The crew, aware they were standing in a lit room with an armed enemy aiming a gun in their direction, hit the floor as one. Everyone but Brakesman, that was. They waited for the inevitable burst of fire.

A single shot rang out. A bullet smacked into the glass.

Ronnie twisted, looked up at the captain. He smiled back. The mess window bore a puckered hole where the bullet struck it.

Gary's voice shook as he confronted the captain. Ronnie was beginning to understand why the man drank.

"Did you ever think about mentioning the bulletproof glass to the rest of us?"

"Hoped we'd never have cause to test it. You can thank me later, boys."

The radios burst into life. A voice screamed to be let in.

"Tony, you're going to have to wait," said Brakesman. "We're being shot at. Hold position at the end of the stacks."

He lifted the radio again. "Sean. On my word, turn on the main bridge lights. Tony, Hicks, stand ready. When the lights come on, get in here. Make it fast."

He took his thumb off the radio. "Gary, go to the door. When I give you the nod, kill the mess lights and get ready to let them in."

Brakesman lifted the radio. Nodded at Gary, who flicked the light switch. The captain radioed his chief mate.

"Sean. Do it."

The bridge lights came on above them, illuminating the containers opposite, providing a crucial distraction. At the same moment, Brakesman yelled, "Go!" and he, Ronnie, and Brakesman watched their panicked crew mates—Tony first, Hicks not far behind

—sprint across the deck to the mess, shoulders hunched in anticipation of a bullet between the shoulder blades.

Once inside, they threw themselves onto the floor. A single round ricocheted off the door as Gary flung it closed, locking the handles in position, sealing them inside.

"Ronnie, Gary, get the shades." The two men obeyed, closing out the night and hiding them from the enemy outside.

At one of the windows facing the stern, Ronnie reached up and stopped. The whole rail was missing.

"Captain?"

Brakesman joined him, looked at where the rail had been yanked from the wall. Shrugged.

"Doesn't matter. Nobody's coming from that direction."

Hicks put his hands on his knees and panted. Tony hung his head and sobbed. He got his breath back first, wiped away tears and snot.

"What the fuck was that?"

Brakesman put a hand on his shoulder. Tony shook it off and faced the captain, pointing a shaking finger at him.

"What the hell is going on? You said all we had to worry about was the Dutch psycho. All that bragging about your research, right? You always know so much about the passengers? When were you going to tell us about the fucking marksman? Would have been good to know before you sent us out there. Fuck. Mike is dead, man. He's dead."

"I'm sorry, son. Truly."

Tony broke down again. He let the captain lead him to a table. The Italian American looked like a scared kid.

Brakesman waved the others over and picked up his radio. Sean's voice came through.

"Be right there, Captain. Before we lost the drone, the cameras were recording. The footage might be useful. OK if I run through it?"

"Do it," said Brakesman. "See what you can find."

Ronnie gritted his teeth. Pictured the drone cam screens during the couple of seconds before they lost it. The sprinting orange and red blob leaping towards the camera, hand held high. It could be anyone. There was no way to tell. And they all thought Tom was dead. No need to panic.

"Tony makes a fair point," said Brakesman. "None of the information I have on Hannibal explains what just happened. He lived with his mother until he was in his forties. According to the report, he only ever handled a gun during his national service, and his commanding officer didn't trust him to point it in the right direction. He's no soldier. He strangled women, then posed their bodies. Sick, yes. Dangerous? Not unless you're female and on a date with him."

He looked around the table. Tony stared out of the window towards the bow and the abandoned body of his friend. Gary sipped at his coffee, both hands wrapped around the cup. Ronnie tried to fade into the background. Hicks, having got his breath back, had an absent expression on his face. It meant he was thinking. Ronnie wished he wouldn't.

"Hicks?" prompted Brakesman.

"If the facts don't fit," said Hicks, "then we must not try to make them fit. We must question our assumptions."

Ronnie was sweating. He didn't dare wipe away the moisture on his forehead.

The captain nodded at the German to continue. "Such as?"

"Such as who might be up there." Hicks counted on his fingers as he spoke. "He is an excellent shot. He can navigate unfamiliar territory in near-silence. He is a superb climber. I don't think any of us would risk that climb in daylight with the ship in dock. At sea—in darkness? He must be exceptional. Sean said we lost the drone. How?"

Brakesman described what had happened.

"Yes," said Hicks. "This fits with the description I have just given. It does not fit Hannibal. Therefore it is someone else."

"Who?" said Ronnie, amazed to hear his own voice come out steady, sounding normal. A vein throbbed in his neck.

"The captain is best placed to speculate, as he has reports on each of them. Tom is dead. Bonnie and Clyde are dead. Miss Felicity is locked in the Hole. That leaves Buster, Clint, and Hannibal."

"Buster is too old and unwell," said Gary. "He couldn't make that climb."

"The best fit is Clint," said Brakesman. "But I put a bullet in his leg. No way he could reach the top of the stacks."

Hicks nodded. "Besides, Miss Felicity told us where Clint and Buster were hiding. You confirmed this, yes?"

"We did. The drone found them close to where she said they'd be. Well. It found two people. We only saw them on thermal cameras." Brakesman picked up his radio. "What's keeping you?"

"On my way," came Sean's voice.

"Then I can only find one conclusion that fits the current facts," said Hicks.

In the pause that followed, Ronnie stopped breathing. A drop of sweat ran into his left eye.

Brakesman smacked the table with the flat of his hand. Ronnie grabbed the edge of his chair to stop himself falling.

"This isn't an episode of Columbo, son. What conclusion?"

"We must have an extra passenger," said Hicks. "A well-trained, dangerous, armed stowaway."

In the silence that followed that extraordinary statement, the only sound was that of Sean's approaching footsteps.

Ronnie wiped away the sweat, brought his breathing back under control.

For a moment there...

Then Sean opened his ugly, loud American mouth, and everything fell apart.

"There's no stowaway, Hicks."

Sean had one of the drone screens in his left hand. He held it the way TV evangelists hold the Bible: first prize in a narcissism contest.

"No?" said Hicks. "You have new information?"

"I sure do, my German friend. You can't tell much from a thermal image, but night vision cams are another story. I found a pretty good mug shot of our stone cold killer before he busted up the captain's drone. And, let me tell you, it's quite the surprise."

Sean twisted the screen around. The picture quality, despite the eerie green and white, was pretty good. Good enough to recognise the big man who couldn't talk, who stared at the floor during the captain's briefing, who no one thought would last long once the game started.

The man whose name on the flip chart had a line through it, and Ronnie's name next to it.

Tom.

Ronnie considered going for his gun, but he saw the throwing knife in Sean's right hand.

"I don't think so, you treacherous little gook bastard."

"Tony," said Brakesman. "Take Ronnie's gun."

Ronnie didn't move—couldn't move—while they disarmed him. He thought of his parents, and of Chul. Of the life insurance money that would follow news of his death. He hoped they would mourn a son lost at sea, proudly display his photograph to visitors, and smile at their memories of him.

The last trace of Brakesman's avuncular manner had vanished. The captain eyed Ronnie as if he could barely prevent himself pulling a gun and emptying every round into his engineer's body.

"Talk," he said.

CHAPTER FORTY

IT'S NOT OVER YET. You can get off this ship.

Commander Dafydd Cadwallader—Clint—had a job to do. A job important enough to track him down in Bavaria, and extract him from a remote farmhouse in the mountains. A helicopter transferred him to Munich and an army plane flew him to Britain.

As soon as he'd walked into the briefing room, he'd known it was the *Trevanian*. Spader's smile meant Brakesman had finally bitten. The fake history constructed for Cadwallader had worked, and it was time for an Atlantic crossing.

Time to find out how a container ship smuggled illegal passengers through rigorous customs checks into the USA or Britain.

He didn't have the information he'd come for, but the events of the past few hours would provide leverage on Brakesman, and that might be enough. If he lived.

The odds against his survival were still long, but a rogue element was helping shorten them.

Whoever shot the two crewmen must have night vision. No other explanation fit the facts. In which case, their guardian angel might be up there now, watching him limp towards the stern.

Who the hell was it?

Not Hannibal. Clint knew a climber when he saw one. The Dutchman was too old, his build was all wrong. Bonnie? Clyde? Possibly, but they'd both have to be top-rate climbers. And they didn't seem like the guardian angel types.

Which left Tom. He didn't have a climber's body—too big, too heavy—but he was strong. Clint couldn't imagine Tom would have the stamina necessary for long ascents, but, in theory, he had the power for short, intense climbs.

But that theory hardly fitted the silent, withdrawn, confused man they'd met in the mess.

Close to the stern, Clint surveyed the area in front of the super-structure. Their anonymous ally had shot out the lights. That would help. When they were functioning, anyone crossing that area was a sitting duck.

There'd been no movement on deck since the brief firefight near the bow. The longer the crew holed up in there with food and water near at hand, the weaker the passengers got.

All Brakesman and his crew had to do was wait them out.

Clint wished there was some way to communicate with Spader—tell him Brakesman's big secret. Spader had spent years coming up with theories for how the *Trevanian* secretly disgorged its illegal human cargo. He'd described it as a magic trick.

A good analogy, thought Clint as he reached the final corridor between the stacks. Like a magic trick, when you know the method, it's obvious. Simple. Disappointing, even. Brakesman's secret was that no one got off the ship. Not in New York, or London. They got off days before reaching land, their bodies wrapped in chains heavy enough to drag them into the inky depths of the ocean. Except... except some passengers did disembark, and their names and faces stared out from every wall of every intelligence agency in the West. How?

The ex-soldier began a series of stretches. His plan might be a long shot, but he wouldn't stand a chance if his upper body and arms were cold. He ignored the dull ache in his leg from the bullet wound. It would heal, given time, but he couldn't put his body weight on it, couldn't rely on it for any help during the next ten minutes. It was worse than useless, actually, because it unbalanced him.

The clouds parted for a few seconds, and Clint saw the waves move, an unhurried rise and fall of the vast body of water, nothing like the choppy surf of Colwyn Bay near his childhood home. This was more like watching a giant creature breathing. Waiting to be fed.

He turned away, leaned against a container and stretched out his triceps.

Between the stacks, objects glittered, reflecting the starlight in the moment before the clouds closed back over. Tiny points of light.

He limped closer. Shell casings littered the deck. From the gunshots earlier. Clint edged around the corner of a narrow aperture between containers. He found two bodies. Bonnie and Clyde.

The corpses were cool.

Why did the crew leave the bodies? To demoralise the others? Or because they came under attack?

The gruesome discovery brought him back to the question of their guardian angel. Clint couldn't accept the logical conclusion. Experience told him the man unable to look anyone in the eye, who struggled to understand the danger, wasn't the same man who saved his life. But if not Tom, who? A rogue member of the crew?

If he was still alive at daybreak, maybe he'd find out.

———

Back at the port walkway, Clint edged towards the stern, getting as close as he dared to the superstructure while remaining unobserved. The floodlights were smashed, but if a crew member using night vision optics checked, it might as well be daylight.

The barbed wire glinted with reflected starlight as the clouds parted again. By blocking access to everything behind and lighting the deck in front of them, the crew believed no one could reach the stern.

He slung the sub-machine gun over his shoulder, across his back, tightening the strap to make sure it wouldn't bounce. The handgun he tucked down the back of his trousers, something only TV gangsters and wannabe hard cases did. But no holster meant no choice.

With one last glance behind him, Clint climbed the railing, lowering himself down the other side. He gripped the lowest rail with both hands and dangled his injured leg off the deck, letting it hang in the dark. Taking his weight on his hands, he slid his left shoe down the hull until he hung from the rail.

Anyone looking at the walkway would need exceptional observation skills to spot Clint's fingers on the lowest rail.

Clint slid his right hand six inches towards the stern, then jerked his left hand along to join it. His body swung out as the ship rode a swell. He couldn't balance the way he needed to. As a climber, he required two hands and two feet. Occasionally, during a tricky ascent, he might have to rely totally on his hands to take his weight. Sometimes only one hand. But only until he found a foothold and relieved the pressure. Not here. There were no footholds. Bringing his left foot up and onto the side of the hull didn't help, because as soon as he moved, he couldn't use his right foot to do the same, and his body swung out over the water, his wrists and forearms screaming.

No. His only choice was to progress hand-over-hand until past the superstructure. Clint estimated the distance at twenty-five yards. Still possible if he kept up the momentum; if he didn't lose his grip on the metal rail, if the ship's constant movement didn't send him swinging too far.

If, if, if.

The hole in his right leg stretched, bleeding every time he moved.

Clint leaned on the lessons absorbed over years of training and experience. He took everything out of his control, every problem beyond his influence to change, shoved them in a box, and buried it deep. Stopped thinking about them. Started thinking about what he *could* control. Which wasn't much. He kept moving as steadily as possible. Right hand sliding along the rail first. Left hand next. Repeat. Right hand. Left hand.

The ship moved as he dangled, legs swinging. A tiny figure on the flank of a behemoth. A toy, a child's action figure. A bit worn out, a bit broken.

Tired.

Right hand, left hand.

Now the most dangerous part. The stretch of the journey where his progress was unobscured by containers or equipment. Where, if a crew member looked, he would be exposed. Helpless. Clint stared at his fingers, imagined them blanched white by night vision goggles. If they spotted him, they wouldn't even have to waste bullets. They could stamp on his fingers, send him hurtling into the water. Would it be cold? Probably not, it being early summer. He wondered how long it would be before his strength faded, before he couldn't keep his head above water and took his first mouthful of saltwater instead of air. He imagined a renewed effort the first time, a determination not to let it happen again. Then, inevitably, another mouthful of water. This time, unable to cough it away. Too weak. A feeble struggle, then conceding to the inexorable, patient power of the water. The spasming body descending into darkness.

No.

Right hand.

Left hand.

He didn't look at the mess and the men inside who wanted him dead. He saw nothing but the dark steel hull an inch from his nose.

Right hand.

His arms got heavier. As if someone were attaching weights to his sleeves.

Right hand.

Right hand?

When his fingers should have found the rail, his weight already transferring, they closed on something impossible to grip.

The crew hadn't ignored the possibility of someone attempting this route. They'd coated the rail with grease.

He slipped.

Hung from his left hand. Body rocking, twisting.

Don't twist.

If he twisted, he'd fall.

Still twisting.

He let his right arm hang by his side for a moment, flexed his fingers. Wiped grease onto his trousers.

Still twisting. Use the momentum, swing like a pendulum. Don't miss.

Swung his arm back up, found the rail this time, six inches beyond the smear of grease. Gripped it. Gripped it hard. The grease was a token gesture, applied haphazardly. They had been sloppy.

Lucky.

Clint let go with his left hand, bending from the elbow, flexing fingers. Wiped more grease onto his trouser leg.

Come on.

Reached up again. Gripped the rail. Wanted to roar his defiance, instead hissing through gritted teeth.

Right hand.

Left hand.

The light faded as he moved past the side windows of the superstructure.

Right hand.

Into the darkness.

Left hand.

He could make it.

The worst was over.

Far enough.

The worst wasn't over.

This was the worst.

He had to pull himself up. Up to the next rail, then pull his whole body far enough to get his left foot onto the deck. With arms that didn't want to play anymore. Arms that were giving up on him.

Pins and needles worse than any he'd ever experienced pierced his armpits; agonising stabs, over and over. Clint pictured tiny beetles burrowing into the flesh of his shoulders and upper arms, tunnelling through tissue and muscle to reach the ligaments and tendons between limbs and torso. Mandibles closing, nibbling, chomping, working through the glistening strands of meat holding his body together.

I can't do it.

I have to do it.

It had seemed straightforward enough when he'd described it to Buster. Hand-over-hand past the unsuspecting crew, pull himself up near the lifeboat at the stern.

Pull himself up.

Three words. Easy to say. Clint had smiled at Buster's incredulous expression. Acted like it would be easy.

Easy.

Clint started a swing, aligning his movements with those of the ship. Another pendulum, subtle at first, the arc soon becoming more pronounced. His fingers numb now. Not sure they would hold.

He'd only get one shot at it. Better make it count.

The pendulum swung again and again. His left toe connected with the edge of the deck.

This time.

Clint's muscles were past screaming their protests. They registered their disapproval with a burst of agony like white-hot fireworks.

His left shoe cleared the hull and slid onto the deck.

At the same moment, the numb fingers of his right hand loosened of their own accord and he slipped.

Fell.

Thought he was about to die.

His left hand took his weight with a jerk and he hung there, from his left toes and left hand, sucking oxygen into his lungs, knowing he couldn't rest.

Clint pulled with his left arm, got more of his foot onto the deck. Then his shin, scraping along the metal. His knee came next.

Balanced for a moment. Slipping again.

His right hand reconnected with his brain, reached up, gripped the rail, allowing him to slide more of his leg onto the deck.

Climbing the rail was easy after that, as if his body had accepted the almost impossible tasks asked of it.

He sat down, rubbing life back into his fingers. He couldn't move. Not yet. If they found him, so be it.

The few minutes it took to get feeling back into his hands seemed endless, but he waited until he could extend every finger, form a fist. The pain was horrendous. Good. It meant he was alive.

He shrugged the sub-machine gun over his head, wincing, and put the strap over his shoulder for easier access.

With all the lights out, the lifeboat loomed as a dark silhouette against a leaden sky. It sat on a ramp, nose pointed at a forty-five degree angle towards the Atlantic. It held up to eighteen people. Once released from its hydraulic clamps, gravity took over, its speed on hitting the water estimated at fifty miles per hour.

Clint had never used one, but he considered himself a fast learner. Besides, the point of a lifeboat was to save whoever needed saving—not necessarily a crew member trained to use it. He hoped for clear instructions, ideally with pictures.

He moved towards the lifeboat, staying low, despite the pain it caused his injured leg.

When he reached it, there were five metal steps to negotiate. No other way in. An unease born of years in war zones prickled across his skin. A single entrance meant a single exit. Not good.

Clint reminded himself of the barriers Brakesman and his crew had erected to make the stern of the *Trevanian* inaccessible. They operated with a skeleton crew and they were two men down, if not more. The chances of them posting a guard back here were slight. Not that it mattered. He had no choice.

He crawled up the metal steps. Undignified, but easier on his leg. At the top, he had to stand. Two handles stood between him and the lifeboat's interior. He stretched up for the upper handle. His right arm howled in protest at having to go over his head again so soon, but he ignored it and gripped the cold metal, ready to twist.

"Bad idea."

He froze. The voice spoke again. "That's far enough, I think."

The voice told him three things. One, its owner was behind him. Too far away for Clint to pull the handgun from his waistband, turn and fire without getting shot. The second thing it told him was that the speaker wasn't Sean, or one of the more dangerous-looking crew members. The unfamiliar voice shook with nerves, or fear.

The final thing was the most useful of all, and gave Clint some hope. The enunciation was sloppy, the word *that's* coming out more like *thass,* the *th* of *think* more like a soft *f.*

The speaker was drunk.

Clint turned slowly towards the voice. The ship's navigator—Barry? Gary?—sat with his back against the superstructure, legs splayed in front of him. It was still too dark to pick out details, but Clint recognised a bottle in his left hand. The uglier looking metal object in his right was a gun.

"Keep your hands where I can see them. Well, look at this. Captain said I should lay off the sauce, but it looks like I just saved his precious little game for him. Good job I keep spare bottles in the lifeboat. Emergency stash, y'see?"

Clint made some hasty calculations. Twelve yards separated him from the seated crewman. Considering the navigator's inebriated state, the bad light, and the motion of the ship, an accurate shot wasn't guaranteed. On the other hand, Clint's position on the top step gave him a serious disadvantage. To reach the deck he could only go forward—any other option was ruled out by the metal handrail on either side.

He still had the sub-machine gun strapped over his back. With two working legs, Clint could have jumped, rolled to one side, and come up firing. Fully fit, he put his chances of success at fifty-fifty. The bullet wound in his right leg lowered his chances considerably.

Gary took a swig of vodka. "You're in luck."

Clint didn't move.

"I'm a bit sick of killing right now."

The navigator took another swig. Drunk and getting maudlin. Clint wondered if he might have time to jump this guy after all. Best to keep him talking.

"It's Gary, isn't it?"

"That's right." It came out closer to *thasrigh'.*

"Mind if I come down, Gary? I want to take the weight off my leg."

"Sure thing, Clint. Come on down."

Clint took the steps slowly, making his limp appear worse than it needed to be, his right hand on the rail, wrist near his hip. He readied himself. On the last step, he would drop left and pull the gun from behind his back.

"Hands up, Clint. I figure that name suits you. Someone's been shooting up the place. Probably you."

Clint did as he was told. What now?

"Like I said, I'm sick of killing, but I don't need to kill you to stop this."

Gary waved the gun around. "Gonna shoot you in your good leg. Then send Sean back here to take care of you. Sorry."

One more swig of vodka for courage.

Clint braced himself to move, but Gary couldn't miss from this distance. So this was how it ended. Shot by a drunk on a container ship a thousand miles from anyone he knew.

The bottle went down.

Clint tensed.

The gun came up.

CHAPTER FORTY-ONE

A SHAPE DROPPED out of the darkness, landing squarely on the navigator's outstretched legs. A cry of pain died before it began, when a heavy fist connected with his head. His skull whacked the wall behind him.

Gary slumped, the bottle rolling across the deck.

The shape took the man's gun and stood up. He was tall. Unfamiliar. It could only be Tom, but Clint doubted his own eyes. Everything about this character was different from the silent, withdrawn Tom. Who was it?

When the man picked up the unconscious drunk like he was a bag of flour, preparing to toss him over the rail, Clint finally found his voice.

"No!"

The dark silhouette paused his run up. He stood as if waiting for a good reason why he shouldn't throw the crewman overboard.

"There's no need to kill him. He's no threat to us now. We can get out of here."

For Clint, there were rules of engagement. After two decades serving his country in various ways, some hard to justify, he kept his sanity by following those rules. There was a line he wouldn't cross, even on missions not officially sanctioned by any government. He'd seen soldiers cross that line, lose their way, go bad. Sometimes it got hard to distinguish between the good guys and the bad guys. Clint knew which side of that line he needed to stand. But he wasn't as sure about the man who'd just saved him.

A shrug of the broad shoulders, and the man dropped the navigator. He hit the deck hard. Didn't move.

The shadowy figure approached the steps of the lifeboat.

Even when Clint recognised his fellow passenger, he still couldn't accept it was him. He seemed bigger, broader. His expression wasn't blank, but guarded, hidden. Calculating. He moved silently, gracefully, with purpose. He reminded Clint of a tiger stalking its prey, its every movement the evolutionary end product of a billion genetic tweaks modified over millennia with one goal: to produce a perfect predator.

Even seeing Tom in front of him, Clint's gut told him it was someone else.

He swallowed, his saliva cold and metallic. Unconsciously, his eyes darted left and right, looking for an escape route. This creature existed to kill, and Clint's instincts had just triggered all the sirens, accompanied by a simple message:

There's no fight or flight option available here. If this thing wants to kill you, he'll kill you, and there's nothing you can do about it.

Then the creature smiled, tight-lipped, showing no teeth. Clint stumbled backwards, anticipating rows of sharpened, bloody molars. He forced himself to look away from those eyes, noting the rifle slung over his shoulder.

Get a grip. It's just a man.

"Thank you. For saving me. Was that you, er, I mean earlier, on top of the containers, did you, uh?"

Clint called on years of training, disregarded the instinctual urge to flee, and brought his tactical brain back to the fore. This man seemed to be an ally. An armed, deadly ally who'd forced the murderous crew to retreat, locking themselves into the superstructure. Saving his life.

He held out his hand.

"My real name is Dafydd. Daff."

The stranger who wasn't Tom shook his hand briefly. It took all of Clint's nerve not to flinch.

"Clint is fine," said the hulking figure. "I'll call you Clint."

"Ok. Fine. Since you're going to call me Clint, can I call you Tom?"

The dark eyes locked on his. Clint swallowed.

"No."

CHAPTER FORTY-TWO

RONNIE OPENED his eyes for the second time in ten minutes and immediately wished he hadn't.

He couldn't see much. The cabin lights were off, the only illumination a flashing LED on the smoke alarm.

Also, he couldn't open his left eye. Not fully. It throbbed along with his pulse, sending lances of agony into the bone of his eye socket, which he suspected was fractured.

Ronnie was curled up on his left side. He couldn't touch his eye to check on the damage because his hands were cable-tied behind his back. His ankles, too.

The eye wasn't the only problem. He couldn't get a full breath—not without needing to scream. Hicks had broken a couple of Ronnie's ribs while he whaled on him like a boxer limbering up. Sean had taken over when Hicks tired, splitting his teammate's lip, knocking out a couple of teeth, and breaking his nose.

Ronnie groaned. It hurt to groan. He frowned. It hurt to frown, too.

He shifted position to ease the pain in his ribs.

Ah, he thought, remembering what had happened ten minutes

earlier when he first came round. *I should try not to move. That's why I passed out last time.*

The bones in his right arm—shattered by the butt of Sean's rifle—sent an urgent message to his brain.

Ronnie passed out again.

When he opened his eyes for the third time, he stayed as still as possible.

He needed a doctor, he knew. But Gary—the closest the *Trevanian* boasted to a doctor—didn't exactly observe the Hippocratic oath, having sent Steve-one to his eternal reward on the captain's orders.

Things were not looking good for Ronnie. Not good at all.

Back in the mess, Brakesman eventually accepted the explanation beaten out of Ronnie by Hicks and Sean. That Ronnie had helped Tom because he felt sorry for him.

"You felt sorry for this guy?" Sean mocked, holding up the screen, the image of Tom's face, half in shadow, but clear enough for any jury, caught a split second before whacking the drone out of the sky. "He killed Cashman and Mike. Probably Stevo, too. But you felt sorry for him?"

Ronnie spat out a tooth in reply. He faded in and out of consciousness. Not that Sean expected a response to his question.

The captain woke Ronnie by holding a lit cigar against the Korean's nipple.

That still hurt. Not as much as the face, ribs, and arms, but it was on the list.

About ten minutes into the beating, Ronnie confessed about the food and water left in the container for Tom. Not that he had been trying to withhold the information. He would have told them earlier if they had given him a chance to speak between blows.

Tom wouldn't be there, of course. He would have moved the supplies, put them somewhere no one would find them. Ronnie had been wrong about Tom; all wrong. He wasn't like his brother, Chul. He still didn't understand how he had been fooled, but the shy, scared, gentle, and silent Tom he wanted to help was a fiction. The real Tom slapped drones out of the air, killed his crew mates, shot out the lights on the superstructure.

Recognising his naivety hurt, too.

The cabin they locked him in neighboured the Hole. He heard its occupant crying after Sean left. The walls weren't thick, and, from the desperate quality to her sobs, Ronnie guessed Miss Felicity might regret her decision to negotiate with Brakesman. Ronnie thought her tactic might still work: greed was a common motivator among the crew, especially the captain. Fifty million dollars was more money than most of them dreamed of, and since she made her offer in front of everyone, Brakesman needed an excellent reason not to take it.

No. Miss Felicity would survive. Smuggling an individual into the USA was easy. Once or twice a year, Brakesman sneaked someone through the border checks in a way that even fooled the sniffer dogs. Not that Ronnie envied anyone who entered the USA via that route. Miss Felicity's betrayal may have paid off, but her ordeal was far from over.

Ronnie's ordeal, however, wouldn't last much longer. He had nothing to barter with. His betrayal meant he wouldn't see New York. Another unfortunate accident at sea. His body couldn't take much more punishment. Another beating like the last one would surely lead to internal bleeding. Or maybe Sean would get bored, and practise his knife-throwing on a human target.

The porthole in this cabin wasn't riveted shut like the one next door. The poor light lent his already compromised vision a grainy, pixilated quality. Dawn was still an hour away. Ronnie had never known a night last this long. He clung onto one last hope: that he might see another sunrise before the crew tossed his broken body into the ocean.

He watched the door. Next time it opened, it would be time to die.

CHAPTER FORTY-THREE

"YOU'RE WANTED UPSTAIRS."

Detective Chief Inspector Barber was in the office early. She hadn't heard back about her request to meet the *Trevanian* on its arrival in New York, but she anticipated a dressing down from Connors—the Met's deputy commissioner—before he signed off on it.

The humiliating arrest of a Tom Lewis lookalike had already taken on legendary status in the Met. A more popular DCI might have got away with it, but the *schadenfreude* around Barber was palpable; everyone—from rookie constables to her fellow inspectors—smirked when she walked past. The only exception, to her surprise, was Cunningham, who had been far less of a pain in the arse since the rubber scar incident.

Upstairs, at best, meant a lecture. At worst, a demotion. A summons to Connors' office before breakfast was so unusual that, in the lift, she wondered if her job was on the line.

"DCI Barber."

Connors didn't offer her a drink or a seat. Two chairs faced the deputy commissioner's desk. She stood behind one of them. He shuffled papers around his desk as she entered, then opened a folder and didn't look up for thirty seconds.

The deputy commissioner of London's Metropolitan Police Service didn't share Barber's reluctance to occupy offices with a view. Behind his ostentatious oak desk, vast windows offered an unobstructed view of the Thames; Hungerford Bridge to the east, Westminster Bridge to the west and—directly across the water—the London Eye. The fact that Connors sat with his back to it told its own story. Yes, access to such a stunning view confirmed his status as the second most senior police officer in the capital, but he was far too important to enjoy it.

Connors continued to ignore her. Barber stared through the gaps in his thinning blonde hair at the pink scalp beneath, then turned her attention to his office. Not that there was much to see. The deputy commissioner adhered to a minimalist interior design ethos in the workspace. A large chair behind a large desk, smaller chairs for visitors, a flat screen television on one wall, and a yucca plant in one corner. The leaves of which were currently being stroked by a stranger.

"This is one ugly plant, Connors. Unwanted gift? Inherited from your predecessor?"

The stranger had an American accent. New York, possibly. Tall and broad, muscle going to fat. He wore a grey suit, the jacket of which would be impossible to button across his generous stomach. A plain blue tie, sloppily knotted. Early forties was Barber's first guess, but she revised it upwards. The deputy commissioner famously adhered to the niceties of rank. Anyone who could speak to Connors with such causal insouciance, and wear his shirt unbuttoned at the neck without comment, must be above the deputy commissioner in the pecking order. No one in their early forties could rise so high. She added a decade to her first guess.

"Barber, this is Special Investigator Spader from the US Homeland Security office attached to the embassy. Agent Spader, Detective Chief Inspector Barber."

"Call me Sam."

Agent Spader's grip was firm, his voice deep, and his teeth symmetrical. The mystery of his casual subversion of Connor's authority was solved. International cooperation between law enforcement agencies often threw up the problem of who was taking the orders and who was giving them. Their American colleague was clearly in charge.

"Sam Spader?" Barber wondered if she were the butt of a private joke between the two men. A glance at Connor's disdainful expression suggested not.

"Yes, ma'am," replied the American. "Parents had a sense of humour, I guess, then I gave them the punchline by going into law enforcement. Glad to meet you. Connors here speaks highly of you."

"He does?" Barber, realising she'd said this out loud, added, "Good. Yes." Not much better.

Agent Spader appeared to be waiting. Barber reviewed the conversation so far.

"Oh," she said. "Call me Barber. Everyone does."

"And your first name is...?"

"Irrelevant."

Spader let that hang for a moment, then gestured towards the chairs.

"Let's sit down, shall we?"

Connors bristled at this usurping of his authority, sitting up straighter and glaring as the American settled his bulk into the chair opposite. If Spader wasn't oblivious of the tension, he did an outstanding job of faking it. He sat back, crossed his legs, reached down to undo the clasp of a leather briefcase at his side. He produced a small tin, unscrewing the lid and offering the contents to Barber and Connors.

"No, thank you." They weren't boiled sweets, but a dozen tiny tea bags. Spader took one and pushed it under his top lip, sliding it to one side. It made him look like a boxer with a damaged gum shield.

"I used to smoke," he said. "Bad habit, unsociable, blah blah. My wife said second-hand smoke was the only thing I ever shared with her."

He chuckled. "Ex-wife, I should say. Guess she might have been right. These things deliver the nicotine kick through the gums. Very big in Scandinavia. Illegal over here. Ah, the perks of diplomatic immunity."

Connors, not bothering to hide his irritation, slammed his folder shut. "Barber, you'll be working with Agent Spader. Temporary assignment, Great Britain, America, special relationship, and so on. For the best, I think. Fresh challenge. Change of scene."

Connors spoke like a nineteen-fifties Powell and Pressburger character. All verbs treated with suspicion.

"Secondment? For how long?"

"Long as it takes."

"As long as what takes?" She caught his glare. "Sir?"

Connors harrumphed—a sound Barber associated with characters from children's books.

"Agent Spader will brief you. That will be all."

———

They waited for the lift. Spader skipped the small talk.

"How many people are involved with the *Trevanian* investigation?"

The container ship Tom Lewis had boarded popped out of her short-term memory.

Barber looked up as if trying to remember, instead considering the ramifications of the American's question. In theory, Homeland Security's international arm protected America's borders through cooperation with friendly nations' law enforcement and intelligence agencies. In practice, they were a box-ticking exercise. Literally. One possible answer in a multiple choice question for the police inspector exam.

"One of my detective inspectors conducted the interview leading us to the port. DI Cunningham."

"No one else?"

Barber gave him a humourless smile. "They're not exactly throwing resources at me right now."

The lift doors slid open, and they stepped inside.

"Yeah." Spader stretched an arm behind his head, and his shirt untucked itself on one side. "I heard about the plastic scar guy. Pretty funny."

Barber said nothing.

Spader tucked the shirt back in. "Too soon to laugh at it?"

Barber didn't reply. Infuriatingly, the American agent laughed anyway.

"Sorry," he said. "Not laughing at you. Remembering one of my own disasters. Back in my NYPD days, I once assembled a SWAT team after a solid tip about a meth lab. We hit them pre-dawn. I run in screaming, guns drawn: the full shock and awe treatment." He laughed again. It was a generous sound. "I kick open the first door I come to, and scream, 'Hands where I can see them, you mother-fucking piece of shit.' Never seen a more surprised nun in my life."

Not renowned for her sense of humour, Barber sometimes doubted she had one. But something about the situation bypassed her defences this time. Relief at keeping her job, the display of inso-lence towards Connors she had just witnessed, or just Spader's delivery— smiling, one hand on his stomach, top lip bulging like a cartoon character. The corners of her mouth twitched. She bit down on the laugh, suspecting she was perilously close, as an ex had once described it, to losing her shit.

But Spader knew his business, and he wasn't quite done.

"The adrenaline's pumping, so I say, 'And who the fuck are you?' The old bird don't miss a beat; she sits up in bed under this huge crucifix, Bible on the table with her reading glasses. About ninety-two years old. Says, 'Me? I'm the motherfucker superior.'"

The lift doors arrived at an open-plan space bustling with activity; officers hot-desking, on phone calls, in impromptu meetings, pinning photographs of suspects onto a cork board. The arrival of the lift didn't usually warrant more than a brief glance, but when the doors slid open to reveal a large man with a protruding lip alongside Detec-tive Chief Inspector Barber—the latter yelping with helpless laughter —the room quietened.

Barber, bent nearly double with laughter, way past the point where she could control it, looked up to see her colleagues frozen in place, staring into the lift. If she had hoped the sight of her workplace, an environment where dedicated officers investigated the city's most serious crimes, might jolt her back to normal, she was mistaken. Instead, the shock on those faces prompted a new level of mirth close to hysteria. She grabbed the wall for support, yipping like an overexcited puppy, tears rolling down her face.

Spader pressed the button for the ground floor, and the lift doors closed, the room beyond now silent.

On ground level, Barber headed for the nearest unoccupied meeting room. While Spader poured three sugars into a latte, she hid behind the coffee machine, facing the wall, her shoulders still spasming with laughter every few seconds. She waited for it to stop. After four minutes, it did.

Spader looked up from his phone. "Better?"

"Much." Barber poured herself a glass of water, wiped her face with a napkin, glad this wasn't one of the rare occasions she was wearing make-up. She felt the need to explain herself.

"I... I don't laugh very often. That was, that was..."

"Necessary, I'm guessing." Spader teased the tobacco pouch from under his lip and flicked it expertly into the bin in the corner of the room. "Thought you might do yourself some damage. I mean, I know I'm a funny guy, but my material isn't *that* strong. You were waiting for an excuse to lose it. I was just the catalyst."

"Maybe."

"No maybe about it. Pure stress release. Good job you let it out. The way Connor tells it, you have a stick up your ass."

He drained the last of his coffee, grimacing. "Go grab this Cunningham guy, and put a lid on your investigation for now. I want the two of you over at my office. Lots to discuss."

CHAPTER FORTY-FOUR

AFTER SHOOTING out the floodlights and sending the tattooed chief mate scurrying back inside the bridge, Jimmy Blue squeezed off a shot aimed between Captain Brakesman's eyes, only to see the bullet stopped by toughened glass.

He rolled back behind a container. Waited, listening.

The two survivors from the party sent to dispatch Clint and Buster approached the mess. Blue came out from behind the container, squatted alongside it near the edge of the stack. Held the gun ready. He didn't need the night vision goggles—the light spilling from the mess was ample.

Brakesman's response—he assumed it was Brakesman—was smart. The man could think on his feet.

When the mess lights went out, Blue responded. He flipped the goggles into place, bringing the rifle scope up to his eye. The bridge lights whited out his vision when they came on. He ripped the goggles away as the two men sprinted for the superstructure below, getting one shot off, firing blind, before the door closed. The bullet hit metal, not flesh.

The element of surprise had gone. Time to plan the next move.

He retraced his footsteps towards the *Trevanian's* bow, past the stranded drone. Blue ripped off its propellers and electric engines, stamping them into pieces. He shrugged off the backpack he'd taken from the man whose wrists and ankles he'd broken. Used Ronnie's flashlight to check its contents. The backpack contained a welcome surprise—two home-made incendiary devices with traditional fuses. He smiled.

He returned his attention to the ship, feeling the vessel's every groan, creak, and stretch through the soles of his feet.

Two people moved below him—one limping. Clint and Buster. At the port walkway, the limp turned left and Buster turned right, towards the bow.

Blue followed the limp.

He tracked the man from the container skyline, leaping across the corridors, landing in a roll and continuing without a sound.

He reviewed Tom's memories. Tom observed everything without judgement, or much understanding. He had feared Sean above the other crew members, considering him the most dangerous man on board. Wrong. Sean might be fit, and quick with a knife, but he wasn't as dangerous as Clint. The soft-spoken Welshman held himself in a way very familiar to Blue. His behaviour in the mess, watching the crew. The calm efficiency when dealing with his injury, and the fact that—even with a hole in his leg—he moved at speed with little sound, all pointed to a level of competence few achieved.

In Bavaria, an exclusive training camp took on a few pupils every year. Those who graduated from its brutal regime were sought after as soldiers, spies, and assassins, whether working for governments, corporations, or themselves. Blue was one of those individuals. He suspected Clint was another.

Near the superstructure, he watched Clint drop over the railing and hang there before moving hand-over-hand towards the stern. Jimmy Blue copied the idea, but adapted it. He jogged over to the starboard side, removed the shoulder strap from one rifle, and looped it around the rail. He stepped over, the churning waves far below crashing against the hull. Blue wrapped the ends of the strap around his hands before starting his journey past the barbed wire. The grease, thick in places, only made his progress even more swift. He bounced on his toes, pushing himself away from the hull, moving the loop a couple of feet each time. Once past the wire, he loped over to the superstructure and climbed two levels before easing around the corner. His progress had been far quicker than the injured Welshman. He watched from the darkness as Clint approached the lifeboat, heard a second voice, and—looking down —spotted the crewman sitting below. Easy enough to drop on the guy.

Now it was just him, Clint, and the unconscious crewman.

When he shook the Welshman's hand, he checked for weapons. As well as the sub-machine gun on his shoulder, his waistband pulled away from Clint's hip, suggesting he'd tucked a handgun behind his back.

Blue pointed at the lifeboat.

"This is your plan? Take this and go? Alone?"

The wounded man shook his head. "Roy—Buster—is waiting at the bow. I'm going to take the lifeboat, pick him up."

"What about the others? The woman. The Dutchman. Going to abandon them?"

"Felicity—Miss Felicity—sold us out. Gave us up. She must have something decent to negotiate with, and she traded our lives to save her skin. Hannibal is probably dead. Bonnie and Clydes' bodies are back there."

"I saw them. And me? You were leaving me?"

"Didn't know if you were alive or dead."

Blue conceded the logic. But he couldn't let Clint take the lifeboat.

"Who are you working for?"

"What do you mean?"

Without warning, Blue swept his right leg across both of Clint's at shin level. As the Welshman fell, Jimmy Blue plucked the handgun from its hiding place, pressing it up against the back of his opponent's neck.

"Don't," he said, reaching over and taking the sub-machine gun, keeping the handgun pushed against Clint's skin.

Most opponents would have continued to struggle. That Clint became still was a measure of his experience. No chance he could regain the upper hand as things stood. Better to wait until another opportunity presented itself. Jimmy Blue respected that, although he knew that opportunity would never present itself.

"I'll ask one more time. Who are you working for?"

"US Homeland Security." Not lying. Another good decision. The Welshman shifted his right leg a little and grimaced. "On secondment from MI5. Look, mind if I sit on the steps? You have all the guns and my leg is killing me."

Blue backed up, let him sit.

Clint shook his head. "Who are you, really?"

No answer. The Welshman surely hadn't been expecting one.

Clint shrugged, stretched out his injured leg. "You guessed I'm working for someone. What gave me away?"

"Everything."

Jimmy Blue knew all about playing games. His years of preparation to avenge his parents' deaths didn't just involve learning how to fight, how to survive. How to kill. He had studied acting, spent eighteen months working short and long cons with grifters on either side of the Atlantic. He could alter his appearance, change his voice, play a part if it got him close to a target.

And he recognised those trained to do the same. Clint was one, but nowhere near Blue's level. Every detail Blue replayed from Tom's memories since boarding the ship combined with the way Clint behaved since the game began added up to a conclusion that didn't fit with Brakesman's suspicions. There was a fundamental disconnect, a hole in the logic. Brakesman offered passage to desperate criminals fleeing the country. He portrayed Clint as some kind of rogue operative, a soldier who'd gone beyond his remit. But Clint's behaviour didn't fit. Clint's best option, once the game was underway, would have been to go solo. Use his training, study the enemy, find weaknesses and exploit them.

But Clint had kept the group together as far as possible. Protected Buster and Miss Felicity until she betrayed them. Even now, he could take the lifeboat without Buster, but Blue had no doubt he intended to go back for the other man.

Taking the lifeboat meant being picked up by another ship. The police would be informed. If Clint was who Brakesman thought he was, his arrest would be followed by a military trial and years in prison.

Blue had Clint pegged. Clint was a Good Guy. A Good Guy pretending to be a Bad Guy. And Good Guys like Clint didn't act alone. Clint had been placed on board to do a job. But by whom? And why?

"Lie to me and I'll know. I'll break a bone every time you do it. Why are you here?"

A simple technique to get the truth, but effective. The Welshman could still lie, of course, if he thought Blue was bluffing. But Clint looked like he'd know when someone was bluffing.

"Combined US-UK operation," he said. "We want to find out how the *Trevanian* smuggles criminals between the two countries. It's taken two years to build up a believable background so Brakesman would buy my story."

"And now you know."

"Yeah. Sometimes the simplest explanation is the right one. The passengers never arrive. Well, not all of them."

"Meaning?"

"We're not as interested in crossings like these. Once or twice a year, Brakesman takes a terrorist. Those guys, he doesn't kill, because they turn up later. A single rogue passenger is easier to smuggle in. But we don't know how he does it. Not yet."

"You don't have enough evidence to bring him down?"

Clint didn't answer immediately. Blue grunted.

"You *do* have enough. If you survive this trip. But that won't help catch the terrorists. As soon as word gets out Brakesman was busted, no one will come near him again. Oh, I see."

Jimmy Blue smiled. Once you understood someone's motivation, they became more predictable. Easier to manipulate.

"You don't plan to arrest him. You'll offer him a deal. Immunity if he cooperates with the authorities. You get your terrorists, and he avoids prison. Despite the people he's killed."

The Welshman tilted his head as if considering something. "I don't like it either. But sometimes bad guys go unpunished."

"That's not the way I work."

"Fine." The Welshman rubbed both hands over his scalp and sighed. "You're the one with the guns. What's your play? You've got the whole crew holed up in there apart from this clown."

Gary still lay on his side where Blue had left him. He was snoring.

"I need to get to America," said Blue. "I'm going to need the lifeboat before we reach New York."

"So come with us. I can't stop you being arrested if you committed crimes back home, but I'll speak up for you, and for Buster."

"No."

Jimmy Blue delivered the word with blunt finality. He didn't discuss, he didn't negotiate, he didn't compromise.

"What, then?"

"We do it my way." He handed back the two weapons he'd taken from Clint.

The soldier raised an eyebrow. "You're going to trust me?"

"You didn't lie. We work together for now. You get to complete your mission and make your deal. I get the lifeboat when we're close to New York."

Clint replaced the handgun in his waistband. "If you have a workable plan, I'm all ears. How do we get in there? There are combination locks on the doors, and the only guy who knows the numbers,"— he nodded towards the unconscious Gary—"isn't much use at the moment."

"You won't need to get inside. They're going to come to you. Tie that fool up with his bootlaces and wait outside the main door to the mess."

Clint eyed the greased railing, flexed his shoulders. "I almost killed myself getting here, now you want me to do it again?"

Jimmy Blue tossed the spare rifle strap at the Welshman's feet. "Use this."

When he realised how much easier his journey hanging from the rail could have been, Clint muttered something guttural in Welsh.

Blue smiled. "Welcome to the mutiny. We're going to take the *Trevanian*."

CHAPTER FORTY-FIVE

AT MAIN DECK LEVEL, every door leading to the superstructure had a combination lock. Five floors above the deck, two more doors offered access from the wings on either side of the bridge. Those doors didn't have combination locks.

Jimmy Blue stared up the white-painted steel walls, pale grey in the predawn light, leading to the bridge. He estimated the climb at fifty feet. Each deck had welds and rivets connecting them to the one above, and small square windows dotted the structure. He stood still for forty-three seconds, mapping out the best route, visualising each move he would have to make.

Blue made sure the AR-15 was secure across his back, pinning the rucksack tight across his shoulders. Shoved the handgun deep in his pocket.

He took a run at the corner of the structure furthest from the mess. He didn't want to be seen. Not yet. His right toes found an inch of purchase on the first window, and he kicked his body up and to the left. For a quarter of a second, he was in the air, then both hands gripped the narrow ledge separating each deck, and his left foot used the top of another window to add a third anchor point.

He paused long enough to shift his weight, get both feet on top of the window, ready for the next short jump; up and to the right. Blue's body was the wrong shape for climbing—too broad, too heavy with muscle—but he had studied with some of the best. The main take-away of his lessons had been to hone his proprioception, the sense of exactly where his body was in space. At its most basic level, proprio-ception allowed someone to shut their eyes and put their finger on their nose. Hundreds of hours of bouldering, climbing buildings, or tackling mountain faces augmented that basic function, turning it into something almost preternatural. An accomplished climber viscerally experienced their centre of gravity at all times, anticipating subtle shifts of balance as their body moved through space, finding secure holds at the very tips of their fingers, arms fully extended, sinews popping.

Blue stayed in motion as he followed the route he'd visualised. Each time he swung from his right toehold to find the window ledge on the left, gravity conspired with his body weight to pull him back. He used that momentum, waited until his body swung back before pushing off and reaching for the next ledge. This jerking, swinging dance took him to the wing in less than half a minute.

He heaved himself over the rail and dropped. Checked below. Dawn wouldn't be long—he easily picked out Clint watching him, the drunk navigator tied up at his feet. They exchanged nods, and the Welshman jogged to the starboard railing, looping the strap over it and beginning his journey back.

Blue stepped up to the bridge door. Not only was there no combi-nation lock, the heavy steel door hung open, a metal hook keeping it there.

Inside the bridge, a sniper rifle with a night scope was propped against a chair near the door. Jimmy Blue picked it up, emptied the magazine and the breech, putting the cartridges in his pocket before replacing the weapon.

As he moved towards the internal door and the stairs, he heard footsteps.

He ducked behind a desk.

Sean didn't even glance in his direction, going straight to the open door, crouching as he went. Either these windows weren't bullet-proof, or the chief mate didn't trust them to do the job. He picked up the empty rifle.

Before leaving, he checked a couple of screens. Like commercial planes, Blue guessed modern container ships steered themselves once out on the open water, needing little input from the crew. A good job, since half of them were dead.

For the first time, Jimmy Blue thought about Ronnie. He recognised the source of this thought, which arrived like an uninvited guest. It came from Tom who—although he could alter nothing, change nothing—occasionally sent up these flares of conscience. He'd done the same with Debbie Capelli. Friendships, emotional ties, and loyalty weren't just useless to Blue, they were dangerous. He couldn't afford to be influenced by anything that might deflect his course. But he couldn't stop the thoughts arising.

Ronnie had tried to help Tom. This removed the Korean from Jimmy Blue's black and white moral universe and placed him somewhere else. Somewhere confusing.

When Sean left the bridge, Blue waited three seconds, then followed.

The chief mate was a big man. Not as big as Blue, but his heavy progress down the metal stairs sent echoes between the hard walls. In contrast, Jimmy's progress was silent. He stayed close to the wall in case the chief mate looked back.

When Sean stepped into the corridor at ground level, Blue picked up his pace, taking three steps at a time. The chief mate turned left towards the cabins.

In the corridor, emergency lighting painted the walls with a monochrome dullness.

Of the remaining crew members, Sean struck Blue as the most likely to cause trouble. Fit, good with a knife, and with a mean streak he didn't bother concealing. Taking him out made tactical sense.

The corridor turned right forty-five degrees as it led to the living quarters. Sean leaned the rifle in a corner. Blue hung back, listening to the chief mate's footsteps. They passed the first cabin, stopped outside the second. A key in a lock. The door opened.

Jimmy Blue rounded the corner as Sean's back disappeared into the dark room.

He accelerated.

Enough illumination reached the cabin to reveal Ronnie lying in a foetal position in the corner, his face swollen, bruised, and bleeding.

Without turning, Sean used his left heel to push the door shut, reaching for the light switch with his right hand.

Neither action had the consequences he anticipated.

CHAPTER FORTY-SIX

SPADER'S OFFICE turned out to be a cafe near the American Embassy. A pair of doors led off the main seating area to what Spader described as a private meeting room, although Barber considered it a misnomer. The floor-to-ceiling window meant every passer-by, of whom there were many, looked straight in at her, the big American, and Cunningham. They sat around a low table containing a jug of black coffee, plates of pastrami and pickle sandwiches on rye bread, and a fully laden cake stand.

"Don't worry about them," said Spader around a mouthful of scone. "They can't see shit. Glass is one-way. Scone? It's real clotted cream."

Both Barber and Cunningham demurred, the latter fidgeting in his chair and looking at his watch. Tutting would inevitably follow unless Spader told them why he had prised them away from their case. The American agent was a hard man to dislike, but Cunningham was giving it his best shot.

"Why are we here?" said the DI, not touching the coffee Spader had poured.

Spader finished his mouthful, took a gulp of coffee. Sighed with satisfaction. "Because I can't think without proper coffee, and this is one of the few places they make it the way I like it. Because scones are the food of the gods, and the reason I'm not ready to go home, because... oh, you mean the case. Sure."

Spader wiped crumbs from his lips with a napkin, refilled his cup from the jug, and pushed another tobacco pouch under his lip.

"Caffeine and nicotine. Probably why I didn't last long at the DEA." He opened the briefcase at his feet, took out a cardboard folder with *Eyes Only* stamped across the front in red ink.

"Homeland Security has a taste for the dramatic," he said. "Lots of *Eyes Only* files. Some of the older ones still say *Top Secret*. Spy versus spy, cloak and dagger. We think all this bullshit makes us look grown up."

He opened the folder, took out two photographs of the *Trevanian*, one of its captain, some long-distance telephoto shots of crew members.

"We've had our eye on Captain Brakesman for eighteen months. Last week, you turned up at Thames Gateway and pulled in one of the crane operators into a police interview room. Why?"

Cunningham folded his arms. "Why watch a container ship for eighteen months taking photos?"

Spader's voice didn't lose any of its avuncular good humour. "Let's not get off on the wrong foot. I'm in charge here. A word from me to your boss, and this time tomorrow you'll be back wearing a tit on your head and giving directions to Chinese tourists. So please answer my questions."

Cunningham unfolded his arms. "Fine."

"Why did you interview Freddy Fullerton?"

Barber answered. "We're pursuing a vigilante. Tom Lewis. We thought we had him in custody, but—"

"Bald head, fake scar, Russian?"

"Yes."

"You think Tom Lewis boarded the *Trevanian*?"

"The witness is credible. We suspect Brakesman offers illegal passage for fugitives, and..."

Barber's routine request for information about Brakesman, his crew, and his ship, had yet to arrive. It should have been routine. "You've blocked my checks," she said.

"Yes," admitted Spader. "Have you spoken to any more witnesses, asked anyone else questions at the port? Have you communicated directly with anyone on the *Trevanian?*"

"No. We don't want to risk alerting Lewis. If he's onboard, the best we can do is wait for the ship to dock, arrest the crew, and search the vessel."

"Yeah. Ain't gonna happen."

"Why not? I've emailed border security in New York to request a joint operation."

"I told them to stand down."

Cunningham muttered something inaudible.

"Anything else I should know?" said Spader. "Any other lines of inquiry concerning the *Trevanian?*"

"No." Barber eyed the folder that had held the photographs. It was very thick. "What have we walked into?"

Spader patted the folder. "Five years ago, I took over a team investigating the movement of international terrorist leaders. We focused on the FTOs—Foreign Terrorist Organisations—who carry out attacks on US soil, or overtly threaten our country. Jihadists, movements like al-Qaida, and officials in states which sponsor terrorism. This last group has become more active over the last few years, infiltrating domestic groups in America and radicalising them. We'd like to prevent these assholes getting into the US, but we're failing. The technology used at borders to identify hostiles is improving, but they found a way past it."

"Container ships," said Barber.

"Right. We tightened checks, but consider the scale of the problem. Eleven million containers enter the US every year. Eleven million. That's the most likely way in. We can't search them all. So we investigated every captain of every ship. When I read the report on Brakesman, especially regarding his crew member's arrest, I knew we'd found our man."

Cunningham stroked his chin and eyed the scones.

"Handling stolen goods?" said Barber. "That was the only black mark on the *Trevanian*'s file? It's hardly uncommon for crew members to get arrested for petty crimes."

"Arrested? Sure. Not uncommon at all. He was a Filipino smuggling cigarettes. Happens all the time."

"So what was different about this one?"

"He got off. Lack of evidence, search procedure followed incorrectly by border officers, misidentification of suspect—they spelled his name wrong—falsification of evidence, suspicion that evidence was planted. The local DA dropped the case faster than Bill Clinton's pants."

Cunningham smiled. "Sounds like a monumental screw-up by your guys if you ask me."

"I didn't ask you. I looked up the guy's lawyer, expecting to find a court-appointed public defender. The Filipino guy washed goddamn dishes on the *Trevanian*. But the attorney who turned up to bail him out drives a Bentley and charges seven-hundred-and-fifty dollars an hour."

Cunningham made a non-committal noise.

Barber was thinking ahead. "Did you follow up on that crew member?"

"Sure did. Take a wild guess."

"Did he suffer a tragic accident at sea?"

"Yes, ma'am, he did." Spader gave her a grim smile. "Mid-Atlantic storm next trip out. Swept overboard. Body never recovered. Three eyewitnesses."

"But Jimmy Blue—whatever else he is—isn't a terrorist."

"Who's that now?"

"It's what Tom Lewis calls himself," said Barber. "He doesn't fit your profile. Last year, he killed most of the criminal gang involved with his parents' murder twenty years ago. Since then, he's moved on to human traffickers and drug gangs. The only common factor linking his victims we've been able to find is that they were all killers.

There's no ideology at play here, no radicalisation. He's a serial killer targeting violent criminals."

"And he's bloody good at it," added Cunningham.

"You admire him," said Spader.

"Nah. Don't put that on me. I'm just saying he's brighter than the average thug. Always a step ahead. He's a thinker. And look at who he goes after: the most vicious bastards imaginable. Really, really nasty pieces of work. Seven murders we know about, but we reckon he could well be in double figures. All that without us getting close."

"You do admire him."

"Whatever. But like the guv says, he's no terrorist."

Spader patted the folder again. "A few years ago, Brakesman expanded his business. He started giving passage to anyone with the cash to buy it, subject to his approval. Good news for us."

"How so?" said Barber.

"More passengers means more chance of working out how he smuggles them in. With these new trips, it can be half a dozen passengers at once. Good money for him, and a better shot at us finding out how they get through border checks. He bribes a few port employees to look the other way when certain containers are unloaded. Customs officers who sign dockets without carrying out proper checks. But he can't avoid random checks, and none of them have caught him. Now he's moving whole groups. We have no idea how he does it."

"Arrest him," said Cunningham. "Lean on him, threaten him."

Barber shook her head. "No. You don't plan to arrest him at all, do you? You want him working for you."

"And that," said Spader, finally opening the folder, "is why she got the promotion and you didn't, bud."

Cunningham coloured.

"We've been working on bringing him over for years. This voyage is our best chance. And then the Met shows up and starts stomping all over our operation."

Spader checked his watch, took a mobile phone from his pocket, and put it on the table.

Cunningham looked at Barber as Spader sipped his coffee in silence. Barber offered an almost imperceptible shrug in return.

Spader slid a photograph from the folder onto the table. It showed a man in his mid to late thirties wearing military fatigues, hanging one-handed from a climbing wall. Clean-shaven, ginger hair cut short.

"A crew member?" said Cunningham.

"Nope. Commander Dafydd Cadwallader, an experienced MI5 agent. The sort of guy you call when queen and country need someone to die in an unfortunate accident. A Welsh, ginger James Bond. Currently working for the Department of Homeland Security. And the reason your investigation needed to stop before it got him killed."

Barber looked at Spader, trying to ignore the protruding lip and the lump of cream half an inch above it.

"You put him on the ship."

"Surely did."

"On his own?"

"It's what Daff does." Crumbs and jam headed off in all directions. "He doesn't play well with others. On his own, he's the best."

Barber sighed.

"You stopped our investigation because Brakesman might find out the Met are asking questions about his passengers."

"You got it."

Barber didn't allow her frustration to show. "Apart from killing our investigation, what do you want from us?"

"To start with, everything you have on this Tom Lewis- Jimmy Blue individual. The one thing you're sure about is that he likes killing violent criminals. Now he's on a boat full of 'em. Plus Daff, posing as one."

Cunningham gave in and took a scone. "Your man is safe. Lewis is on the run. He's hardly going to draw attention to himself before he gets to America, is he?"

Spader looked at him evenly. Cunningham looked from the American to his boss. "Is he?"

Spader picked up the photograph of the Welsh agent. "Daff calls in every two hours to deliver a code word. He missed the last one."

He tapped the mobile phone on the table, looked at his watch. "And the latest call was due five minutes ago."

CHAPTER FORTY-SEVEN

RONNIE SNAPPED awake from a fitful sleep at the sound of footsteps in the corridor.

He'd been dreaming about his brother, about their days fishing off the dock after school. Chul loved the thrill of the twitching float, the taut line, and the splashing of the fish as Ronnie reeled it in. But as the distressed fish got closer to the net he held, Chul's excitement gave way to empathy with the thrashing animal he lifted from the water. He'd talk to the fish, stroking its side as he removed the hook before returning his prize to the sea. Ronnie never brought home a single catch from their trips. He complained, of course, but he didn't mind, not really. He remembered the silver flashes as the fish squirmed in Chul's hands before relaxing as he whispered to them.

Ronnie had only got close enough once to hear what his brother said to calm the terrified creatures. Chul apologised to them. He apologised, then wished them a long, peaceful life. Ronnie had almost laughed, but he'd stopped himself, flushing with shame at his first reaction. On the way home that day, he'd draped his skinny arm across Chul's big shoulders, proud to call this caring, gentle soul his brother.

He smiled now as the door opened. For a moment, he was ten

years old, in his bedroom, reading a comic book, waiting for Chul to brush his teeth and come in. They'd look at the pictures together, Ronnie telling his brother what the words said. Sometimes they'd make up their own stories to go with the pictures.

Ronnie's smile faded at the sight of the silhouette in the doorway. His left eye, glued shut with dried blood, blurred what was left of his vision, turning the chief mate into a threatening smudge. His injuries dialled up their signals to his brain, reminding him he needed medical attention.

Not going to happen, he tried to tell his broken arm, his ribs, his face, his eye. *This is the last human being I'll ever see. A bully. A killer.*

No. His grip on consciousness remained tenuous, so he could choose to be elsewhere. Fragments of his dream remained; amorphous wisps of memories. He'd been a happy kid. Chul, too. Better to go back there, abandoning this reality, this pain, this body.

Just as his good eye was about to close, he saw it. Woke up, eye wide open, blinking moisture away. A second figure stood behind Sean.

It happened so quickly, and the image was so unlikely, he wondered if it were another dream.

Sean kicked the door shut, but an extended foot from the shadow prevented it closing. A huge hand closed on the chief mate's wrist and prevented him turning on the light.

The shadow stepped into the cabin, closing the door. The room returned to near darkness.

In the dim light of the smoke alarm LED, two figures grappled. There were no words, no threats, no entreaties. This was no bar brawl or altercation between stir-crazy crew mates too long at sea. This was a deadly encounter only one would survive.

Ronnie, eyesight compromised, brain confused, straining to make sense of reality, listened and watched.

At some level, he understood the two men must be Sean and Tom, but that wasn't what he saw. Ronnie saw Street Fighter II, the arcade game he and Chul played obsessively, spending their pocket money. Ryu versus Blanka. Ryu looked like the Karate Kid on steroids. Blanka was a green-skinned, orange-haired berserker with the face of a Japanese demon.

Ronnie didn't hear the snap of a bone, the thump of a fist on soft tissue. He heard the cartoon-like soundtrack of his childhood, each blow an 8-bit sample nothing like a real punch. He saw his score racking up in the top left corner, the looping lo-fi soundtrack, the identical, repeated grunts as Ryu took punishment from the unstoppable Blanka.

At one point, a solid *thunk* pulled Ronnie out of his vision and he recognised the quivering blade six inches from his face. One of Sean's throwing knives. A series of heavy blows followed, then a lull, punctuated by gasps of breath.

The floor vibrated as a heavy body landed a few feet away. The face of the stricken man faced Ronnie, stale beer and gum on his breath. Sean.

Unsure if he was mixing his arcade games up, and well past caring, Ronnie whispered, "Finish him."

A hand pulled the throwing knife out of the floor before returning it to its owner - blade first, between the ribs, into the heart.

Sean twitched like one of Chul's netted fish. There was no whispered apology for Sean. Just one last violent shudder, a rattling cough, then silence.

"How badly injured are you?"

Ronnie recognised Tom's voice. He should be terrified of the stranger who had just killed Sean with his own knife. But he couldn't muster enough energy to be scared.

"Pretty bad. Ribs broke, nose, maybe jaw. Right arm, too."

"I'll get you some help." Not even out of breath.

Sean's killer opened the door. "Wait here."

"Sure," breathed Ronnie as the big man left the cabin, leaving the door unlocked. "Like I have a choice."

CHAPTER FORTY-EIGHT

HICKS CONSIDERED HIS FUTURE: long-term, medium-term, and short-term. Long-term centred around buying a nightclub or two in Berlin —a dream since his teens. Medium-term had shrunk to cover the duration of this Atlantic crossing. He intended surviving it, then leaving the *Trevanian* for good. Short-term was the sticky one, and everything relied on it. Short-term meant winning the game. At least one passenger had proved deadly, and was out there now, armed, dangerous, hunting the hunters.

He looked around the darkened mess. Just him, Tony, and Brakesman. Tony, slumped on a plastic chair, head in hands, was no help. Hicks caught his boss's eye. They were both thinking the same thing.

Brakesman stood up. "Sean's taking his sweet time."

The *Trevanian's* captain had lost much of his Southern drawl, and the relaxed demeanour that accompanied it. He waved his cigar at Hicks.

"And when did you last see Gary? The man is a liability. Gary?"

He shouted this last word. No answer. Brakesman tried the radio with the same result.

"With me," he told Hicks. The two of them drew their handguns and walked towards the corridor leading to the galley, sickbay, and cabins.

The corridor was darker still. Hicks ducked to the left side when a large shape moved in the near-blackness. Brakesman responded, moving right, pressing up against the wall. They flanked the opening to the corridor, weapons held ready.

"Sean? That you?"

No reply. Hicks and Brakesman waited, listening. The silence, like the darkness, was oppressive, heavy. Why didn't the chief mate answer? Something smelled wrong about all of this. Hicks hissed the name again.

"Sean?"

The voice that replied was a stranger's. Deep, flat, emotionless. No discernible accent. Tom. "Sean is dead. I stabbed him in the heart. The game is over. You lost."

Then the voice sang.

"Well what is this that I can't see
With icy hands takin' hold of me
Well I am Death, none can excel
I'll open the door to Heaven and Hell"

Hicks held his breath, the hairs on his neck, arms, and hands lifting away from his skin. Brakesman froze, both hands wrapped around his gun. Hicks fought against the same instinct.

"Incorrect," said Hicks, his voice tight and strange. "The only way in here is through this doorway. We have enough weapons and ammunition to kill you a hundred times over. You have merely delayed the inevitable."

He hoped it sounded more convincing than he felt. He just wanted to provoke a response.

It worked.

"Wrong," said the voice, but Hicks didn't listen. He raised his gun, kept his body where it was, only his hand emerging from cover, firing blind, sending bullets into every corner of the corridor beyond. After the silence, the sound was obscenely loud, each shot echoing down the metal-lined corridor, ricochets ripping chunks of paint and steel from the walls, the flattened slugs dropping to the floor, bouncing and rolling across the hard surface before settling.

Then silence again, other than a ringing in his ears, the gun hot in his hand, the air rich with the acrid stench of propellant.

"Missed."

No triumph in that voice, no mocking undertone. Tom spoke as calmly as before. Brakesman nodded towards the flashlight hanging on the wall by Hicks. He nodded back, lifted it down. There were three doorways along the corridor. The galley and the sickbay on the left, the bathroom on the right opposite the stairwell. If they knew where their attacker was hiding, they could come out firing, pin him down.

"As I was about to say," continued Tom from the darkness, "you have overestimated your chances of survival."

Brakesman held up three fingers with his left hand, his right hand tight on the gun. Hicks shrugged the sub-machine gun from his shoulder, braced it against his hip, ready to follow up Brakesman's shots with enough automatic fire to stop a rhino.

"In a few moments," said the emotionless voice, "you will go outside. Or you will die."

Two fingers. One.

"You'll have five secon—"

Hicks clicked on the flashlight, leaned out into the doorway at the same moment Brakesman swung into view, already firing.

He saw Tom. Only for a fraction of a second. Half in, half out of the sickbay door, Tom's hand jerked back behind his neck, then moved forward in a blur. The image came and went as fast as subliminal advertising frames spliced into old movies. Then the flashlight was spinning back into the mess, and Hicks was back against the wall, fingers twitching, his forearm pumping blood along the hilt of the throwing knife buried half an inch away from the artery in his wrist.

The voice returned. Still calm. Still triggering the instinct to flee. "Don't interrupt."

Hicks, breaths coming short and fast as he looked in disbelief at the knife—one of Sean's—in his arm, backed away, his left hand aiming the sub-machine gun at the corridor. The moment that crazy bastard appeared, he'd tear him in half.

Brakesman retreated, too. He'd only squeezed off two shots. His hands shook.

"Five seconds is an estimate," said Tom. The flashlight had skidded back into the room, its beam illuminating the far wall. "I could give you a more accurate countdown if I made the devices myself, but there you go. We work with what we have."

The two men backed into the room. Brakesman upended a table to use as cover. Hicks did the same, crawling behind it. His arm sent jolts of agony throughout his upper body with every movement. He ignored it as far as possible and kept his attention on the doorway, kneeling behind the table, bracing his weapon on it. He had no idea what the crazy passenger was talking about, but it didn't sound good.

And that was when Tony, who Hicks had forgotten about, went crazy. As if zapped by a cattle prod, the young Italian-American leaped to his feet, sending his chair skidding backwards.

Brakesman waved a hand at him from behind his table.

"Get down, for Chrissakes. Find some cover."

"He killed Mike." Tony's throat was tight, his voice pushing its way out as if he were being strangled. "He killed Mike."

He took a step towards the darkened corridor, gun held tight in both hands, the barrel shaking.

"Tony," hissed the captain. "I told you to find some cover. It's three against one. We'll kill him. Together. Don't do anything stupid. Get down."

If he heard his boss, Tony didn't react, but kept moving, approaching the entranceway at an angle, still out of sight of the enemy.

Hicks pushed another table over. "Come on, Tony. Get behind this."

Tony ignored him, too. At the point just before he would be visible to anyone waiting in the corridor, he stopped moving.

Hicks puffed out a relieved breath. For a second, he thought his crew mate had lost his mind.

"Tony. Come on."

"Die," said Tony, quietly. He repeated the word, a little louder, then again louder still.

"Tony! Whatever you're thinking of doing—"

"DIE."

Tony ran into the corridor, screaming and firing as fast as he could pull the trigger.

After the third shot he stopped screaming, then he stopped firing.

When Tony's gun hit the floor, Hicks and Brakesman looked at each other, then back at the corridor. They lifted their weapons as someone approached.

Tony stepped backwards into the mess, hands at his throat, blood spurting between fingers failing to stem the flow. He couldn't speak, his voice emerging in wet, wordless gasps. He shot a desperate silent appeal at Hicks, who waved him over without leaving the cover of the overturned table.

Two shots rang out, so close together they were almost simultaneous, a flam on a snare drum, the sound echoing in the corridor. Tony's chest blossomed with a blood-red rose, his head twitched and he flopped forward, face-first, twitched once and was still.

"Great," said Brakesman. "Just great, Tony."

Tony's killer spoke as if reading aloud from a particularly uninteresting book.

"One of your crew made these two devices. I broke his ankles and wrists to prevent him taking any further part in the game. He was already unconscious, and it seemed unnecessary to kill him. But I found his body a few minutes ago. Looks like your captain doesn't want to carry any dead weight. As it were."

Hicks looked over at Brakesman, who shook his head in response. Not that Hicks had any trouble believing Tom's accusation. He already knew the captain for a ruthless bastard.

He considered pulling the knife out of his arm, but feared it would cause him to bleed out.

"However, your recently deceased companion had a couple of home-made pipe bombs in his backpack. Probably full of nails, screws, bolts, broken glass. Standard fuses, pretty short. Like I said, I reckon you'll have five seconds, but that's just a guess. Might be ten. Might be three. You should check how close you are to the door. How long it will take you to open it. It's your only way out. Alive, that is. I guess you could run towards me."

Both men heard what came next. The flick of a lighter, the hiss of a lit fuse.

"Five," said the voice, "four, three..."

The bombs sailed through the doorway, bounced on the floor, and rolled. One came to rest in the middle of the room, the second up against the table where Hicks crouched.

"Fuck," said Brakesman.

They ran. Hicks reached the door first, fumbling with his left hand. Brakesman shouldered him aside, got the door open, and the pair of them burst onto the deck, the sky now lightening with the dawn.

The expected explosion didn't come. Either Tom had been bluffing, or the fuses were longer than he'd anticipated.

A man waited outside, his back against the first row of containers. Clint. An AR-15 pointed at them.

"Well, well," said Clint. "He's a man of his word."

He fired and Brakesman fell, his knee shattered. Clint turned the gun on Hicks.

"Drop it."

The Berlin nightclub was never going to happen. Hicks eased the sub-machine gun strap from his shoulder, ready to comply. Then every window in the mess blew out, and he dropped.

Bulletproof glass could absorb the impact of a small projectile, but not a thousand of them blowing outwards simultaneously. Flying shards of glass accompanied hot shards of metal as the pipe bomb exploded. Clint cursed and dived for cover.

The second device hadn't exploded yet. Hicks saw an opportunity. Took it. Ran.

Not fast enough.

Shots. Rapid-fire, controlled. Clint fired from the ground, lying on his side, the rifle tracking Hicks as he sprinted away. The *thwock* of metal on metal, ever-closer.

The port side walkway. Close. So close. Five more steps? Six?

A bullet sliced a sliver of flesh from his right buttock. Hicks stumbled, screamed in pain, anger, and frustration, knowing the next shot would likely shatter his hip and put him down, where the follow-up would finish him.

The second device exploded.

A white-hot flash from the mess. Clint couldn't have been expecting it, as his next few shots sprayed wide, and, hardly believing his luck, Hicks put a row of forty-foot steel containers between him and the Welshman.

He ran for his life while screws, bolts, nails, and glass dropped from the sky onto the deck, some hitting his head and shoulders. The pipe bomb sent its payload in every direction, but the walls of the mess stopped most of the deadly shards. The trajectory of the remaining pieces took them up and out until, at the mercy of inertia, they fell like hail.

Hicks dodged into the first corridor crossing the width of the ship, checked right for danger before continuing his run towards the ship's bow along the starboard walkway.

The knife in his arm meant his short-term plans had taken on a new focus. He couldn't remove it. Hicks remembered enough from first aid courses to know the blade plugged the wound. He needed a doctor standing by to stop the bleeding and sew him up. Which meant Gary—if he was alive and sober enough to do it.

Once he cleared the last row of containers, Hicks used the grey light of dawn to examine his forearm, which had gone worryingly numb. The blood still seeped along the metal blade. He took off his belt, wrapped it around his upper arm, slid the leather under and over to make a knot. Not a perfect tourniquet, but good enough. His fingers were leeching colour, the tips whiting out, a photograph left in direct sunlight.

He'd lose the arm if he didn't get help soon.

He put his fingers on the seat of his torn trousers and winced. The wound on his backside hurt, but it wasn't serious.

He looked up at the forecastle. Sailors once used it to defend their vessels against attackers. The forecastle, with its huge reels of rope, easy to hide behind, might keep him alive long enough to start thinking again about those medium and long-term plans. One man could hold off many others there.

A sound strategy, but Hicks wasn't the first to think of it. As he reached the top of the metal steps leading to relative safety, something moved in the half-light.

CHAPTER FORTY-NINE

BUSTER LOOKED at his watch and cursed.

"Of all the bloody times to pack in, you cheap piece of shit."

He waggled his arm as if it might make a difference, might cause the grey screen to display an accurate time instead of flickering, then dying again. He'd always liked digital watches. Wore them first time around, when they were cool, carried on wearing them for the twenty years when they were considered uncool, then found himself back in the vanguard of male timepiece chic once again. And that, thought Buster, told him everything he needed to know about fashion.

Only now the bloody thing had given up the ghost a thousand miles from the nearest shop.

He looked at the sky. A good sight lighter than when Clint left. How long ago? His body clock told him an hour, maybe more, but he didn't want to believe it. Didn't want to think about what it meant.

Twice, he left his hiding place behind a massive coil of rope in an even bigger metal reel, crawled over to the side, looked down at the waves. Nothing to see but the constant oily spasms of sea water sliced aside by the *Trevanian*, nothing to hear but the engine of an enormous lump of metal thundering through the water followed by a thousand slaps of liquid against the hull.

Like the ocean is telling the ship to piss off.

But nothing else to see or hear. No lifeboat. No Clint.

Buster had followed the Welshman's instructions. The gun—horrible bloody thing—lay by his side. He visualised what he'd have to do if Clint failed. If the crew came after him. Brace the gun against his hip. Aim for the midriff. Don't stop firing until they're down.

He listened for the lifeboat engine again. Didn't hear it. But he heard the explosions. First one made him drop his ciggie, and it rolled out of sight.

Clint had said nothing about explosions. Couldn't be good, could it? Not on a ship. Not anywhere, really, but particularly on a ship, floating god knows how many thousands of feet above the cold sea bottom, halfway between London and New York. Explosions. Fires. Not what you want at all.

But what did it mean tonight? On a ship where the crew were trying to kill the passengers? It could be a new tactic. A blunt weapon to finish the game. Or it could be the work of the mysterious figure who saved him and Clint.

Buster risked a glance over the top of the reel. Nothing. Just a million sodding containers. No glow in the sky suggesting a fire.

He sat down again, took out his tobacco pouch, rubbed the pungent strands between yellow-stained fingers, dropped them into the paper. Licked it, sealed it, lit it. Took three goes to get a flame. His thumb wouldn't cooperate, jerking wildly. He waited the spasms out. They'd pass soon. They always did.

Nothing like a good roll-up to settle the nerves. Buster smiled. Plenty of people—his doctor, his sister, his first wife—had told him the ciggies would kill him. Cancer sticks, that's what they called them. Government stopped tobacco companies advertising them, locked the packets away in shop cupboards. Made the companies stick photographs of diseased lungs on the packaging to discourage smokers.

Still let folk buy 'em, and still slapped a load of tax on 'em, though.

He took a long drag, let the smoke fill his lungs, sent twin plumes out of his nostrils.

Ironic that when a terminal illness did show up, it wasn't cancer. Buster told people that's what it was, because it stopped any further conversation, particularly when they saw him light another cigarette.

Truth was, Buster had Huntington's disease. Progressive, incurable, and not much fun. A genetic lottery ticket with a fifty-fifty chance of being inherited. Mum died of heart disease a decade ago, so the Huntington's probably came from the dear old dad he'd never known. The first symptoms turned up on a job in Cobham. An involuntary twitch when dialling in the combination of a nice, solid, old-school safe, and he'd sent the spindle well past the mark. Added nearly a minute to his time. No one else noticed, but, for a moment, Buster had lost control of his fingers.

Paid for a diagnosis from a Harley Street quack. Another grand for a second opinion confirmed it. A death sentence.

"You're a lucky man," the second over-privileged prick intoned. "You're already in your late fifties. Most Huntington sufferers present in their thirties."

Oh yes. When you put it like that, I feel very lucky indeed. Arsehole.

If he took an average prognosis from the two docs, he could expect four or five years before the symptoms became bad enough to need day to day care.

Buster dry-swallowed a couple of the antipsychotic pills that helped calm the twitches.

He'd planned on being dead before the daily care stage. Not on a container ship, though. That hadn't figured in his various imagined death scenes. Sandwiched between two hookers, off his head on drugs, ideally. Not hiding on the front bit of a boat. Not in imminent need of a poo.

Oh well.

It would take a few minutes for the pills to settle the spasms. In the meantime, his right hand twitched. Not just his hand, Buster noticed. His arm jerked a few inches.

Just wait it out.

That's when he heard footsteps coming up towards the forecastle.

Buster spat out the cigarette, got on his knees, picked up the gun, trying to stay quiet. His arm spasmed, and the barrel of the weapon smacked against the metal cylinder.

Bugger it.

The footsteps stopped. No one called out. Not Clint.

He looked down at the safety mechanism. Seven red bullets. Fully automatic. That's the setting he needed. When he reached over to twist the knob, his arm jerked the weapon away.

Buster had never paid attention to the precise time it took the pills to work, but, now, with someone about to kill him, he was sure of one thing: too bloody long.

Buster dropped the weapon to the deck, pinned it under his right knee, keeping it in place while his left hand twisted the knob. Safety off. Fully automatic.

The tremors subsided. Buster was right-handed. He'd never fired a gun in his life. And now that he had to, his good hand wasn't cooperating. He stared at it, willing the spasms to stop.

A watched kettle, mate.

The footsteps resumed. Slow, cautious, but not silent. And he could hear the man breathing. Not breathing normally, though. Buster knew the sound of someone in pain. They were wounded. Good. He needed every bit of help he could get.

It went quiet again. What was happening out there? He'd have to risk a look.

Buster leaned out. Scanned the forecastle. Saw his man, visible from the eyes up, gun braced on the deck, looking for him.

Buster got lucky. The crewman was checking the starboard side, and Buster had chosen the port, following Clint's instructions.

The tremors stopped. Almost immediately, Buster heard running. Panicking, he leaned out from cover, firing as soon as the muzzle was in clear air.

Clint hadn't been kidding. The first shot might have hit someone if he'd been pointing it in the right direction, but the crewman wasn't where Buster thought he would be—running towards him—instead sprinting across the deck towards cover. The recoil took Buster by surprise and sent the rest of the bullets into the sky, dangerous to no one apart from any passing seabirds.

The crewman, still running, responded by sending a far more accurate burst of shots his way before reaching another cylinder and taking cover.

This ain't no good. No good at all.

Buster had been a successful gambler all his life. He had a head for numbers, lots of patience, and a personality that doesn't get kicks from placing silly bets. Buster played the long game, and he made money. The key was understanding the odds and knowing when to walk away. The only terrible odds he'd been on the wrong side of were the ones that handed him a terminal genetic condition.

His gambling brain kicked in as the crewman settled behind the starboard cylinder. Despite his injuries, the man could still run, and, unlike Buster, his skill with a sub-machine gun meant he presented little risk to birds. No. When this guy came out firing, Buster's time was up.

Only one way to even things up. Do something surprising. No point thinking about it.

The gap between tremors was longer. Long enough? Buster couldn't be sure, but, well, in the words of Saint Francis of Assisi...

Fuck it.

He stood up, gun held ready. No sign of the injured crewman. *Probably reloading.* That's a thought. Clint hadn't shown him how to reload. *Better make whatever's in the magazine count. Is that what they call it—a magazine? Or a clip?* Buster tried to concentrate, but his mind ran through an unending list of trivia.

Hang on—is it a cartridge? Nah, that would be weird. Pens have cartridges.

He put one foot in front of the other, walked away from the coiled rope out onto the open deck.

But magazines are for reading. Autosport is a magazine. Why do dentists always have car mags? Are all blokes supposed to be obsessed with cars?

Buster didn't head towards the crewman's position. He moved

diagonally, the gun pointing towards the spindle, waiting for his enemy to come into view. If his luck held, the man would be facing away from him. If his luck held.

Cosmopolitan, *that's a good read. If you're lucky, there'll be a mucky article or two in* Cosmo. *Do people read magazines these days, with the internet an' all?*

Buster's stream of consciousness dried up all at once, like a twisted tap. He saw the dark outline, the back of the man's jacket.

Push the gun into your shoulder. Aim for the midriff. Be ready for the recoil.

His luck held. The man didn't turn, didn't see him coming. He was leaning, looking for Buster.

It's you or him, mate.

Buster's luck ran out.

As his finger tightened on the trigger, another spasm rolled through his arm, sending random electrical impulses through his muscles. His right arm twitched and his bullets hit the stacked containers.

The crewman responded immediately. Buster watched it all in slow motion, the man turning, the sub-machine gun in his right hand held against his hip, a knife sticking out of his forearm like a bloody 3D tattoo, the sweat on his upper lip falling, the wide pupils mirroring his own fear. Just another bloke, really, when all was said and done, but somehow they'd ended up here, facing off, each offering nothing but death to the other, like millions before them in tribal clashes, in battles, in fights over money, love, or religion.

Buster fired again. No tremors this time. His bullets found their mark, opening the crewman up from chest to neck, knocking him off his feet.

Buster took a few steps backward as he fired.

Hang on. Cartridge is another name for bullet, ain't it?

He let go of the trigger. The man fell awkwardly on one side, the knife hilt in his arm hitting the deck first, pushing the blade all the way through his flesh. He didn't complain, and he didn't move.

Still don't understand why they call the other bit a magazine, though.

Buster's stomach cramped. His bowels were about to open, whether he liked it or not. He fumbled for his belt. Gasped in pain. The cramps were agonising. Unstoppable.

He tried to push his trousers down, but the pain became white-hot and he dropped to his knees, fell onto his side.

I've shat myself. Like a bloody baby.

His fingers found his belly in an attempt to relieve the pain. They came away wet, sticky, warm. He held them in front of his eyes. Red.

He got me, too. Jammy bastard.

Buster tried to get comfortable, but every movement caused more blood to pump out of his wounds.

Sure I read somewhere that being shot in the stomach is the most painful way to die.

His breathing hurt now, so he kept his inhalations short and shallow, which made him light-headed.

Or was that drowning? Yeah, maybe drowning's the most painful way to die.

A gap between breaths, then another. Three very short gasps to get more air, followed by no breaths for a few seconds. The pain receded as Buster became sleepy.

Who did they interview to find out the most painful ways to die? Did they use a ouija board or what? Load of old bollocks.

His right hand rested on his stomach. The blood pumped out through his fingers, slower and thicker now. He closed his eyes.

And where the hell did I read that, anyway? Wasn't Cosmopolitan, *that's for bloody sure.*

The gaps between breaths got longer and longer, the breaths themselves becoming tiny, silent goldfish gulps. His lips dried.

The last thing he heard was his own throat rattling; his final thought concerned his ex-wife. All told, the poor girl had put up with a lot, not least his snoring.

CHAPTER FIFTY

BARBER RETURNED to New Scotland Yard and delegated ongoing cases unrelated to the Jimmy Blue problem. A fraud investigation into a prominent investment bank, a Yorkshire murder suspect now thought to be living on the streets in London; reports of a turf war breaking out between rival drug gangs over the territory once controlled by Douglas Penrose. No one mentioned the Russian fiasco, but she knew her authority had taken a knock, so she made sure every officer left their meeting with no doubt that DCI Barber remained very much in charge.

Throughout, Barber's thoughts returned to Tom Lewis and the *Trevanian*. Spader's briefing was a courtesy he had been under no obligation to offer. He could have just killed the investigation. He claimed to have brought her and Cunningham in out of professional respect. Either that, Barber mused, or he'd just wanted an up-close look at the woman who'd spent a hundred thousand pounds of Metropolitan Police resources to bring in a clown with a rubber scar glued to his head.

When Spader's call came in, Barber put it on speaker and leaned out of her office, waving Cunningham over. He shut the door quietly behind him as the American's distinctive rumble emerged from the phone.

"Dafydd Cadwallader missed all subsequent check-ins. So it's Plan B."

"Which is?"

"Which is a complete screw-up of a two-year operation. I'm way over budget already, and Daff was my last roll of the dice. If he's compromised, my orders are to forget about using Brakesman's network to infiltrate criminal organisations. That's over. We bring him in. We bring them all in, and go over the *Trevanian* inch by inch until we find out how the passengers get into the country. It's due in New York in three days. 'When they dock, we'll be there. Which means you can come pick up your boy. I've shaken some expenses out of your boss. Joint operation. I'll see you in New York."

When the call ended, Barber treated her subordinate to a rare smile. His own was much broader.

"Trip to New York for the arrest, eh? On expenses? Very nice. Ticket paid for by the taxpayer, I assume? Disgusting waste of public money."

"Oh. I planned on getting two tickets," said Barber. "But I assume your principles stand in the way of you accepting?"

"Just this once, I shall attempt to rise above my personal distaste, and join you on this crucial Anglo-American operation. Business class, I assume."

"Don't push it, Cunningham."

"Guv. When do we go?"

"Well. Today's Friday. The *Trevanian* docks on Monday."

"So a nice, relaxing weekend to catch up on some much-needed sleep before a Sunday evening flight, giving us plenty of time to arrest Tom Lewis when the ship arrives in New York?"

Barber said nothing. Waited. Cunningham shrugged.

"Or, considering the fact that Jimmy Blue, a dangerous criminal, managed to escape with every London police officer looking for him, we get the next available flight. Am I getting closer?"

"You are," said Barber. "Remember the bookseller?"

"So we're going to spend the weekend pursuing one tiny lead. In a second-hand bookshop."

For the second time, Barber didn't answer, and Cunningham filled the silence.

"I'll go fish out my passport, then."

CHAPTER FIFTY-ONE

JIMMY BLUE STOOD in the doorway of the cabin, watching the *Trevanian's* medical officer work.

Besides the lump on his head, Gary now boasted a red right cheek already turning purple, where Blue had backhanded him hard enough to knock him off his feet. The *Trevanian's* navigator had made the mistake of asking for a drink.

"Well?" Blue stepped closer, and Gary flinched. The drunk had given Ronnie painkillers, but the Korean still passed out when he set the broken arm.

"I'm doing the best I can, I swear. But I'm no doctor, not really. He needs a hospital to fix that eye. I've cleaned it and dressed it. Nothing I can do about the ribs. They'll heal on their own. It'll take a few weeks. He's gonna be ok."

Blue stepped over Sean's corpse.

The Korean stirred on the mattress Blue brought in for him. He opened his good eye, blinked, and took in the reality of his changed circumstances. Jimmy registered the mixture of fear and gratitude in the injured man's expression when he saw his rescuer, but he offered no smile, no words of comfort. Fear was good. Better to be feared than liked, or respected.

"Are you going to pass out again?"

Ronnie shook his head, then winced. "No. I don't think so. What's happening?"

"The game is over," said Blue.

"I tried to help you," said Ronnie. Gary mumbled something about not killing anyone.

Jimmy Blue said nothing in reply, letting the silence fill the tiny room. The crew mates who hadn't personally killed any of the passengers were hardly guiltless, and Ronnie had only helped Tom, no one else. Blue let the two men reach their own conclusions about how he viewed their participation. The chief mate's body, cooling on the floor between them, was a reminder of how Blue dealt out justice.

They all reacted to the shots from the bow. A burst of automatic fire, then a second.

"Turn around and put your hands behind your back," said Blue. Gary obeyed, shaking. Blue found cable ties in the bathroom. He secured the man's wrists, then pushed him away. Gary tripped, landed hard on one shoulder, shuffled back until pressed into the corner.

Blue took a handgun from his jacket pocket. Both men paled. He emptied it of ammunition, pocketing the bullets, leaving a single round. He handed it to the Korean.

"If he tries to leave, shoot him."

Another two bursts of gunfire.

Blue stepped into the corridor, closed the door. Didn't lock it.

On deck, Clint had tied a tourniquet around Brakesman's upper leg. The captain leaned against a container, looking smaller; older. Blue recognised that look: defeat. No fight left.

Clint had piled weapons at his feet, ammunition removed. He looked up when Blue emerged from what was left of the mess. The deck was littered with debris from the pipe bombs.

"The gunfire," said Clint. "It must be Buster. He's hiding at the front." He nodded towards the captain. "Watch him, will you?"

"I'll go."

Clint, limping away, stopped, looked at Blue. Nodded in agreement. "Hurry."

Jimmy was already gone.

———

Climbing the stacks, following his memorised route to the top, Jimmy Blue used the time to think through the changed situation. Six hours ago, the crew had set out to murder their unarmed passengers. Since then, the balance of power had shifted somewhat.

Six levels up, he leaped across the width of a corridor, landing and rolling.

They had the *Trevanian*. Three more nights and they arrived in New York. But Clint worked for the US and UK governments. His communications with his superiors would dictate, to some extent, the ship's reception when it arrived in America. Clint's bosses wanted Brakesman working for them so they could catch their terrorists. That meant no helicopters, no SWAT teams boarding the *Trevanian,* tearing it apart, searching every container, arresting or shooting anyone they found. No. They'd board without drawing attention. With Brakesman alive and compliant, Clint and his bosses still stood a chance of getting what they wanted.

Hardly a satisfactory outcome for Blue, though. He was a wanted criminal in Britain, and as soon as the American authorities discovered his identity, he'd be on the next plane to London, hands and legs cuffed, a US marshal on either side.

He needed to check the lifeboat, and sabotage any tracking device onboard.

Towards the bow, Blue came to a halt, brought his breathing under control, became still and silent. He listened. Brought his attention to the different levels of sounds around him, from the constant splash of waves, the droning engine, and the stretching and contracting of steel, to the relatively tiny humans who scurried across the decks.

And he heard nothing from the forecastle. No scrape of shoe on metal, no struggle, no gasps of pain. He listened for a couple of minutes until sure, then followed one of his routes down to deck level.

The sun was a low orange ball on the horizon now. Some might consider the rich, buttery yellow light that bathed both sea and ship beautiful, but Blue ignored it. His distrust of daylight, and of those who lived there, was deep-rooted. He carried the darkness with him, never fully alive during the day, always yearning for night, when the creature at his core could unfurl, stretch, flow out, and be free.

No one breathed on the forecastle. Nothing lived beyond those metal steps. He climbed them silently nonetheless.

He spotted the first body. Face-up, eyes open, seeing nothing. A sub-machine gun still clutched in his hand. Bullet holes like ragged stitches tracing a vertical line from sternum to neck. Sean's knife, thrown by Blue, sticking out of the corpse's forearm, the bloody blade lit by the rising sun.

Beyond, curled into a foetal position, Buster. Eyes closed. Skin grey. Belly punctured by four, maybe five bullets. Still warm, but not breathing.

Jimmy reviewed the current roster of crew and passengers. Of the passengers, besides himself, Clint and Miss Felicity were alive. Hannibal might have made it through the night, but Jimmy doubted it. He had found no trace of the Dutchman, and there were few places to hide—the crew made sure of that before the game began.

As for the crew, Blue had killed most of them. By his count, Brakesman, the drunk navigator, and Ronnie were the only survivors.

Three more nights on the Atlantic. Three nights to form a plan. Not that he needed it. The only way off the *Trevanian* before landfall waited at the stern. The lifeboat was his ticket out of here. Wait until they were close to the American coast, then launch it.

Halfway back to the superstructure, Jimmy Blue stopped dead, went to the port railing and leaned out, hoping the sound he heard didn't mean what he thought it meant. A heavy, deep splash. Something else, too. He strained to listen.

There it was. An additional note alongside the ship's engine. Like a harmonic in a musical chord, subtle but unmistakable. Rising in pitch now. A second engine. Smaller. Mid-Atlantic, only one thing could account for that sound.

He saw it then, a luminous orange square on the waves, heading away from the *Trevanian* towards the rising sun.

The lifeboat. Gone. And with it, his only escape route.

CHAPTER FIFTY-TWO

————

Once he'd established the *pain in the ass Brit cops* not only didn't have a warrant, but lacked any legal authority, Don Viola, the warehouse manager at Bookbart, laughed in their faces. He poured himself a coffee without offering any to his visitors, settled his considerable bulk behind a metal desk, and leaned back in a swivel chair which emitted a squeal of protest. After his cowboy boots thumped onto the desk, he took a slurp and regarded Barber and Cunningham with an expression that didn't pretend to be anything other than a sneer.

"You woke my boss up in the middle of the night to ask about a goddam parcel, now you want me to help you find the books that were in it? Let me check my schedule, see if I can help you out."

He hadn't asked them to sit down, so Barber and Cunningham stood in silence. Cunningham, Barber noted, had resisted reminding her that he thought trying to track down Tom Lewis's parcel of books was a colossal waste of their time.

Viola tapped a key, and the computer brightened, the blue-white light making shadows of the folds of skin between his chins.

"Ok. Here we are. Eight-thirty to nine-thirty, I'm drinking three cups of coffee and reading the sports pages. Nine-thirty to nine-forty, gonna take a shit. Five minute break, then I'm scratching my balls for twenty minutes. And it looks like the day is full of appointments more important than you. Busy, busy, busy. Shut the door on your way out, will ya?"

Barber and Cunningham were too dispirited to bother with a comeback. They had no authority on US soil. They trudged down the warehouse's external metal staircase and back into the parking lot.

Their rental car, an anonymous Ford, waited in the vast concrete lot. They had driven ninety minutes to the outskirts of Phillipsburg, a good location for a twenty-four hour, seven days a week, three hundred and sixty-four days a year business that relies on regular deliveries by road, but, thought Barber, a grim place to work. Especially with a miserable slob like Viola for a boss.

Bookbart bought its stock in bulk, mostly from thrift stores. Literary merit was not a proviso for Bookbart purchases. They paid by the kilo. The boxes went to the nearest warehouse, of which there were seven, dotted over the United States. Around eight percent of the books were recycled, the rest catalogued and stored, ready to be picked and sent to the next online customer.

A truck was unloading when they'd arrived. It was leaving now, and a yawning woman in her thirties was taking a smoke break at the loading bay.

Barber nudged Cunningham, and they diverted, heading over to the employee, who regarded them with little interest.

"Good morning. My name is Detective Chief Inspector Barber from the London Metropolitan Police. We're investigating the theft of some valuable books. Mr Viola has been helping us, and he suggested we speak to you."

The woman's eyebrows creased in disbelief. Barber wasn't surprised. She doubted Don Viola ever lifted a finger to help anyone in his life.

"Me?"

"Absolutely." Barber was hamming up the British accent. The cliché had proven true so far—most of the cops they'd met found her and Cunningham exotic. Might as well use it in their favour.

"Well. OK, sure." The woman dropped her cigarette and ground it under her heel. "Whaddya wanna know?"

"Is this how all the books arrive? Delivered by lorry, I mean."

"Sure. Trucks come in day and night. We unload them, catalogue them, put them on the right shelf."

"We're interested in a box posted from the United Kingdom. Sent by air, should have reached you,"—she consulted her notebook—"last Tuesday."

"By air? You sure?"

Barber nodded. "Is that unusual?"

"Lady, we buy books by weight. Like onions. If you mailed us a box from out of state, you'd make a loss. Who the hell would pay for air freight?"

"So someone might remember the box?"

Barber couldn't help the note of excitement in her voice.

"I guess. That would be Al. Hold on."

The woman unhooked a walkie-talkie from her waist. "Hey Al, it's Shawna. Got a second?"

A man's voice answered. "What do you need?"

"You remember a box coming in last week from Britain? Sent by air?"

"By air? Yeah, sure I do. Crazy. Arrived on the mail truck, all on its own."

Cunningham stepped forward. "What was in it?" Shawna relayed the question.

He and Barber held their breath until the voice came back.

"Well, it was the weirdest thing. I opened it myself. Thought if someone paid a couple hundred bucks to send a box from England, it was gonna be a signed Jane Austen box set at least. Nope. Just a bunch of books we've seen a million times before. Hardbacks, good condition, but nothing special. Real popular titles, all of them. Quick to sell. We've probably sent half of them out already."

Barber had her mouth open, but Shawna got there first. "You remember any of the titles, Al?"

"Sure. *7 Habits of Highly Effective People. Catcher in the Rye. Harry Potter. To Kill a Mockingbird.* Like someone looked up the twenty most popular used books in America and sent them over. Like I said, weird. That all you need?"

Shawna looked questioningly at Barber, who gave her the nod. "That's great, Al. Thanks."

She shrugged at the police officers. "You need anything else? I gotta get back."

"Yes," said Barber. "One thing. These books. Al said some of them will probably have gone already. What about the others? Do you know where they're being stored? Could you find them?"

Shawna coughed out a proper smoker's laugh, pushing the sound through layers of sediment.

"What's so funny?" said Barber. The warehouse worker didn't reply, instead climbing the four steps behind her and beckoning them forward to the loading bay door. When they joined her, she held a pass in front of an electronic lock, then pushed the door, holding it open with a foot.

Barber and Cunningham stood at her shoulder. Looked into the warehouse. Saw more shelves than they'd ever seen in their lives, forklift trucks driving between them.

"Nine million books," said Shawna to their unasked question. "Good luck finding the ones you're looking for."

A shout came from behind them.

"Hey! You wanna take a look inside, you come back with a warrant."

Viola, a cigar clamped between his fingers, scowled at them from the top of his staircase. "And you—back to work."

Shawna kept her head down. The warehouse door shut behind her. Barber and Cunningham returned to the car under the baleful eye of the warehouse manager.

They didn't speak until they were back on the freeway.

"What difference does it make?" said Cunningham. "We know where he is and—more importantly—we know where he'll be tomorrow evening. Does this even matter now?"

Barber clicked on the cruise control at a steady fifty-five. "Yes, it matters. You think stopping him will be as easy as stepping onto the boat with a pair of handcuffs?"

"Why not?"

Barber didn't reply, her fingers tapping the wheel as she stared ahead. She was thinking of the Russian with the rubber scar.

CHAPTER FIFTY-THREE

MONDAY. Four miles out of New York.

———

Dafydd 'Clint' Cadwallader watched Manhattan appear like a mirage on the horizon; a homogeneous glow separating into a million distinct pinpricks of light.

The *Trevanian's* engines sang a new song now, as the vast ship's progress dropped to a crawl of eight knots. Clint looked out across the black water for the tiny vessel they were expecting to meet them.

Forty minutes later, Ronnie opened the shell door as the pilot boat pulled alongside—a minnow on the flank of a whale. Under normal circumstances, the pilot alone would climb the ladder to join them, but the present circumstances were hardly normal.

Ten experienced crew and six armed officers boarded the *Trevanian* and followed the limping Korean to the bridge. They'd all been briefed by the agent leading them, one hand on the butt of his pistol.

From the bridge, Clint watched the new crew head for their stations, ready to bring the vessel into port. Normally, the captain would remain in command, advised by the pilot, but not this time, as the captain was a murdering, terrorist-helping arsehole with a bullet in his knee.

Although Clint's leg would heal well, the bullet having missed the bone and any major arteries, Brakesman's shattered knee was a different story. The captain might be about to negotiate a deal that kept him out of prison, but his ruined leg would be a constant reminder of this trip. Clint took some comfort in that.

He bent down to speak into Brakesman's ear.

"You're sure it's set up?"

"I'm sure."

Clint got even closer. "Remember what I said. You mention anything about Tom to anyone, ever, and I will kill you. I'll do it slowly, too. Trust me, I know how."

A familiar face headed the group of agents who entered the bridge. The man's official title was Special Investigator, but he wielded a great deal more authority than the rank suggested. Clint knew him by one name.

"Evening, boss."

"Good to see you, Daff. Real good." Sam Spader clapped the Welshman on the back and squeezed his shoulder. "It's not how we planned it, but you got the job done. Congratulations. How's the leg?"

"Sore."

Spader was a talker; Clint, not so much. He'd sent his reports from the *Trevanian* once he'd assumed control of the vessel, and had little to add. He wanted one question answered, though.

"Any news on the navigator and Miss Felicity?"

Spader looked blank.

"The lifeboat," clarified Clint.

"Her real name is Rita Chabouri. A cruise ship intercepted the lifeboat two nights back. I guess the pair of them hoped to bump into another container ship, where Chabouri could buy the crew's silence for a few million dollars. No chance when the whole thing got posted on YouTube by hundreds of passengers. We stepped in pretty quickly and made sure the press got a different ship's name for their stories.

Wouldn't do for Captain Brakesman's future clients to see the *Trevanian* on the news."

Brakesman, slumped in a chair in front of a panel of instruments, barely registered Spader's comments. Clint had fed him a regular supply of ibuprofen and paracetamol since shooting him, but the captain wouldn't be out of pain until a surgeon had salvaged what they could of the knee. He might never be pain-free, which Clint saw as a bonus.

"How's the leg, Brakesman?"

Spader leaned over and smacked the captain's knee. Brakesman screamed, then bit down hard, regained control, and glared at Spader, who smiled back.

"My bad," he said, pointing at Brakesman's good leg. "I thought it was that leg. I was mistaken. It's this one, isn't it?"

He smacked the leg again, and Brakesman shrieked.

"Must remember that," said Spader.

The pilot radioed orders to the crew, and Clint stepped away from the instrument panels to let him work. One officer was a medic and had already injected Ronnie, who, white-faced and sweating, waited at the far end of the bridge.

"We'd be dead if not for him," said Clint.

"I read your initial report. We will take his actions into consideration. He might avoid prison."

"I hope so." Two officers hung back from Spader, waiting their turn. A woman in her forties, her male colleague a few years younger. Neither looked at ease in Kevlar vests and baseball caps.

Spader stepped aside.

"Daff, this is Detective Chief Inspector Barber and DI Cunningham from London. They have a few questions about our mysterious friend."

"Ah," said Clint, as the woman stepped forward. "You mean Tom?"

"Yes." Barber was all business. Single-minded, focused. "Are you sure he's dead?"

Clint shrugged. "Did you read my report?"

"I did. But I want it in your own words. Any minor detail might be significant."

"There's little to say. He helped us take the *Trevanian*, killing at least four of the crew. Last time I saw him, he went to investigate gunfire at the front of the ship. The forecastle. He never came back. It was the same time the navigator escaped with Miss F—with Rita Chabouri."

Clint had heard the lifeboat detach with a hiss as its hydraulic clamps released it, then the splash before it raced away. He'd found Ronnie Leong alone in the cabin, a handgun on the bed next to him. "I couldn't shoot Gary," said the Korean. "Not in cold blood."

"And when you investigated the gunshots?" said Barber.

"I couldn't. I had to watch our friend here." He nodded towards Brakesman. "Tom never came back. That's it. I wish I could help, but there's nothing to tell."

The detective chief inspector kept looking at him. Waiting for him to break the uncomfortable silence. Russian Federal Security Service officers had once interrogated Clint for six days and nights straight. The DCI could stare at him all she liked. He looked back, expression neutral. Waited for her to speak again. Which she did.

"We searched the front of the ship before coming up here. Found two bodies. Neither of them are Tom Lewis. Can you explain that?"

"Either he's still alive, or he got shot at the rail, and fell overboard."

"Convenient."

"Is it?"

DCI Barber held his gaze, waiting for more. When it wasn't forthcoming, she turned aside. The man beside her stuffed his hands in his pockets.

"We're searching the ship, guv. If he's still here, we'll find him."

"Not necessarily. We've only got a few hours."

"True, but even if we don't find him now, we have dogs checking every container that comes off. If he's here, we'll have him. But he's probably dead."

That sentiment earned Cunningham a sceptical shake of the head from his boss.

"Thing is," she said, "I don't believe it. Lewis is alive."

"He's human, guv. Doesn't matter how clever he is, how well-trained, if someone shoots him, he'll go down."

"You'd think so, wouldn't you? But I'll believe it when I see a body. Don't forget he's been shot before. In the head. That would kill most people. It just made him angry."

―――――

It was stretching the bounds of normal procedure, but a random drug check of incoming vessels wasn't unheard of. They just weren't usually this thorough.

US Customs officers opened a dozen randomly selected containers, checking their contents against the manifest. Nothing untoward turned up. Brakesman covered his criminal activity by scrupulously observing the regulations in all other areas.

But for locating a concealed human being, nothing beats the olfactory superiority of a dog. If a canine can't sniff it out, it isn't there.

As a light rain soaked into their fur, sixty dogs examined the containers unloaded from the *Trevanian* into the holding area, a vast concrete expanse as big as a small town.

Barber and Cunningham drank instant coffee from plastic cups in a supervisor's office overlooking the action. In the loading bays below, the dogs ran from one forty-foot container to the next, pushing their noses against the doors before moving on.

Each cleared container left the port as scheduled, hundreds of haulage company trucks rumbling away to every corner of the country with a hiss of air brakes and a belch of diesel. Some contained consumer goods: televisions, refrigerators, washing machines. Others held the belongings of families, looking for a new beginning. Some contained furniture, or the raw timber to make it from scratch.

But, according to the canine task force assigned to the job, none of them contained a dangerous killer by the name of Tom Lewis, otherwise known as Jimmy Blue.

"It's over," said Cunningham, taking a last sip of coffee and pulling a face. "He's dead. Fish food. A shame we didn't collar him, but at least he can't kill anyone else. The worst criminals in America can sleep a little easier tonight, cos Jimmy Blue won't be coming for them."

Barber didn't turn from the window. The sound of barking grew fainter as the dogs were rewarded with treats and loaded into the back of vans.

"The dogs are lucky. They don't care either way, do they?" It wasn't a question requiring an answer. Cunningham waited for her to continue. "Find a criminal, or find nothing. They get a biscuit when they're done, a scratch on the head from their handler, and they're happy. They won't lie awake tonight wondering if they allowed the most dangerous man I've ever encountered to slip through their hands."

"Paws, not hands," corrected Cunningham, only to regret it when he saw the look on her face. "He's dead, guv. Let it go."

When she didn't respond, Cunningham left her standing at the window and plodded downstairs to wait in the rental car. She joined him five minutes later, and they drove back to the hotel in silence.

CHAPTER FIFTY-FOUR

RONNIE WOKE from a dream about Chul. More of a memory, perhaps. The two of them sharing a clandestine beer in their hideout; an unused garage under a neighbouring apartment block. Ronnie, like most fifteen-year-olds, couldn't wait to transition to adulthood, and saw alcohol as a shortcut. Chul, by then only a few months away from being legally allowed to drink, showed little interest in beer, but dutifully swigged at the lukewarm bottles to please his brother. After their fifth bottle, Chul rubbed Ronnie's back as he vomited acidic liquid onto the concrete floor.

"You're smiling. That's a good sign. How are you?"

The man Brakesman nicknamed Clint sat next to Ronnie's bed.

"I feel..." Ronnie fished around for the word he needed. "Drunk. I feel drunk." That explained the dream. Since that initiation into the joys of beer in a dark, damp garage, Ronnie had been teetotal. But this light, floaty, carefree sensation reminded him of the brief, pleasurable period between opening the first bottle and throwing up.

"Yes," he confirmed. "Drunk."

"That'll be the morphine." Clint pointed at the drip next to the bed. "Because your injuries weren't treated immediately, the doctors re-broke your arm to make sure it heals properly. Painful. But they tell me you'll be fine in a couple of months."

Clint stood up, paced around the room, shut the door, and sat down again. For a man recently shot in the leg, he looked in good spirits.

"How drunk?" asked Clint. "I mean, can you follow what I'm saying?"

"Yes." The only trouble Ronnie had understanding the man came from his strange accent.

"Good. Pay attention. I only have a few minutes. The local goons will be along to interview you later. I've briefed the boss and here's the offer: a new name, a new identity, and six months' back pay from Brakesman. They'll ask you to fill in any blanks in your statement. You understand what you need to say?"

"Yes. I understand."

"Excellent. Good luck, Ronnie. You have a second chance. Make the most of it."

Clint stood up to go. Ronnie stopped him at the door.

"Have you heard anything? I mean—"

"I know what you mean. No. And I don't expect to. Stick to your statement. No need to add details. Your injuries will explain any gaps in your account. Rita Chabouri—Miss Felicity—escaped in the lifeboat. Every other passenger died during the game. I'm the only survivor. Keep reminding yourself of that and it'll become the truth. Because that's what happened, got it?"

Even through the morphine haze, the memory of Sean returning to the cabin to beat Ronnie to death remained clear. He owed Tom his life.

"Got it," he said. "I wish I could thank him. I will thank the gods instead."

Clint shook his head. "Not the gods. The *deus*."

Ronnie stared at the door after Clint left. Wondered what would happen to the man who won the game, outmatching Brakesman and his crew. They believed themselves predators, the passengers their prey. Until they met a real predator.

269

Ronnie closed his eyes. An image appeared: the gigantic man following Sean into the dark cabin, bringing death. Ronnie turned his thoughts away from the memory and drifted back into dreams of his youth.

CHAPTER FIFTY-FIVE

DWIGHT S. PEARSON JUNIOR, as director of the logistics business founded by his father, still got behind the wheel of a company vehicle a couple times a month. His employees thought it denoted a rootsy desire to stay in touch with the sharp end of truck driving. The real reason had made Pearson Junior a multimillionaire, a fact known only to his private accountant.

Many of his trips in a company rig were innocuous. They provided cover for the ones that counted.

Dwight's day to day work clothes favoured linen and cotton blend shirts and handmade suits. Jeans, a baseball cap and a button-down company shirt transformed him into a trucker.

Pearson Logistics' headquarters was located less than three miles from Port Newark. The dark-red Pearson trucks were a familiar sight at the port, dropping off and picking up containers.

This afternoon's pick up followed a phone call from a satellite phone two days ago. Dwight's contact had never given him a job on such short notice. The agreed code words eased Dwight's doubts. He gave up a day on the links he had been looking forward to, but a fifty grand bonus made up for missing an afternoon practising his swing.

Along with a bunch of disgruntled drivers, he endured the three-hour delay before being allowed to load the container onto his flatbed. Not the most comfortable few hours Dwight had ever spent. Rather than join the other drivers smoking and muttering by their cabs in clusters of three or four, he stayed in his vehicle, pretending to be asleep. He might look the part, but most people in the logistics business would recognise Dwight S. Pearson. He preferred anonymity.

Eventually, his pretence of sleep turned into the real thing, until a blast from a neighbouring truck's air horn jolted him awake. He started the rig's diesel engine and joined the queue rumbling into the port.

The usual paperwork and checks followed, then the line of trucks formed up as if waiting to start a drag race. Called forward one at a time, and waved into position, sidelifters deposited the correct container onto each waiting trailer.

That was when he saw them—the dogs and their handlers. They'd finished checking the containers, including the one waiting for Dwight S Pearson. Despite this, a cold bead of sweat meandered down his neck.

It all took longer than usual, and everyone he encountered, from the other drivers to the customs officers and forklift operators, seemed—to Dwight at least—more than usually thorough.

He smiled when necessary, said little, spoke when spoken to. Brakesman had warned him this might happen. Random checks were a fact of life in a business handling international logistics. But this didn't look random to Dwight. Not random at all. Had someone tipped off the customs officers? Was he heading into a trap?

Even after getting the paperwork stamped and driving through the exit gates unchallenged, Dwight's heart rate stayed high. Maybe they would wait until he left the port, then surround him, a dozen screaming sirens forcing his vehicle off the road, making him wait in the back of a cop car while they dismantled the container.

But it didn't happen. No sirens, no flashing lights, no loudhailer demanding he pull over and exit the cab with his hands in the air.

The last opportunity for disaster came eighty-seven minutes after leaving the port, when Dwight steered the rig onto an exit ramp and into the parking lot of a shabby rest area.

A tired-looking diner, a bathroom block you could smell from a quarter mile away, and not much else. Most drivers chose a more attractive place to take their break. But it served Brakesman's purposes, so Dwight backed the forty-footer into a space at the far end of the lot.

Dwight earned the three hundred grand a year retainer and the fifty thousand dollar a job bonus during these ten to fifteen minute stops at the rest area. If caught, he'd never be able to claim the *Trevanian's* captain had duped him. What he did here made him complicit.

He sat in the cab for five minutes. Everything looked normal. Four trucks, a bunch of cars. Lights on in the diner, the faint sound of country music.

Mouth dry, he pushed open the heavy door, stepped down. Listened. Stretched his hamstrings as if tired from a long trip, while scanning the area for anything out of the ordinary. Nothing to see.

After one last roll of his neck, Dwight grabbed a water bottle from the inside door pocket, walked to the back of the truck, released the bolt, and opened the container.

The usual sight greeted him. A container full of Scandinavian lumber, the trunks stacked neatly, filled the interior. A spider might stow away between the tightly packed trees, but nothing any bigger could hide there.

Dwight held his breath. Still nothing. He put on his work gloves.

Three logs up, two over from the right. Grabbing the end of the log, he unscrewed it, lifted away the section of modified trunk, the brass thread inside catching the last of the afternoon light. Dwight tapped six digits into the keypad revealed in the hollowed tree. Pressed enter. Stepped back.

A concealed locking mechanism clicked, and Dwight grabbed the handle under the keypad with both hands. Braced a foot against the tailgate and pulled. A heavy steel door opened to reveal the hermetically sealed space behind. They could send a hundred sniffer dogs to check out this container. No air meant no scent, no minuscule human traces for an excited beagle to yap about.

Dwight had followed the same procedure on four previous occasions, waiting as instructed to make sure the occupant of the hidden compartment survived the ordeal. Four occasions, four survivors: men who'd scrambled out of a space not much bigger than a coffin, dropped to the ground and spent a couple of minutes rubbing their limbs, shivering, and drinking the water Dwight supplied. And that was the end of his involvement. Each man stepped over the low fence behind the truck into the trees behind the parking lot. Dwight would seal the compartment, closing the door on the scuba tanks lined up along one side of the tiny space. After calling the number supplied, letting it ring twice before ending the call, he'd leave. He tried not to think about his passengers again. He didn't need to know who they were. Didn't want to know.

Some nights he'd wake from nightmares of being trapped himself inside the compartment, breathing through a scuba respirator, seeing the sky disappear inch by inch. Sealed inside. The worst nightmares ended with him finishing the first tank of air, feeling for the next in the pitch black, putting the rubber device between his teeth, twisting the valve for air and... nothing. Someone made a mistake. He needed twelve hours of air, but one tank was empty. He'd run out of air with a few hours left before reaching safety. He'd die in the dark. No point screaming in a soundproof, airtight coffin.

Dwight blinked, peering into the dark space, the outline of a man coming into focus. A big man. Real big. Head down as if praying. Bald? Black? No—a dark bandana pulled tight across his head. Not moving.

Christ. Not moving.

What if this one had died, run out of air? What if Dwight's nightmare came true? What then?

"No, no, no. Don't be dead, you can't be dead. Don't do this to me."

He'd have to seal him back inside. What other choice did he have? No way he could dispose of a body. Let Brakesman throw it overboard. Other than that, just follow the usual procedure. Change the paperwork tonight, send the lumber back onto the *Trevanian* tomorrow, the manifest showing it as arriving from Georgia yesterday.

What a mess.

Maybe he should check first, make sure. What if the guy had passed out? If Dwight sealed him back in, he'd be condemning him to a horrible death.

Not his problem.

But better to make sure. It would be better for everyone if the passenger survived. Brakesman might baulk at paying a bonus for a corpse.

Dwight steeled himself, took a deep breath, leaned forward, his right hand reaching for the figure's neck. He'd never checked a pulse before, but how hard can it be?

As his outstretched fingers touched warm skin, Dwight let out a breath.

The flood of relief lasted under a second before being replaced by terror.

The man barrelled out of the container, a human torpedo, the black bandana-covered head hitting Dwight's left side as he pivoted away. The impact spun him around, and he lost his footing, ending up sprawled face-first in the stones and dust.

"Hey," he croaked, spitting grit. He got to his knees, put a hand to his cheek, saw blood on his fingers where tiny stones had torn his skin.

Once back on his feet, Dwight dusted himself down, coughing. Found the water bottle against a tyre. He opened it, rinsed the cuts, swigged a mouthful, and spat it at his feet. Looked into the trees. No sign of the passenger.

"Hey," he repeated, voice clearer, but—to his dismay—higher than normal, with an old-timer's thin, querulous tone. He coughed again, tried to pitch his next utterance lower.

"I'm on your side, man." As if to prove this, he replaced the top on the bottle, and placed it where concrete gave way to dry, unhealthy grass. "Water. For you. I have to leave now."

The man in the bandana watched him from the trees. Hidden in the shadows somewhere. Dwight didn't try to spot him. This passenger didn't want to be seen. Fair enough.

He resealed the compartment, screwed the fake log back into place. A perfect illusion. Locked the doors, climbed into the cab without a single glance at the trees. Drove away.

Ten minutes back on the freeway, and Dwight whistled along with the radio, his thoughts turning to the game of golf he'd lined up for Saturday.

Didn't think about the sensation of something deadly watching him from the shadows between the trees at the parking lot. Nope. Didn't think about that at all.

CHAPTER FIFTY-SIX

BARBER WAITED for Spader outside the utilitarian three-star hotel.

A June heatwave meant she sweated underneath her suit, but she had nothing else to wear. She was here on police business, and that meant dressing the part, remaining professional.

When Cunningham rounded the corner wearing jeans and a T-shirt, red-faced and puffing with a shopping bag in each hand, she couldn't decide whether to ignore him or issue a verbal warning. She opted for the former as he offered a cheery salute from the hotel steps.

"I'll just grab my bag, guv. Thought I should pick up souvenirs for the little 'uns. Wouldn't hear the end of it if I got home empty-handed."

Barber's neck prickled and flushed. She'd forgotten Cunningham's family. She wasn't the only one making sacrifices. Not for the first time, she wondered if she'd misjudged him. Too little too late, perhaps, but they made a good team this trip. A shame about the transfer. Maybe she'd talk to him about it when they got back to London. They wouldn't be able to discuss it on the flight. Not now they'd been recruited as babysitters.

Cunningham reappeared and bumped a bulging wheeled suit-case down the steps.

A dark saloon with too many aerials drew up. The window rolled down and Spader's smiling face leaned out, upper lip pushed forward by the nugget of tobacco behind it.

"Hey, Barber, what's up? Hope you managed to fit in some sightseeing."

He, at least, had something to smile about. Robust gag orders now protected the details of the *Trevanian*'s murderous voyages. The criminal passengers boarded without papers, leaving no trail for anyone looking for them. Their deaths would go unreported. Barber preferred honest police work, where murderers got punished. She understood the need for compromise to crack open a terrorist organisation, but she didn't have to like it.

Captain Brakesman and his ship would continue as before, the only difference being his employment status. He might still sign his emails as director of a shipping company, but in reality he now reported to the Department of Homeland Security, and the *Trevanian* was crewed by its agents. In a year or less, they hoped to net at least one of the most wanted global terrorism leaders by exposing their networks.

The trunk popped open and Spader stowed their luggage, wincing at the weight of Cunningham's case. He caught Barber's eye.

"Please don't tell me you spent your time here chasing a ghost. He's dead, Barber. It's over."

Barber said nothing. Spader motioned towards the passenger door.

"You're shotgun. DI Cunningham, you're in back with the prisoner."

They got into the unmarked police car, which smelled of air freshener and sweat. Barber twisted to see Rita Chabouri, the financial fraudster who brought an investment bank to its knees. The woman scowled back. Her hands were cuffed. Lank brown hair framed a thin face with frown lines like speech marks between her eyebrows.

"Ms Chabouri, my name is Detective Chief Inspector Barber. Detective Inspector Cunningham and myself will escort you back to Heathrow where we will hand you over to officers from Operation Falcon—the fraud and linked crime online team. You will be cautioned at that time, but I will inform you that anything you say to DI Cunningham or myself may be used in evidence."

Cunningham swigged water from a bottle. "So probably best for all of us if you keep your bloody trap shut. I'm knackered, and I intend to catch up on some kip during the flight."

Chabouri shot Cunningham a contemptuous glance. Spader, amid the obligatory horn honking, pulled into the New York traffic, heading south towards Brooklyn Bridge and John F. Kennedy International Airport.

On the famous bridge, Cunningham took out his phone to get photos for his kids. Spader kept up a genial running commentary about historic crime scenes, giving them a bloody and violent guided tour. Drug busts, murders, a bank robbery with hostages that ended badly. A jumper from a skyscraper who landed on a salvation army band, taking two of them to the afterlife with him.

Barber tuned his voice out to think about Tom Lewis. Died en route. Body lost at sea. Case closed. Only she didn't believe it. Wouldn't believe it. She once watched a senior detective lose his perspective and his job, determined to crack a cold case and bring a child killer to justice. His obsession coloured his judgement, made him a liability. Ruined his career. Barber wouldn't end up like that. This was different. If the *Trevanian* hadn't been off-limits because of the deal Spader made, she'd be on board now, scouring every inch. She'd find the evidence. She'd find it, then she'd find Lewis. Bring him in. See justice done.

"They're digging up the road by the piers," said Spader, leaning on the horn again as he crossed lanes. "We'll take Flatbush and cut back through Sixth back to the freeway."

It was a foreign language. Still, at least Spader's monologue didn't require more than an occasional nod in response. Barber looked out of the window. The architecture over the bridge featured low brown and grey buildings a far cry from Manhattan's mirrored skyscrapers. Not so many tourists, either. A sleeping man stretched out on a cardboard bed in front of an empty building next to a pawnbroker with the flashing sign, *Checks Cashed 24/7.*

She seethed at how easily the dangerous killer had eluded them again. Lewis proved, over and over again, to be precociously intelligent, resourceful, and lethal.

"I'm serious, Barber."

"What?" Spader had stopped talking. "I'm sorry, I didn't catch that."

He wore driving gloves. The only other person she knew who wore driving gloves—Grandad Peters—died thirty years ago.

"Sure," said Spader. "You're still thinking about Lewis, right? I get it. But at least consider the possibility that you might be wrong. It happens to all of us. Might happen to me one day."

He laughed as he turned right onto Sixth Avenue. Brownstones, stoops, mature trees. This was the New York of a thousand movies.

"I grew up a block from here," said Spader as they crossed a junction. An imposing red-brick church loomed on their right. As Barber turned to admire the stained glass windows, a loud bang made all of them flinch.

The car lurched to one side, then the other. Spader fought to correct it. From a speed of twenty-five miles an hour, the police vehicle came to rest in a few seconds.

Spader cursed. "Goddam blow out. Would you believe it?"

A motorcyclist pulled alongside the driver's window, visor down. Voice muffled.

"You folks OK? Need a hand?"

Spader wound down the window a few inches while reaching for the radio. "We're fine. Police business. Please move on. Thank you for your concern."

Barber reviewed what had just happened. The bang came from the rear. Not underneath the car. Behind it.

The motorcyclist's hand came up with a gun in it.

"Put the radio down."

Spader did it. Under his jacket, Barber could see the butt of his handgun. No one else carried a weapon.

"You." The motorcyclist tilted his head towards Barber. "Wind down your window."

The air outside was much warmer than the air-conditioned car.

"Big guy. Take out your gun between thumb and forefinger, and pass it to your girlfriend."

The motorcyclist spoke with a bland American accent: generic, the tone even and calm. Barber couldn't place it. Spader handed her his gun, warm and heavy. She'd never liked the things.

"Toss it out the window, over the church wall."

The wall in question stood about three feet high. She lobbed the gun over it.

"Now your phones. All of you. Hurry. Over the wall."

Barber noted the motorcyclist only asked for the driver's weapon. Did he know who Barber and Cunningham were? Why else assume they were unarmed? Their phones joined Spader's gun. Chabouri held up her hands to display the cuffs. "No phone."

"The radio. Pull out the handset by its cable."

Spader did it. Passed it to Barber, who looked into the dark visor and said, "Over the wall?"

The motorcyclist dipped his head. She threw the handset out after the rest.

"Hands on your heads. Big guy, unlock the rear doors."

"Listen, son," began Spader, but stopped when the barrel of the gun touched his forehead. He released the rear door locks, and the motorcyclist pulled open the door next to Chabouri.

"Get on the bike."

Not a tough decision for a woman facing a long prison sentence. Rita Chabouri stepped out of the car and mounted the bike, grabbing the back of the rider's jacket.

"Car keys. Handcuff keys, too." Spader handed them over.

The motorcyclist twisted the throttle and roared away, weaving through the other vehicles, none of which stopped during the two minutes they were stationary.

"Shit," said Spader before opening his door and scrambling around the front of the car, onto the sidewalk and over the low wall to pick up his gun and phone.

"On the bright side," said Cunningham from the back seat, "at least we don't have to babysit that miserable cow for six hours. And the New York police will get all the paperwork."

Barber didn't hear him. Her eyes followed the biker's route, recalling every detail she could. Rita Chabouri was about her height, or a little taller. Five-foot seven, say. But she looked like a little kid clinging onto the huge, broad man who shot out their tyre.

It couldn't be. It had to be.

"Lewis," she breathed.

CHAPTER FIFTY-SEVEN

JIMMY BLUE FOLLOWED his planned route, dumping the bike in an underground parking lot. He and Chabouri transferred to an anonymous panel van stolen that morning.

He took his helmet off, tossed it in the back, and started the van. The woman beside him stared in shocked recognition.

"Tom? But... I mean, how... who?"

"No questions." He pulled on a baseball cap and eased the van out of the parking space, through the automatic barrier, and back into the Brooklyn traffic.

Chabouri evidently didn't like being told what to do, and the sudden freedom emboldened her.

"What the hell? I mean, thank you for getting me away from the police, but you can't expect me to—"

Jimmy Blue looked at her for the first time. She met his gaze, whimpered, and stopped talking. Her eyes dropped to the floor She stayed that way for the rest of the journey.

Had she looked up, Rita Chabouri may have been surprised by their apparent destination. The van crossed Brooklyn east to west, picking up Linden Avenue at East Flatbush. Twelve minutes later, Blue took the ramp for John F. Kennedy Airport.

Ignoring the signs for arrivals, departures, or parking, he guided the van to a cluster of three-star hotels on the perimeter of the airport. The anonymous grey vehicle blended with hundreds more in constant motion around the hotels, and Blue headed for a poorly lit service road.

Jimmy unzipped the top of a backpack. There wasn't much cash on the *Trevanian*, but the contents of Brakesman's safe, augmented by what he found on the dead crew, provided enough short-term cash for his purposes.

He pulled out a laptop and entered the internet password found online for the nearest hotel's broadband. Budget hotels might skimp on luxuries, but no one wanted to stay anywhere with a slow internet connection.

When he placed the laptop on Chabouri's lap, she looked up, but not at his face. She stared at the screen.

"Why did you rescue me?" she whispered.

"Fifty million reasons."

Chabouri took a few seconds to process his words, then shook her head. "I can't. I mean, it's impossible. If you want money, I can get about twenty thousand straight away. There are systems to stop people moving really large amounts, you see."

When he didn't respond, her voice grew louder as she regained some confidence.

"If you need more, it will take about a week to set up. I'll transfer the twenty thousand now and send the rest later. I need somewhere to hide in the meantime. They'll be looking for me."

She stopped talking with a gasp when Jimmy Blue shifted in his seat, leaned over, and put his face close to hers. He waited. She started shivering, the laptop bouncing on her legs. It took ten seconds for her to look at him, her eyes seemingly forced against her will to find his. When they did, he let the mask slip away. He showed her the darkness.

When he sat back in his seat, he spoke quietly.

"Lie to me again and I'll kill you here and now."

Once Jimmy Blue had picked up the laptop, he spent a productive few hours researching Rita Chabouri's financial crimes. While some of the money was recovered, over fifty million was still unaccounted for. Despite their best efforts, the investigative body couldn't find any trace of the missing money.

She'd tried to bribe the ship's crew. If she told them they'd have to wait a week to get it, she'd be at the bottom of the Atlantic instead of in a van parked outside a New York airport hotel.

"One million dollars to this account." Blue reeled off the numbers. Chabouri noted them, opened a new tab, and started a download.

"What are you doing?" Despite his even tone, Chabouri shrank away from Blue, her breaths coming faster.

"It's automated. I wrote my own code. I need to download it. Won't take long, I swear."

She installed the package, and Jimmy Blue watched as her fingers flew over the keys. Even allowing for her shaking hands, she navigated the laptop like a concert pianist. Her program required a series of passwords. She'd introduced a novel security measure. The passwords needed to be entered at different speeds. Chabouri slowed her keystrokes substantially for some and almost mashed the keys for others. Jimmy filed away the concept for future use.

When done, Chabouri pressed ENTER and automated dialogue boxes populated the screen, filling up with characters, then disappearing again. Too many to keep track of; hundreds, maybe thousands. Each accessed a bank account and transferred small amounts to his account.

"Done," she said. Blue opened the online banking app on his phone and checked the balance in the international account. A satisfyingly large figure appeared.

"Good. Forty-nine million into this account."

A few more minutes and it was done. Jimmy Blue had no way of checking whether the money arrived, but Chabouri didn't know that. He had no doubt that a certain British charity set up to help the victims of human trafficking just received a significant, and anonymous, donation to help fund its work.

Blue shut the laptop and replaced it in the backpack.

When he leaned across the seat, Rita Chabouri squeaked like a trapped rodent. A big hand closed on hers, and she stopped breathing entirely. The double click of the handcuffs springing apart sounded loud in the enclosed space, and she stared at her wrists.

"If you get rearrested, tell them I dropped you a few blocks away in Brooklyn. I kept my bike helmet on. You never saw my face. You have no idea who I am. Got it?"

She nodded, licking dry lips. He leaned close to her ear.

"I'll be watching. Tell the police about me, and I will come for you. Now get out."

She shuffled fast along the seat, pulled at the handle. A blast of hot air puffed into the van from the air conditioning units lining the back of the building.

When she stood on the road, Chabouri found a scrap of courage and knocked on the van window. Jimmy Blue pressed the button, and the glass slid down.

"What about me? I have nothing now. What am I supposed to do?"

"You're a thief," said Blue. "Steal something."

He jammed the shift forward and drove away, glancing in the wing mirror once before turning back onto the exit road. Rita Chabouri hadn't moved.

CHAPTER FIFTY-EIGHT

IT TOOK THREE DAYS. Three days of giving statements and asking questions. Three days of windowless New York police interview rooms and surprisingly poor coffee.

It could have been over in few hours, had Barber's account tallied with those of Cunningham and Spader. But, despite never seeing the face behind the mirrored visor, she knew the motorcyclist was Tom Lewis. And she wouldn't leave town until they took her seriously. She told them as much. After a couple of terse discussions with senior NYPD officers, Spader himself delivered the bad news. They weren't taking her seriously, and she was going home.

"I'm sorry, Barber." The special agent handed her an airline ticket an hour after she'd called the leading detective on the Chabouri case a moron. "Time to go. I volunteered to drive you. No one else would do it."

He chuckled as he led the way to his car, but Barber didn't join in. She could see, and judge, her actions objectively, an ability which had been instrumental in her rapid career advancement. Not so helpful now, though. Not when she saw an obsessed burnout getting close to sabotaging any chance of further promotion. But she couldn't stop herself, even though there was no point being right when no one else agreed. Her claims hung on a hunch. She couldn't prove a thing.

They hadn't even found Chabouri yet, let alone the hijacker. The bike turned up half a mile away in a car park, where the trail ran cold. Stone cold. No one was dead, and Chabouri was a UK problem, so few NYPD resources were made available to pursue the matter.

Cunningham waited in the car. Spader paused before opening the door.

"Look Barber, don't forget this is a win. A huge win. I copied your boy Connors in on my initial report."

She almost smiled at the thought of the uptight, self-righteous, Eton and Oxford educated Deputy Commissioner Connors being referred to as her 'boy'. But Spader was wrong. Lewis had won. Lewis had won, and Barber couldn't bear it.

Spader's good humour continued during the drive.

"Daff—Commander Cadwallader—said he wouldn't have survived without your friend. Lewis took out most of the crew before being killed."

"Allegedly killed. And he's not my friend."

Cunningham pointedly looked out of the window. Spader ignored the interruption.

"So we owe him. And if you hadn't been chasing him in London, he wouldn't have boarded that ship. We owe you, too. Which is why I didn't include your claims about Chabouri's hijack in the report. And I leaned on the NYPD chief to stop him filing a complaint. No need to thank me."

"I wasn't about to."

Spader chuckled and pushed a fresh lump of tobacco under his lip. Nothing would dent his good mood.

Barber ignored Spader during the drive to the airport, and Cunningham kept his own counsel.

In fact, DI Cunningham barely spoke until they were in the air. After the announcement that the Dreamliner had reached its cruising altitude, he lined up three beers and three miniature vodka bottles on his tray table. He slid another three vodkas onto her table.

Cunningham downed the first vodka, opened the beer, and took a long swallow. Only then did he turn to her.

"Thing is, boss, it's possible you're right."

Barber was staring at the clouds. Now she turned to face Cunningham.

"That might have been Lewis," he said. "It's not impossible. But you have to admit it doesn't make much sense. On the face of it, I mean. Guv, how did he get off that ship? And even if he got off, he'd be insane to grab Chabouri like that."

"Your support is less than overwhelming."

He smiled. It was the closest thing to humour she'd attempted for seventy-two hours.

"Guv, if anyone could have pulled it off, it's Lewis. I'll give you that. But what's the point?"

"The point of what?"

"Of hanging on to this. You're a brilliant police officer. You deserved that promotion. I'm sorry for being such a prick about it. Don't throw it away over one case."

My god, she thought, *wisdom. From Cunningham, of all people.*

"Guv, even if he's out there, he's screwed. It's a foreign country, he's pretty bloody distinctive looking, and he's not so great at keeping a low profile. You think he'll give up smacking bad guys around because they're American?"

Barber recognised a question that didn't require an answer when she heard one. "Go on."

"When he screws up—and he will—you'll get a call. Until then, forget him. Right?"

Barber shrugged. Cunningham unscrewed her vodka miniature and poured it into the plastic cup.

"Right?" he repeated. "Now have a drink."

She hesitated, then mirrored Cunningham's actions and downed the liquid, the flush of heat that accompanied it warming her throat.

Ninety minutes later, Cunningham snored on her shoulder while she stared back out across the endless sunlit clouds.

She kept thinking about the books. Why the books? With the

police closing in on him, Lewis posted a parcel of popular, best-selling, second-hand books to one of the biggest online sellers in America. Why?

For once, Barber's gut refused to pull together the disparate elements of a case and provide an answer. It was a mystery.

Detective Chief Inspector Maisie Barber hated mysteries. She stared out as the sky darkened, her lips pressed tightly together. She drank another two vodkas, frowning. An hour after the cabin lights were dimmed, she fell asleep. When the steward pulled the thin blanket over her shoulders, she was grinding her teeth.

———

After leaving Rita Chabouri, Jimmy Blue drove the van three hundred yards to the next airport hotel, used a stolen phone to connect to the Wi-Fi, and distributed the million dollars into twelve personal accounts. The banks he'd chosen were international, the money accessible at any time. Each deposit was small enough not to raise any queries.

The phone went into the Hudson, but not before he'd signed into an app which brought up a map of America. A flag appeared in Wyoming.

He signed out, then back in again, using an almost identical user-name. The only difference was its suffix: *deadwinter02*. The map appeared again, this time showing a suburb of Chicago. He signed out again, repeating the process with a new username.

deadwinter15 proved the charm, bringing up a map of New York State, a green dot pulsing on a location a hundred and twenty miles west.

He memorised the address and checked his watch. He'd be there by nightfall.

CHAPTER FIFTY-NINE

"MR ZAMBRANO, with all due respect, I will not open a case file until you explain what crime has been committed."

Benjamin Zambrano slammed his cane onto the counter. Sergeant Angel Coffrey—plump, sassy, and his junior by half a century—didn't so much as flinch. She raised an eyebrow and leaned forward. In four years at the front desk of Scranton Police Department, she had developed an air of Buddha-like calm. Nothing rattled Angel, and those who tried her patience fell before her thousand-yard stare like wheat before the scythe.

"Would you like some time to calm down, sir?" She treated the red-faced octogenarian to a faint smile and pointed down the hall. "Grab a cup of water, perhaps? Think about what you want to report, because, right now, it sounds like you might be wasting police time."

The red complexion darkened to purple. The whites of Zambrano's eyes, more yellow than white, were streaked with tiny red veins. He drank too much. Always had. Angel knew this because everyone in the neighbourhood knew it. And it hadn't started when his wife died twenty years ago. Nope. Zambrano had been buying pints of cheap whiskey every day since... well, since forever. Folks speculated that the smile on Mrs Zambrano's face in the chapel of rest was one of relief.

"Wasting police time?" Spittle hung from his lips. His hair, of which precious little remained, formed wispy grey clouds above a parchment skull. He took a mint from his pocket and slid it between his lips, sucking on it until his cheeks hollowed.

"That's correct, Mr Zambrano. And wasting police time *is* a crime, as I'm sure you're aware."

Rapid blinking accompanied a yellowing tongue darting out to lick cracked lips. Zambrano clenched and unclenched his fists, picked up his cane, and gave Angel a brisk nod.

"My privacy has been violated, Officer Coffrey." He said the word *officer* as if it were an insult. He treated other human beings as though their existence inconvenienced him. "A thief broke into my house. I might have been murdered in my bed."

His voice tightened and rose in pitch. "Murdered."

"Goodness." Angel twirled her ballpoint pen between her fingers. Looked at the report sheet. She had yet to write anything other than the old man's name. "Well, you are still very much alive, a blessing for which the Scranton Police Department, as well as the wider community, are very grateful."

Zambrano's milky eyes narrowed as if suspecting sarcasm, but Angel's blank expression gave him no ammunition to pursue it.

"But I was robbed. And that's a crime. I want to report it."

Angel looked over his shoulder. Midweek, mid-morning. No one waiting. All quiet.

"Robbed. Right. Tell me again."

"It's just as I said on the phone."

"Humour me."

The fury in his glare competed with Angel's patient boredom and, after a brief scuffle, conceded.

"I watched a little television last night before bed. All the doors were locked. I always make sure they're locked. The whole neighbourhood has gone bad these past twenty years. Not what it was. Not at all. Full of bad types. You know. Low life. Taking drugs, living off welfare cheques. Fallen women."

"Fallen women?" Angel associated the expression with romance novels set in the nineteenth century.

"That's right. You know exactly what I mean. No one feels safe anymore. And they're all, well, you know. What do you call them now? Coloureds? People of colour? That's it. People of colour."

"I'm a person of colour, Mr Zambrano."

He jumped a little at that, leaned closer. "You sure?"

"Quite sure."

"Oh. Well. You're not, I mean, you're only... anyhow, you've made something of yourself. Got a job. Not living off handouts."

"I'm mixed-race, Mr Zambrano. Let's try to steer clear of any potentially racist remarks—hate speech is a crime—and focus on last night. You had gone to bed."

His mouth opened and closed.

"Yes. This morning, I got up at six-thirty. I don't spend half the day in bed like young people do."

Probably had to drag himself up to empty his wizened old bladder. And start the day with another drink. The mints he sucked couldn't conceal his sour, rotten, booze-tinged breath.

"And that's when I saw it. The bathroom window. It was open. And someone had pushed everything on the shelf below to one side. That's how he got in."

"You said the bathroom is on the second floor of your house. At the rear. Is that correct?"

"Yes."

"It's the room next to your bedroom?"

"Yes. I told you already. He must have climbed the drainpipe, forced the window."

"But you heard nothing?"

An alcohol-induced semi-coma will do that. Angel suspected the high school band could hold nightly rehearsals in his bedroom and Zambrano wouldn't notice.

"You checked to see if anything had been taken?"

"I did."

"Do you have any valuables? Any money on the premises?"

Like most misers, Benjamin Zambrano displayed few signs of the fortune inherited from his father, the founder of a national newspaper. Zambrano junior surely owned a few valuable items.

"Well, well, this and that. Nothing worth stealing. A little cash."

"But no money was missing."

"That's not the point. He was in my house. My house! While I was sleeping. Not just that—he was in my bedroom. That's where he stole my property."

"The book you claim was stolen."

"Claim? Claim? It *was* stolen. Taken from my bedside table by some drugged-up, er, loser, ah, of colour, so he can sell it to get his next fix."

Angel kept her voice level. "But whoever took it left the cash."

"Yes, well, maybe he heard a noise, got nervous. I don't know. That's your job, isn't it? Not that the Scranton police are what they used to be. When I was a young man, we respected the police. And the police respected us. These days, we hardly see you. Did you come when gangs were selling drugs outside my door? No. But when I confronted them, you people turned on me!"

Angel had been on duty that night, too. Zambrano had been cautioned for screaming racial abuse at a group of ten-year-olds riding their bikes. He had been drunk. The kids' parents hadn't pressed charges.

"This book. Was it valuable?"

"Is that relevant?"

She left a pause. He muttered.

"Well, not particularly. But it only arrived last week. Bought it through the internet."

"Price?"

"Ah, well, er, ninety-nine cents. Nearly four dollars with shipping."

Angel put the pen down. "Four bucks."

"Yes. But he was in my house. And I haven't finished reading it yet."

Angel remembered what her sixteen-year-old daughter said when things weren't going her way. FML. Angel had taken to saying it herself for a few months until a fellow officer told her it stood for *Fuck My Life.* Still, nothing else seemed to fit the occasion better.

"FML," she said, sliding the report sheet off the desk and into the basket at her feet.

"What's that?" Zambrano stuffed another mint into his foul mouth.

"It's police code, Mister Zambrano. It means we'll keep an eye out for your stolen property. If it turns up, we'll call you."

"Hmm. I should think so."

"What was the name of the book? You know, in case we find it being fenced on the ninety-nine cent books black market."

Angel didn't know if his hesitation could be attributed to an unreliable memory, or if Benjamin Zambrano was reluctant to share the information, but it took a while for him to lean in and whisper the title.

"*How To Win Friends And Influence People.*"

CHAPTER SIXTY

IN A NEW YORK'S Port Authority Bus Terminal restroom stall, Blue turned to the last page of the hardback book he stole in Scranton. The geolocation app had guided him to an old house, paint flaking and peeling. The Southside neighbourhood was run-down, but the houses were a good size. Most front and back yards boasted mature trees, one of which gave him easy access to a bathroom window.

Using a craft knife, Jimmy sliced a line across the inside back cover, tearing away the paper to reveal a shallow hidden compartment. He removed the SIM card first, the one that had led him to Scranton. He snapped it, wrapped it in tissue, and flushed it away.

Blue turned the book over, tipping out a driver's licence and social security card. Superb forgeries, indistinguishable from the real thing. Made by a talented, and expensive, specialist in London. Twenty of them, concealed in hardback books which, by now, had arrived in homes all over America. Each ID, if run through a database, linked to a real person. Dig deeper, and the illusion unravelled, but it would be enough to satisfy a curious cop. ID would help Tom find a job. Settle down.

Jimmy Blue craved the darkness. He had been in control for too long. Tom's parents were avenged. Robert Winter—even if he didn't die at Blue's hand—was gone. Jimmy's murderous spree through London's underworld left some very bad people either dead or terrified.

The plan had always been to return to America, where, a few years before tackling Winter and his crew, Tom had been happy. No language barrier, and nearly four million square miles in which to lose himself.

Blue played his part. Planned the escape, got Tom to America. Not the easiest journey. Now he could rest. Let Tom flourish while he slipped back into the womb-like darkness that cocooned him.

He stared at his own face on the driving licence. *Tom Maddox.* The fake IDs all shared the same first name. Tom couldn't answer to anything else.

He tucked the ID and social security card into his wallet, exited the stall. While washing his hands, he looked in the mirror. The eyes that stared back were blank. Not friendly, not threatening. Empty. When Tom looked in a mirror, he saw himself. A person. A human being who experienced pain and pleasure, who enjoyed a good movie, or a walk in a park.

Blue didn't envy Tom. The qualities that made Tom human also made him weak. Unfocussed. Predictable. Not so with Blue. His mind and his body, driven by his unshakeable will, made him unique. He answered to no law, no societal moral code. Other people found life complicated, but it was simple. Jimmy Blue looked at the world and saw good and bad.

He punished the bad.

But it was time to sleep. Time to let Tom live again.

When he walked out of the restroom, the next long-distance bus on the departure board listed Miami as its destination. He bought a ticket, boarded the waiting bus, took a window seat halfway down, his rucksack on his lap.

Most seats were taken when the bus engine coughed into life. No one sat next to the six-foot three man whose bulk encroached on the empty seat beside him.

The bus station had been dark, but as they exited the building, afternoon light flooded the vehicle's interior. Blue winced, pulled down a blind, turned away. Closed his eyes.

Slept.

CHAPTER SIXTY-ONE

A HISS OF AIR BRAKES, a door opening.

Eyes sticky.

Mouth dry.

Legs cramped, tingling.

Tom rubbed and scratched at the sleep in his eyes before opening them.

"You back with us, then? Thought you ain't never gonna wake up, son."

He blinked back at a smiling face—wrinkled, missing a tooth. She looked a hundred years old, grabbing the backs of seats for support as she made her way to the front of the bus.

"Mm?" his voice, rusted, croaky, strange. Even simple words drifted out of reach. His lack of conversational skills didn't bother his new friend.

"I been on since Washington. After the first five hours, I took to wondering if you'd upped and died on us. Pity, I thought, a fine strong young man like that, taken in his prime. But I reckoned the snoring meant you weren't departing this life just yet. How d'ya feel? You need the bathroom? We're stopping for twenty minutes. The speed I move, by the time my ass touches the plastic, I've gotta get up again."

She laughed.

She'd said Washington. He'd made it. America.

The old woman cackled as she moved away. Tom called after her.

"Mm, mm, w-w-where, mm?"

She didn't turn, but shouted back as she continued towards the door.

"Charlotte, South Carolina. My sister-in-law lived here in the seventies. They call downtown uptown, and that's all you need to know about folk in South Carolina. This your stop?"

The old woman's comment now made up Tom's entire knowledge of the city of Charlotte. He stood up, shuffled out into the aisle, backpack held close. Stretched tight and aching muscles. Rolled his neck until it cracked.

Tom had been to America before, but there was no one he could call, no one to help him now. Jimmy Blue had been awake for most of the last America trip, not Tom. There was one period when Tom woke up. A few weeks with a kind woman who helped him... somewhere warm. Somewhere near the ocean. But he knew he couldn't go back wherever it was.

He'd known a girl called Charlotte when he was a child. Infant school in South West London. Pigtails, dimples. Once ate a worm when dared to do so.

This would do as well as anywhere else.

He fished out his wallet, saw an unfamiliar card with his face on it. Recognised *Tom*, but the next word was wrong. He couldn't read it, but Blue had prepared for this, so the word echoed in his head as he stared.

Maddox. Tom Maddox.

Tom Maddox alighted in Charlotte as the last of the evening sun dipped behind the horizon.

Everything he owned was in the backpack. He slung it over his shoulder.

Alone.

Scared.

Safe.

A new start.

Along with the fresh ID, the wallet contained a few hundred dollars. Tom joined a line by the roadside and waited for a cab. When his turn came, he slid onto the back seat.

"Where to?"

Tom said the word silently first, making sure he got it right. Then he looked up, met the driver's eyes in the rear-view mirror.

"Mm, u-uptown."

The driver started the meter, turned the wheel, and joined the evening traffic.

fusebooks.com/aviolentlife

AUTHOR'S NOTE

I've loved telling the story of Tom Lewis's revenge. I've already written three Jimmy Blue novels. And I know there will be more to come.

Please leave a review if you can—it makes a big difference.

If you haven't signed up for your free Jimmy Blue story yet (and the occasional email from me), you can find it here:

fusebooks.com/ian

I have a website imaginatively named after myself, and I can be found in the usual social media places. I don't post photos of my dinner there, I promise.

Thanks for reading,

Ian

Norwich, 2021

Printed in Great Britain
by Amazon